Stocking STANDOFF

MELODY TYDEN

For all the women who like to be in charge.

Chapter One

Last Night in Ecuador

~Eve~

Tears glistened in the eyes of the women standing in a semicircle in the small office space, making it harder for me to try to keep my composure. In some ways, it felt like I'd just arrived, and yet, somehow, my incredible year abroad had come to an end. My car had just pulled up outside and everyone had gathered to say goodbye.

"You'll come back and see us, sí?" Maria asked. Only a few years older than me, she had been one of the first women I met when I arrived in Ecuador the previous December. Since her home had been in her husband's name and he died without warning, she and her three young children were evicted and left with nothing. Friends stepped in to take care of them, and one of those friends told her about our office dedicated to helping women in need. She showed up the next day with her kids in tow and all her belongings in the world on her back, and what she lacked in formal education or training, she made up for in sheer determination. One year on, she had a nice apartment a short walk from our office and her children's school, and she'd just been appointed to take my place as project manager when I left. I couldn't think of anyone better qualified.

"I'll come back whenever I can," I promised. My future looked a lot less defined than hers did, but after seeing first-hand what could be done with the right people and resources, at least I had a few ideas. A proposal to my father would be the next big step, but first, I had a few other stops to make.

After one last round of teary hugs, with several of the women taking one last chance to touch my flaming red hair that they found so unusual, I managed to make it out the door to where the car waited to take me to Quito, the capital city. After a meeting there the following day with the new head of the charitable organization I'd spent the last year volunteering with, I would be heading to Toronto to meet up with my father on a business trip before returning to New York for Christmas with my whole family. Looking out the car window at the countryside as the town that had been my home for the last year disappeared behind me, New York felt a world away, and so did the woman I'd been when I left there.

Arriving in Ecuador had been a culture shock, but I had a feeling that returning to the casual excess of my life back home would be an even bigger one.

In Quito, I checked into my hotel and headed out into the city, eager to explore one last time in relative anonymity. No one there knew who I was. Although I stayed at a Stamer hotel, I checked in under the name I'd been using for the last year: Sudlow, my mother's maiden name. That had been my dad's idea. He'd been afraid that if people saw the Stamer name, it might attract someone who wanted to take advantage of my connections. He had outlined nightmare scenarios where I could be kidnapped and held for ransom if people knew just how much money my family had.

Although I thought he exaggerated out of protectiveness, I didn't mind going incognito. It had been a nice change to have people treat me just like everyone else, and I had to admit I would miss it when I got back to New York. There, nothing about my life could be called anonymous.

"Eve?"

I've just taken a seat on a bench in the Plaza Grande to rest my feet when someone called out my name, and I looked over to see one of the women I'd worked with a few months earlier rushing over to me with a big smile. Her long, dark braid hung over one shoulder and her dark eyes shone with excitement.

"What are you doing in Quito? You should have told me you'd be here."

"Hola Sara." I got up to give her a hug and a kiss on the cheek. She looked nothing like the broken, bruised woman who had turned up at our office door eight months earlier, before we'd helped her get out of her abusive relationship. "What a nice surprise! I'm only here for one night, I'm afraid, that's why I didn't get in touch. I didn't want anyone to go to any trouble."

I didn't add that I had planned to use that night to prepare for my meeting the next day; it would sound rude. No one would choose to be alone when they could spend the evening with other people instead; that had certainly been the credo of the women I worked with.

"It's no trouble. You could have stayed with me," she admonished me. "There's no need to waste money on a hotel."

She didn't know I didn't have to worry about money, or that my family's company would get the profit anyway.

"At least let me take you out tonight," she pleaded. "We can have so much fun!"

My plans for a quiet night quickly disappeared, as I knew it would be impossible to say no, and I gave in as graciously as possible. She gave me the address of a restaurant we could go to later and I promised to meet her there after a quick nap. It looked like it wouldn't be an early night after all.

Several hours later, wearing an elegantly casual black dress that I'd brought along with me and not worn at all in the last year, I followed Sara into another club. We'd already eaten at a restaurant and tried out one club, but she decided that one didn't have enough handsome men in it. "You need one last fling before you leave Ecuador," she told me with a laugh. "So you can leave with a smile on your face!"

Honestly, men and sex had been the last thing on my mind during my time there. I'd decided when I got there that not only did I want to get to know who I was without my trust fund, I wanted to live without the pressure of pleasing a man either. My discreet toys helped me out when I needed a release, and I hadn't encountered very much temptation, not when most of the men I'd encountered during my stay had been the ones our clients were trying to escape, like the one who'd beaten Sara before we helped her relocate to Quito. Nights like the one she had in mind hadn't been part of my agenda at all.

Sara's experience didn't seem to have slowed her down any, I was glad to see. She flirted and chatted with the men around us in multiple languages, looking confident and at ease. The particular club she'd brought us to seemed to attract an international crowd, and I heard several familiar-sounding American accents.

The one that caught my attention wasn't American, though. It had a French lilt to it as it drifted over my shoulder as we waited at the bar to order a drink.

"No, thank you, I don't need another...I have a lot of work..." His refusal seemed to fall on deaf ears as his companion ordered another round, obviously ignoring his protests. "...and he's not even listening to me. No one is listening. I'm just talking to myself now."

The self-deprecating tone made me smile, and I turned my head just as he turned away, so I only saw the back of his head. "I'm listening, but I'm afraid that doesn't help you get out of here."

His face turned back to me, and an almost-forgotten zing of attraction shot through my body. Warm, intelligent brown eyes met mine from beneath tousled brown hair, a stubble shadow lining his jaw, and his lips spreading into a warm smile as he took me in, obviously liking what he saw just as much as I did. He was older than me, but not much, probably no more than thirty.

"I think it helps a lot," he corrected me. "Someone as beautiful as you could definitely distract everyone while I make a break for it."

His words were completely unexpected, and I had to laugh. He managed to compliment me without hitting on me; very few men managed to pull that off so smoothly. "And you would leave me stuck here when I have to work tomorrow too?"

"Ah, I didn't realize we both need to escape. That changes things, then." His accent sounded even sexier as he leaned closer to me conspiratorially. "I don't suppose you know any magic tricks?"

"Just one. Follow my lead." I gave him a wink before taking his hand and putting his arm around me. The closer I got, the better his cologne smelt, and the heat his body gave off warmed me in a very comforting way. Leaning into him, I turned to Sara first. "I'm going to go now. Enjoy the rest of your night. It was great to see you."

It took her all of two seconds to eye up the man with his arm around me and determine that I had a good excuse for leaving. "Have a *great* night!" she whispered in my ear as she hugged me goodbye. "Travel safe."

With that taken care of, I turned to my new friend's companion. "Is it okay if I steal your friend for the rest of the evening?"

The man's jaw dropped as he looked at me and his friend's arm around me. "Yes, of course. Monsieur, I will see you tomorrow."

"Yes, thank you." The man next to me did his best to keep a straight face though I could see his lips twitching. "Good night."

That was all it took, and he kept his arm around me until we were out the front door and home-free, at which point we both began to laugh.

"So simple, but effective," he marvelled.

"I've found the people here to be very direct, and they respond well to directness. Don't try to be polite, they won't take the hint. I'm guessing you haven't been here for long."

"I just arrived yesterday, so that's very good advice, thank you." Taller than me, but not too tall, and strong-looking in a lean, wiry way, his brown eyes looked even warmer beneath the streetlights in the warm night air. The temperature never really changed in Ecuador; despite being December, it was still just as warm as July. "Would you like to share a taxi?"

Perhaps I could blame it on the drinks I'd had, or the fact that I was leaving the country the next day, or maybe just that I hadn't met anyone I found so attractive in so long, but something about the situation brought out my bold side. "I'd like to share a taxi back to where you're staying, if you're interested."

His eyebrows raised in surprise as that same slow smile spread across his face. "I appreciate a woman who knows what she wants. Are you always this take-charge?"

I couldn't argue with that assessment. "Would it be a problem if I said yes?"

An even greater appreciation filled his eyes. "Not at all. I would be happy to take instruction from you."

I believed he meant it, and the arousal that had been building in my body ever since I laid eyes on him got even stronger. Very few men that I'd encountered actually liked being told what to do, especially when it came to the bedroom, but I had a feeling he might be different. If my gut instinct about that was right, I had a feeling the night might end up being very satisfying for the both of us.

~Julien~

The night had just taken a very unexpected turn, and I couldn't think of a single reason to complain about it. In Ecuador at the tail-end of a whirlwind South American business trip, I would have happily spent the evening preparing for my meetings the next day, but the office director had insisted on taking me out to 'show me a good time'. Explaining to him what I considered a good time wouldn't be possible, so I agreed to go for one drink. When he told me he was getting another, I tried to protest, unsuccessfully, and that was when the gorgeous redhead entered the picture.

I'd rarely seen anyone so flawless, so perfectly suited to my personal tastes. Thick, gently curling red hair framed her heart-shaped face, with eyes so dark I instinctively wanted to move closer to see into them better. It felt like it would be easy to fall into them completely. Her friendly and open smile suggested good humour and confidence without a hint of arrogance, a rare combination in anyone, but particularly someone so physically blessed.

Despite her stunning beauty, I didn't have any intentions of making a move on her at first. Beauty only went so far. I'd had enough disappointing sexual encounters with attractive women to know when not to waste my time.

However, when she took control of the situation, my body immediately responded, and by the time she invited herself back to my hotel, my plans for the evening had completely changed. She said she liked to take charge and I hoped she meant it. As long as she kept that attitude once we got back to my room, it could turn out to be a very good night indeed.

Only after I flagged down a taxi, held the door for her and got settled next to her did I realize I didn't even know her name.

"What should I call you?" I asked, inhaling her classy, feminine perfume in the close confines of the taxi's back seat. I had no idea what the scent was, but it gave off the same vibe of understated confidence that she herself did. It suited her perfectly.

Her eyes moved over my body shamelessly, turning me on even more. It couldn't be any clearer what she wanted from me, and we were definitely on the same page. "We don't need to bother with names. This won't be more than one night, right?"

She had a point. I would only be in Quito for a couple more days, and she must have been a tourist with her bold American accent.

However, I hadn't asked for her name. "That's not what I said. What should I *call* you?"

Her eyebrows raised at my impertinence, making my cock jump. Not a thing about her suggested she would back down. Nothing gave me a hint of submission, just as I wanted it.

"You can call me E." Her sultry voice made me even harder, especially when combined with her next words. "When I say you can speak, that is."

Oui, calisse. My instinct about her had been right on the money, and although it surprised me to run into someone on my level in a random nightclub far from home, it excited me far more.

It had taken me a while to figure out the dynamic that I craved in the bedroom: a strong, confident woman telling me exactly what to do. In my job, I managed people and projects. Everyone came to me for answers, and though I never sought dominance, control usually rested with me. In private, I relished putting myself in someone else's hands and letting my natural desire to please come through. Had she guessed that about me from our brief interaction at the bar? Or had it really just been a lucky break that we stumbled across each other that night?

"Oui, Madame E." I gave my agreement in my native French, partly because arousal as strong as I felt at that moment sometimes made interpretation impossible, and partly because American women generally responded well to it. She didn't let me down, the look in her dark eyes growing even more intense with my words.

She had to be younger than me, probably by about five years, which surprised me. Normally, I went for older women simply because they knew what they wanted and were less intimidated about telling me.

Intimidation didn't seem to be in E's vocabulary.

"Can I touch you?" The taxi seemed to be taking its time meandering through the dark streets of the capital. Christmas decorations hung across the streets despite the warm evening that felt nothing like the Decembers of my snowy childhood. I had no idea how far we were from the hotel, but any distance seemed too far when the smooth skin of her crossed legs beneath the short skirt of her black dress looked more enticing with each passing second.

E smiled, letting me know she approved of me asking permission, even if she denied my request. "No. Not yet. You can touch yourself, though."

I stifled the groan in my throat, aware that we weren't yet fully alone. The driver seemed to be ignoring us, humming along to a local song on the radio, and I shifted my body as naturally as I could in the seat, spreading my legs open wider as I pressed my palm against my rapidly-stiffening cock within my tan pants. My eyes remained fixed on E as I ran my hand slowly down the length of my cock, my breathing growing shallower by the second.

She held my gaze, not watching my hand but my reaction to it instead. "Very good," she murmured in that low, commanding tone of hers. "Now, stop."

Immediately, my hand moved away. No matter how much my body urged me to continue, my mind responded to her words instead. She was testing me, I could tell, seeing how well I could follow orders, and I had no intention of disappointing her.

"Señor?" The taxi driver's interruption made me realize we had stopped moving. I'd been so caught up in my companion that I hadn't noticed. "This is right?"

We were indeed in front of my hotel, and I hurriedly grabbed some US dollars out of my wallet to pay the fare. Doing my best to cover my awkward state of arousal as I stood up, I offered my hand to E to help her from the car. She accepted gracefully, saying goodnight to the driver in Spanish before closing the door behind her.

"This is... different." She eyed the small, family-run hotel in front of us curiously. "Not where most businessmen would be staying."

Since her tone held no disapproval or condescension, simply observation, I had to agree. "I chose it myself. I like to help out local business owners when I can rather than feeding more money into large international companies."

Her face tightened for just a moment, so quick that I almost missed it, before she turned to me with a sly smile. "I hope the walls are thick enough."

My cock twitched yet again. "That won't be a problem. Please, follow me."

Using my key, I let us in through the front door. Thankfully, the reception desk was empty so I didn't have to make any awkward conversation with my hosts about the woman I had brought back with me. When I booked the hotel for myself, I hadn't anticipated having any guests.

The room itself was clean and functional, with hand-made decorative touches, and E looked around with interest as I turned the lamps on and emptied my pockets onto the dresser next to the door. Outside, the street lamps provided a little extra light, but the streets were empty and quiet. We weren't in a busy or touristy part of the city. Besides the dresser and the queen-sized bed, the room had a small TV stand with a TV and a sink for washing. The bathroom and showers were communal for the floor at the end of the hall. Hopefully, E wouldn't mind.

It didn't seem to be a concern at that moment when she turned back to me, sizing me up once again. About four paces separated us, her at the end of the bed and me still standing by the door. Her lithe, firm body looked amazing in her pretty black dress and high heels. "You're clean?"

Obviously, she meant more than just hygiene.

"Yes." I always got a full physical before travelling, including an STD test, just to be safe. "I have the papers if you want to see them."

Her eyes widened in surprise before she gave a throaty laugh. "No, that's okay. I'll take your word for it. I am too. You have condoms?"

"Yes." I appreciated that she took the time to ask before things got too heated. It demonstrated yet again that she knew exactly what she wanted and what she would and wouldn't accept. To make it clear I took things just as seriously, I pulled open the top drawer of the dresser and pulled out the package to show her.

"Good." She nodded in approval. "And you don't have any problem with doing what I say?"

Although our conversation in the car gave her some clue about that, I appreciated that she wanted it stated outright. Consent was always important. "I'm at your service, E."

A satisfied smile spread across her lips that made her look even more beautiful than before, and a thrill of anticipation ran through my body. If she looked that good to me while simply standing there, I couldn't wait to see what she looked like when she came. I couldn't wait to help her get there.

"On your knees, then."

My knees bent almost before she finished giving the order, buckling beneath the weight of my arousal. Lust clouded my vision, my whole body responding to her authority. Every muscle tensed as I waited to see what she would tell me to do next, my cock still trapped within the tightened confines of my pants.

"Are you hungry?" Her dark eyes were cool but her smile stayed warm, the combination drawing me in but keeping me on edge at the same time.

Clearly, she didn't mean food.

"Starving," I answered honestly. Just the possibility of tasting her had my mouth watering.

She knew exactly how to draw out that anticipation. Moving slowly, her eyes on me at all times, E reached up beneath her dress. It almost felt like slow-motion as she pulled down the black lace panties underneath it. In the dim light of the lamps, I could just make out the dampness of the fabric, the slightly darker spot that had been between her legs, letting me know that despite her cool control, she found our situation just as stimulating as I did.

Slowly, she pulled the thin lace fabric down her legs and stepped out of it, one foot and then the other, her black heels clicking on the hardwood floor and reminding me of the firmness of that same floor beneath my knees. I didn't mind, though. A bit of pain would be worth it for the reward she offered.

Using just one finger, she held up the discarded panties and my tongue darted out reflexively, licking my lips as I tried to get a hint of her scent, even from that distance. The movement made her smile as she hitched up her dress just a touch and sat down on the end of the bed, spreading her legs to give me my first glimpse of her gorgeous pussy.

Her neatly trimmed hair matched the red on her head and her lips glistened with her arousal. I leaned forward unintentionally, desperate for a closer look, and her expression immediately hardened. "Did I say you could move?"

"Non, Madame E." My back straightened again as I slipped back into French. The words sounded thicker, my voice heavy with lust. *Crisse*, I wanted to please her.

My disobedience deserved punishment, and punish me, she did. As I knelt there watching, she took her own finger and swept it through the wet folds between her legs. It shone with her moisture as she lifted it back up, her eyes still on me as she placed it between her own lips, her tongue licking it clean.

My cock strained painfully against my clothes, but I forced myself to remain still and silent, fighting against every desire in my body.

"Good," she praised me when I didn't move a muscle. "Come closer, on your hands and knees."

Keeping my movements slow and measured in case she changed her mind, I bent down so my hands reached the floor, crawling towards her as I kept my eyes on her to show my submission. Her eyelids looked heavier as she watched me. If her heart beat even half as fast as mine did, she must be throbbing for me. Hopefully, I could give her an orgasm she would remember, because I had no doubt I would enjoy every second of it.

When I reached the foot of the bed, I paused, waiting for her permission. As I inhaled, the sweet scent of her pussy reached me and my eyes closed briefly in bliss. She smelled even better than I could have imagined. I could bury my face between her legs and live on that smell for days.

But it wasn't up to me; I'd do it only if she let me.

After making me wait for what felt like forever, E finally took mercy on me. "You can eat."

Dieu, merci. She hadn't put any restrictions on me, perhaps wanting to see what I would do, and I took that responsibility seriously. I was determined to make her proud.

My first taste must have been what it felt like when a kid ate sugar for the first time. I'd been with my share of women before, and I liked oral sex a lot, but never had I tasted anything quite as sweet as her. It had been a while for me, probably a few months since my new job demanded so much of my time, but that didn't entirely explain it. Some of it must have simply been her.

My tongue explored her thoroughly. Wide swipes were followed by deeper darts into her pussy, teasing her and tasting her before I moved on to her clit. E moaned as my tongue swept over it, and I kissed her deeply, sucking and licking as my lips and tongue gave her all of my devotion. Her head had tilted back, making her gorgeous red hair hang even further down her back, her eyes closed to focus on the sensations I gave her. Each action brought me pleasure too, knowing it pleased her, and I paid as much attention as I could to how she reacted, trying to learn all her personal likes and pleasure points. Each woman had their own personal turn-ons; there were no one-size-fits-all solutions.

When I thought I had the right combination, I truly set to work. I fucked her with my tongue, as deep as I could go, thrusting and licking all around the walls of her entrance before moving back to her clit, licking and sucking it until her legs began to tremble.

My ears were tuned the whole time in case she gave me any other instruction, but she seemed happy to let me do it my way that first time, and so I did, sucking her hard until she came. As her body convulsed, I quickly licked my way back down to lap up any sweetness that she shared with me.

Calisse, was I glad I let myself be talked into going out that night.

~Eve~

Waves of pleasure washed over me as my orgasm echoed through my body. The man's face was still buried between my legs, his tongue still lapping at me even as my body surrendered to the effects of his attention. I didn't even know his name and he'd just given me not only the best orgasm of my year but one of the best of my entire life, using only his mouth.

Part of it had to do with how turned on I'd been to begin with. Having him submit to me so completely was incredibly sexy. I'd played around with that dynamic before with other partners, but they never committed to it so fully, or for very long. Sooner or later, they wanted to be the one calling the shots, and I didn't push it since it would only be fun if they were into it too.

Kink had never been a dirty word in my house growing up. My parents had their own dominant and submissive relationship, though, unlike me, my mom preferred the submissive role. When I turned eighteen, she let me look inside their private playroom, offering to answer any questions I might have. I asked about a few of the items, but overall, like most teenagers, I didn't want to spend too much time thinking about my parents' sex life. The message I took from it, though, was that whatever turned me on would be okay. I would encounter no judgement from my family, and whenever I thought about that room afterwards, if I pictured myself in a similar situation, I would be the ones holding the reins, literally and figuratively.

In real life, though, I had never gone as far as I did with the sexy stranger, ordering him around and making him crawl to me. Maybe the fact that I didn't know him and would never see him again after that night gave me a greater sense of freedom. Maybe the way he responded to me naturally drew out my more assertive side. I couldn't say for sure; I only knew that I loved it just as much as I always thought I would.

"Thank you, E." The stranger's brown eyes were fixed on me as I opened mine, looking down to see him still only a breath away from my clit. If he stretched out his tongue, he could probably still reach it. "You are delicious."

No one had ever thanked me for the chance to go down on me before, and his French accent made everything sound even sexier. The shot of arousal his words sent through me made it clear I still wanted more. Would he protest, though, if I ended things there? How much control would he let me have, really?

Curious to find out, I sat back up, placing one of my high-heeled shoes gently against his chest to push him back. Staying on his knees, he moved back and looked up at me in anticipation, awaiting further instruction, his lips still wet with my pleasure.

"You have a very skilled tongue," I told him truthfully, and he flushed at the praise, adorably. "How many languages do you speak?"

"Four fluently," he answered readily. "A few more conversationally."

Good with his tongue *and* smart, not to mention devastatingly handsome. What a shame I didn't run into him sooner during my stay.

Still curious about how far his submissiveness would stretch, I got to my feet and pulled my dress down, still clutching my panties in one hand. "Well, it's been a pleasure, Monsieur. I hope you enjoy your stay in Quito."

Disappointment flashed across his face, there could be no doubt of that, but he stayed on his knees, making no move to stop me as I walked towards the door, my heels tapping on the hardwood floor. "I enjoyed meeting you too. May I call you a taxi?"

His response answered my question perfectly. He would let me go, leaving him unsatisfied, if I wanted to, but he still showed concern for my safety, bearing me no ill will. I couldn't have dreamt up a man more suited to my personal preferences, and since he passed that test so flawlessly, I had no intention of leaving him hanging.

"Maybe I could stay a little longer, if you make it worth my while."

The light immediately returned to his eyes, a smile of relief and excitement spreading across his face. "What would you like me to do?"

My eyes drifted down to his pants, straining along their seam. "Well, you've already had a look at me, so I think I'd like to see you too. *All* of you."

While I stood there, he quickly got to his feet, eager to comply. His shirt went first, his fingers swift and sure as they undid each button, gradually revealing his body to me. Yet again, he was just my type. A light smattering of chest hair, pecs and abs that were defined but not overdeveloped, and a trail of hair leading into his pants that had me almost licking my lips in anticipation.

"You're in great shape," I complimented him, and as I'd hoped, he blushed again, his hair flopping over his forehead as he looked down to pull off the sleeves of his shirt.

"My job involves a lot of physical labour. Or it did, anyway. I was just promoted, so now, I'll be working mostly in the office. I guess I'll have to find a new routine."

"Congratulations on your promotion." It didn't surprise me to know he was successful in whatever business he did, but I did wonder if he was as naturally submissive in the workplace as he was in the bedroom. It could go either way; my mom had always been a leader professionally, running her own business when she was my age. No one who met her in the office would guess she liked to be tied up, but other people carried over their submissiveness into the rest of their lives too. Which camp did he fall into, I wondered?

Before I had a chance to ask, he undid his belt and pants, pulling them down to reveal his stiff cock, and all thoughts of his job immediately flew out of my head.

I'd seen bigger dicks, to be fair, but bigger didn't always mean better. His looked like the perfect size; wide enough that I would definitely feel it, but not so much that I couldn't get it down my throat if I wanted to.

The metal buckle of his belt thudded against the floor as he tossed his pants aside along with the rest of his clothes, leaving him standing there completely naked and exposed to me as he waited for my next instruction.

Partly to draw out the tension and partly because I simply enjoyed the view, I circled him slowly, examining his body. It looked damn near flawless. His back looked as firm and strong as the men I'd seen working shirtless out in the fields during my visits to the more rural parts of the country, supporting his previous statement about doing manual labour. The only mar on the landscape of his body was a white raised scar running diagonally across his lower back.

"What's this?" I ran my fingers lightly over the long-healed skin and he shivered at my touch.

His response came as a complete surprise to me. "A former lover got a little too enthusiastic with her punishment."

Seriously? He obviously wasn't as new to this kind of situation as I was. That scar had to be several years old. What had she struck him with to cause a scar like that? How did he respond when it happened? How did she? Had they been in a serious relationship? Did they stay together afterwards?

Though my questions multiplied as my imagination kicked into gear, I kept them all inside. We were there for pleasure, not to exchange our life stories. I appreciated that he'd answered me honestly and openly, and I left it at that.

Moving back around to the front of him, my eyes fell again on his cock. I would love to taste it, and tease him while I did, but dropping to my knees for him as he had for me would alter the balance of power in a way that neither of us wanted. Unless... unless he couldn't see me do it?

"Open your mouth," I commanded. "You're going to stay nice and quiet."

As his lips parted, I bunched up the panties in my hand and shoved them into his mouth as a makeshift gag. The sight of him with the black lace in his mouth, and the pleasure he took from it, made obvious by the way his cock jumped, had my body humming in excitement again.

"Close your eyes."

Immediately, he shut them, placing himself entirely in my hands, and with his eyes closed and his mouth full, I got down on my knees to give his cock the attention it deserved. When I took hold of his base, his sharp inhale above me made me pause, but he made no further sound, taking my instruction to stay quiet seriously.

With long, languid strokes, I licked my way up and down the length of his shaft, exploring every inch of him. Just as he did to me, I took my time to learn his particular pleasure points and I paid careful attention to his state of arousal. As soon as I thought he might be getting close to release, I backed off, leaving him on the edge of his orgasm and wanting more.

I'd never been shy, as anyone who knew me would agree, but sucking a stranger's balls into my mouth while he bit down on my panties had to count as a new level, even for me.

He took my command to stay quiet seriously. The only signs I had of how much my efforts affected him were the state of his cock and the fidgeting of his fingers and toes as he tried his best to stay quiet and still.

Minutes passed, and more of them, but I couldn't guess how long I teased him. Through it all, he kept his poise, taking what I gave him and not demanding anything else. Just as I'd decided he'd earned his reward, a loud, shrill noise filled the room, startling us both.

"What's that?" I asked, still with the man's cock in my hand.

He reached up and pulled my panties from his mouth. As his eyes blinked open, he squinted against the lamplight, even though it wasn't very bright. "I think it's the fire alarm."

As much as I wished he was kidding, the alarm suggested otherwise. "We have to go outside?"

"I think so." His regret couldn't be clearer, and it mirrored my own. I hadn't meant to leave him in that state. "May I get dressed, E?"

"Yes, of course." Had he been with women who would have said no? My curiosity about him grew even stronger with every glimpse of his life he gave me.

Quickly, he pulled his clothes back on and escorted me back out onto the street where the other guests had already gathered. An older man with short dark hair and a friendly face spoke quickly to him in Spanish, and my mystery date answered back just as fluently. Spanish must be one of his four languages, it seemed.

As the conversation drew to a close, he turned to me. "He says it might be a while, they have to wait for the fire department to come and give the all clear. I can't ask you to wait, so he will call for a taxi for you."

Every word he said made sense but my mind rebelled against it anyway. I didn't want to leave yet, not until we'd finished what we'd started. Realistically, though, I still had my meeting in the morning, and a long flight afterwards. Returning to my hotel would be the reasonable thing to do, so I nodded my agreement, against my will.

"I hope you enjoy the rest of your time in Quito," I said as he held the taxi door open for me when it arrived.

"And you." His warm brown eyes crinkled as he smiled down at me. "I won't forget you, E."

"I won't forget you either."

We both knew there would be no point in dragging things out further, and he closed the door gently, giving me one last wave before turning back to the other people on the street. Only when I got back to my hotel and pulled my dress off did I remember that I hadn't taken my panties back from him, and the thought made me smile. Maybe he would keep them as a memento. I liked the idea that somehow, no matter where he went, he would carry a small part of me with him as proof that our short, wonderful encounter truly happened.

Chapter Two

CHARITY MEETING

~Julien~

E's perfume lingered in my room when I opened my eyes in the morning, instantly filling my memory with tantalizing images from the previous night and stirring my desire once again. Walking outside during the fire alarm with my dick still painfully hard had been agony, but a good kind of agony. The kind that held the potential of the best kind of release. The kind that made me feel alive. Even when I got back to my room by myself after I sent E away, I didn't do anything about it. Laying in my bed, I thought about her, about the classy perfection of her and the way her lips felt around my dick, and I got almost as hard from the memory as I had from the real thing. Without her there to satisfy me, I wallowed in the incompleteness of it and the longing for more. Self-denial could be a powerful turn-on, at least for me, and our encounter had given me enough ammunition to last for months.

Unfortunately, with the morning sun, I had to get back to reality, and after a quick shower in the communal bathroom, I pulled on a pair of dress pants and buttoned shirt, formal enough to make it clear I was in charge but not as stuffy as a full suit. After a quick glance in the mirror to make sure I looked the part, I headed into the office to prepare for my day.

Despite having stayed out later than me, the office director already sat at his desk, greeting me with a smile when I walked in. "Good morning, Monsieur Labrecque. I hope you had a good evening?"

The curiosity in his eyes made it clear he would love to hear more about the beautiful woman I'd left the club with, but sharing those kinds of details had never been my style. I simply gave him a nod instead. "Thank you for your hospitality last night. I'll take my files into the meeting room for the day."

I didn't have a desk since I was only visiting for a few days to meet the key people in the region. Any of the staff would have given up their desk for me, but I didn't think it necessary. I could work just as well in the meeting room without disturbing anyone. People seemed to have certain expectations of the chief executive of any business, even a charity, but I never played into that stereotype if I could help it. Having a certain job title didn't make me any better or more important than anyone else. We were all working toward the same goal.

My promotion to global operations director had come as a surprise to just about everyone. I'd only joined the organization a year earlier after cutting my teeth for several years with a charity that looked after underprivileged children around the world. That followed years of volunteering myself, during which I spent time on every continent, immersing myself in local cultures and problems as much as I could.

As satisfying as it had been to help children, the time I spent on the ground convinced me that we could make even more of an impact by empowering women. By giving them the tools to be financially secure, they could provide better homes for their children, with better educational opportunities, and provide strong, solid role models for the next generation. It was better 'bang for the buck' as the Americans said, and so when a job opening came for an assistant director with a charity that specifically focused on helping women, I jumped at the chance.

Eight months later, the global operations director decided to leave, and the board approached me to ask if I would like to take his place. I agreed on the condition that the salary be cut in half and the budget for all of my travel be funded directly by the board rather than coming out of the charity's donations. I didn't do the work to get rich or to live well off the contributions of others. In my view, money should be used to help those who needed it, not to line the pockets of people who already had enough.

That morning, I had a meeting with a volunteer who had just finished a year-long assignment in the north of the country. I'd heard great things about her and was eager to pick her brain about what had worked and what could be improved before she left the country.

First, though, I had time to go through a few emails and get caught up on any issues in the rest of our offices around the world. My assistant, Claire, had emailed me, as she did first thing every morning, with an update on my upcoming schedule.

Your flight back to Toronto is booked for tomorrow, arriving Thursday evening. Don't forget that on Sunday, you have the charity reception at the new Stamer Hotel. I've rented a suit for you and will drop it off at your house.

A groan rumbled out of me at the reminder. My least-favourite part of my new job had to be attending the extravagant receptions thrown by our donors. The head of Stamer Hotels had just made a sizable donation to us, though no one knew for sure why, and was even throwing a party to raise additional funds. People would attend just to suck up to him, not caring about our work at all. I knew I shouldn't complain when we got money out of it, but the whole world those people lived in felt grotesque to me, and spending even one night among them left me feeling dirty, not in a good way. Just one of the watches the men wore could cover several of my programs for a year, putting food in people's bellies.

"And the jewellery... mon Dieu, don't get me started on the jewellery. Comment peuvent-ils dormir la nuit?"

I hadn't realized I'd started muttering out loud, wondering how the super-rich could sleep at night in French, until someone chuckled softly from the door. "So, you talk to yourself regularly, I see."

The sound of the voice sent a shockwave through my body, and I looked up in astonishment to see the beautiful redhead from the night before smiling at me. Her hair was swept up in a messy bun and she wore a casual suit in a deep green colour that complimented her hair and colouring perfectly. It certainly contrasted with the ravishing, elegant dress she'd had on the night before, but if anything, she looked even better in the cold light of day.

What in the world was she doing there?

"Can I... help you?" Had she tracked me down on purpose? How? Why? The idea that she might want more of the same had my body buzzing, but it could also be a red flag, not to mention that I had to remember where I was. I kept my work and personal life separate, always, both for my sake and the charity's.

"You must be Julien Labrecque." She stepped forward, extending her hand confidently. "I'm Eve Sudlow. We have an appointment."

I knew that name; I'd just been looking at it on my schedule. *She* was the volunteer I was supposed to meet? The odds of that must have been astronomical, and though she smiled at me, looking cool and in control, I could see the surprise in her eyes too. She hadn't known we shared a professional connection any more than I had, and in that room, our roles were reversed. Technically, I was her boss. The power rested with me.

"It's a pleasure to meet you. Please, have a seat and we can begin."

~Eve~

My first clue that fate might be having a laugh at my expense came when I walked into the office and immediately recognized the man from the bar the night before; not the one I'd left with, but his friend who I'd helped him brush off. The friendly older man greeted me as I walked into the charity's Quito office, and from the greeting he gave me, I could tell he didn't recognize me from the club. It had been dark, I'd had the other man's arm around me, and he'd only gotten a glimpse of me. Perhaps his gaze had been focused more on my dress than my face. Whatever the reason, he gave no indication that he knew me, but it didn't take a genius to connect the rest of the dots.

The two men had seemed like acquaintances rather than good friends, and the man I went back to the hotel with told me he hadn't been in Quito for long. It made sense that a work colleague would have taken him out, so reason dictated that the man whose face had been buried between my legs not that many hours ago might also be there in the office that morning.

My dad said there was no such thing as a coincidence. If someone kept popping back up in your life, like my mom had in his when they first met, it meant something. An opportunity lay behind it if you were smart enough and brave enough to recognize it.

"Monsieur Labrecque is in the meeting room just there," the man, who introduced himself as Luis, told me as he pointed to a small room at the end of the hall. Its door sat open but I couldn't see anyone inside. "Would you like some coffee?"

"Yes, please." I'd mastered the art of using a drink to buy me time to think during a presentation or interview situation. This meeting would technically be neither of those, but in a way, it would also be both. I wanted to highlight the work I had done and make a good impression on the global director so that if my dad agreed to the proposal I planned to make to him, I would already have a good relationship set up with the charity's head.

"Go on ahead and I'll bring it to you," Luis promised. "Don't be shy, Monsieur Labrecque is very approachable."

That was good news. I'd done a little research on him prior to that morning, though I couldn't find much about him online. The charity website had no photos of him and there were too many Julien Labrecques on social media to be able to guess which one he might be, since none of them mentioned the charity's work. The details of his career were easy enough to find, but anything more personal proved elusive. He seemed to dislike having his picture taken, but that would have to change now that he'd taken on his new role. Public relations were part of running a business, even if that business was charitable. Maybe I could give him a few pointers on that as part of the deal I hoped to strike.

Looking forward to learning more about the elusive Julien, I made my way down the hall, ready to greet him with a confident smile, but my steps slowed as I heard someone speaking. At first, I hesitated because I thought he might have someone else with him or be on the phone, but as a few more words drifted out to me, a jolt of recognition hit me.

The sexy French accent and timbre of his voice would have been familiar to me anywhere, and as I stepped close enough to realize only one person was in the room, the realization hit me with full force: the man I had come there to see was none other than the man whose mouth I had stuffed with my panties the night before.

In all my business training, they'd never covered how to deal with *that* particular situation.

In the split second that I hovered by the door, a hundred different thoughts flew through my head at once. Would he regret what happened between us once he knew who I was? Should I say something about the night before, or pretend we'd never met? Even when it occurred to me that he might work for the charity, I never pegged him as the director, but as soon as I made the connection, I couldn't say why it hadn't crossed my mind. His confidence and his intelligence had been clear to me the night before, so why *shouldn't* he be running a major international charity?

Nothing that happened between us the night before had been un-pleasant to either of us, so why should I act ashamed of it? He seemed perfectly at home in that world, much more so than I did, so I didn't think he would hold it against me.

More intrigued than ever, I quickly put on a smile and made a gentle joke to announce my presence and break the ice. Disbelief flashed across his face as I introduced myself, but he kept his composure just as I did. As he gestured to the seat across from him, I took my spot at the table with as much grace as I could, pulling out my file folder and pen to maintain an air of professionalism. Luis brought my coffee in, gave us both a smile, still not recognizing me, and closed the door behind him, leaving Julien and I alone in the private, enclosed space.

Julien spoke first, getting straight to business. "I understand you've been a project manager for the last year, Ms Sudlow. Your office has been mentioned repeatedly to me as a success story, so before you leave us, I wanted to get a chance to find out what worked so well, and if you have any suggestions on how we can make improvements."

Those warm brown eyes of his looked sharp and astute in the meeting room's natural light. A large window overlooked a small garden behind the building, shared between all the buildings on the block, and the morning sun streamed in, highlighting his handsome, chiselled face and the light stubble along his jawline. It took all my concentration not to let my gaze drift downward as I remembered how he had looked standing naked in front of me.

Tapping the folder in front of me, I leaned forward. "I do have a few ideas, actually, and I was delighted when I found out you would be in town to go over them. The timing couldn't be better, but please, call me Eve."

His lips twitched as he tried not to smile, obviously putting together what the 'E' had stood for the previous evening. "Very well. Let's see what you've got, Eve."

For the next forty-five minutes, I went through the documents I'd prepared, showing which of the programs I've worked on had been most effective, which ones hadn't worked as well, and which I thought still had more potential. Along with the charts showing our results, I also had projections of what could be done with increased funding and manpower, not only in Ecuador, but throughout similar parts of South and Central America.

"This is very impressive," Julien told me when I had wrapped up my planned presentation. "What's your academic background?"

Since he could find it on my personnel file, I listed off my Ivy League school, the same one my father had gone to, and his father before him. "I studied business."

His eyebrows raised, but I couldn't tell if the reaction was a negative or positive one. "Not many people would give up a year of working after such an expensive degree to come and volunteer their time."

He could hardly have given me a better set-up, and though I hadn't planned on saying anything until I spoke about it with my dad first, the words spilled out of my mouth anyway. "Actually, I think they would if it could be positioned to them in a more mutually beneficial light. I've had an idea for an internship program that combines volunteer work with charities like this one with a more traditional internship within a business. Businesses would sign up to be part of the program, their potential employees would be exposed to far more of the world, and businesses get candidates who are more socially aware and not afraid of a little hard work. I don't have the numbers here with me today, but I think a program like that could meet the extra personnel demands in the plans I've shown you, and if the businesses make a contribution to the charity as part of taking part in the program, it offsets the charity's costs. From the business' point of view, they get good publicity. Everybody wins."

My hope that he would greet that idea with the enthusiasm I thought it deserved turned out to be misplaced. Wariness clouded Julien's expression instead. "I'm not sure I love the idea of a bunch of spoiled rich kids using us as a stepping stone to prove their virtue."

That stereotype seemed a little harsh, but I could understand his concern. I'd met the odd person in my social circle who would be useless in a field office, but as a whole, my peers weren't quite as vapid as he seemed to think. "I think you'd be surprised how many of them would actually enjoy it, but ultimately, that's not the point."

"And what is 'the point'?"

He mimicked my accent good-naturedly as he repeated my words, and I couldn't help smiling before returning to my argument. "The point is that you would get free, well-educated labour from people who want to make a good impression, and additional funding from the participating businesses. You would need to hire extra people to run the program and coordinate the logistics, but I'm convinced it would more than pay for itself. I even have a couple of large businesses in mind for a pilot project."

All of that was true; I hoped that in the next few days, I could convince my dad that Stamer Hotels should be one of them.

"And do you have someone in mind to run this pilot project?" His eyebrows raised as if he might have already guessed but I answered with full confidence anyway.

"I thought that I would. As long as you hire me."

~Julien~

Eve turned out to be nothing like I expected and exactly what I thought she'd be all at the same time.

Poised, confident and well-spoken, she looked just as in control in the meeting room as she had in the bedroom. When I pushed back against her in any way, she stood her ground, offering me clear and thoughtful responses in a respectful tone. As much as she acknowledged my authority, she showed no signs of being intimidated by it. I honestly couldn't imagine what it might take to intimidate her.

And yet, she seemed to possess an idealism I wouldn't have expected. Most new volunteers finished their time feeling more sober and realistic about the very real challenges faced by the people we helped, but Eve radiated a natural optimism that only became more pronounced as she outlined the idea for her program. Genuine enthusiasm sparkled in her dark eyes, drawing me in and making me almost want to believe what she suggested could be accomplished as easily as she made it sound. Unfortunately, after ten years in the field, I'd become a little more jaded, especially when it came to the type of privileged people at the heart of her plan.

Her admission that she had gone to one of the most prestigious colleges in the United States took me by surprise most of all. How did she afford that? I could easily see her charming her way into a scholarship, and she had the intelligence to back it up. Had she worked while studying to pay her fees? Did she have debts that she'd put off for the year she'd just spent with us? I wanted to ask, but in the context of our professional meeting, it didn't seem appropriate.

Those concerns quickly left my mind anyway when she announced that she thought I should hire her to run the program she'd proposed.

In some ways, it shouldn't have surprised me. It couldn't be more of a classic business school move to make herself indispensable: identify a potential solution that only she could solve. I admired both the chutzpah behind her suggestion and the twinkle in her eyes that let me know she was completely aware of just how cheeky it sounded. If she'd said it with no self-awareness, it would have come across as arrogant; instead, with her natural grace and good humour, it struck me as charming.

And I'd be damned if the idea of hiring her didn't appeal to me. Any program like the one she'd outlined would be run from our head office in Toronto, meaning the person in charge would be working right alongside me. The thought of seeing her in the office and spending much, much more time with her appealed to me far more than it should have for someone who had always made it a point to never mix business and pleasure before.

Just like I couldn't stop staring at the strands of hair that had worked their way loose from her updo and curled around her neck, almost begging to be touched.

Clearing my throat, I tried to bring my thoughts back into focus. "We're a long way off making any hiring decisions for a program that doesn't exist, Eve, but if you're serious, of course I would be willing to hear a full proposal, along with the charity's board."

She drew in a quick breath as I said her name, the first real hint she'd given me that she might also be thinking about our encounter the night before, and my heart rate immediately quickened.

Her next words didn't slow it down any. "How quickly could you set up a meeting? I'll be in Toronto all of next week and I would be happy to meet with all of you then. The proposal is nearly ready."

She would be coming to the city where I lived? Once again, the odds seemed almost inconceivable, and I had to take a deep breath of my own to try to stop my body's natural reaction to the thought of spending more time with her, showing her around the city, and showing her my home, including the room in my basement...

Crisse, I needed to concentrate.

"What are you doing in Toronto?" I managed to ask without sounding too flustered.

"My father has some business to do there and he invited me to join him. It seemed like a relatively calm way to ease back into my old life since things will be full steam once I get back to New York. I leave for Canada this afternoon."

It didn't surprise me in the least to learn that she called New York home, but the idea of her in Toronto for a whole week still had my body humming. I would like to hear her proposal, but more than that, I wanted to spend more time with her outside of the office. Would that influence my decision about whether or not to back her proposal? The board would make the final decision, but they would certainly ask for my input. I thought I could keep my personal and professional feelings separate, but I'd never been put to the test quite so directly.

"Have you been there before?" Tentatively, I turned the conversation down a more personal path, and as I hoped, Eve willingly followed me down it.

"I have, but not for years. Not as an adult. I'm sure there's a lot I haven't seen. When do you go back?"

The invitation in her words couldn't be clearer as she set me up perfectly to offer to show her around. She gave the illusion of leaving the decision in my hands while she had actually arranged all the pieces. That kind of graceful maneuvering, that subtle domination, might feel pushy to some men, but not to me. To me, it felt perfect. I knew what she wanted, and to please her, I simply had to give it to her. She'd removed all the guesswork for me.

"I get back on Thursday. I have Friday off and I'm free most of the weekend. If you have any time available, I would be delighted to take you to some of my favourite places."

Eve's satisfied smile sent another shot of anticipation through me, reminding me of the state she'd left me in the night before and calling to mind a dozen ways we might return to that kind of situation.

Business still had to be taken into consideration, though, so I added a disclaimer. "I can let my assistant know about your request for a meeting. If it's possible to set something up next week, she will. Anything we do on the weekend would be completely separate, as friends, not potential colleagues."

"Of course," she agreed, her voice low and warm like a purr. "On that basis, let me give you my number."

My phone sat next to my computer, so I unlocked it and pushed it across the table to her. Watching the sure, confident way she handled it set my heart racing even faster. As incredible as our short time together the night before had been, I knew without a doubt that we could have a lot more fun with a more open-ended encounter. We'd need to set some ground rules first, but it felt like we were still on the same page, and I already knew I had another long, exquisitely painful night ahead of me, dreaming of her and what might happen in just a few short days when we were reunited half a world away. No torture could be sweeter.

"I'll be expecting your call." Eve's words sounded almost like an order as she passed the phone back to me, an order I had no intention of disobeying. "It's been a pleasure to meet you, Julien."

She hadn't said my name yet, and the sound of it almost sent a shiver down my spine until I remembered where we were. "Thank you for the hard work you've done here, and I appreciate your time in speaking with me this morning."

Even though she bowed her head in acknowledgement, her eyes remained on me, letting me know, as subtly as everything else she did, that despite outward appearances, she still held the upper hand.

I walked her back to the office door, shaking hands with her professionally in front of the other people in the office, and as I walked back to the meeting room on my own, I couldn't help wondering what they would think if they knew I'd been on my knees for her the night before, and fully intended to be again, just as soon as she'd let me.

Chapter Three

TORONTO

The smile stayed on my face as the taxi wound through the sun-drenched city streets on the way to the airport. I wouldn't have imagined it could be possible, but after our meeting, I found Julien even more attractive than I had before. Passionate and committed could be added to the rapidly-growing list of his positive qualities, joining the others I'd already chalked up from our evening together: intelligent, sexy, good with his tongue, and very good at following orders.

He had an understated charisma that drew me in, and I imagined it worked on others too. Without even trying, he could command a room not by being the loudest or the boldest, but through his sense of purpose and quiet confidence. Someone with his skill set could easily be running a Fortune 500 company, but he had chosen not to. He used his talents to help those who needed it instead, and I admired that more than I could say.

We had more in common than just our sexual preferences, but our compatibility in that area and the idea of being alone with him again to explore them even further was what had me smiling most of all, especially when my phone buzzed with a text before I even reached the airport.

I don't think you fully appreciate what this does to me.

Beneath it, he attached a screenshot of the entry I'd left in his phone: my number under the heading "Madame E".

Biting my lip to keep my grin from growing too wide, I sent back a quick response. *On the contrary: I know, and I want you thinking about it until you see me again.*

His reply was two simple words, all the more effective for their directness. *It's working.*

When Sara took me to the club the night before, she said she wanted me to leave Ecuador with a smile on my face, and in that, she had most certainly succeeded.

My dad had booked my flight, so naturally, he'd bought me a first-class seat for the short flight to Panama and the longer one to Toronto. The flight attendant offered me champagne as I sat down, and I had to keep from grimacing, trying not to think how the flight probably cost more than what most of the women I'd been working with in Ecuador made in a year.

"Heading home for the holidays?" the man next to me on the flight from Panama to Toronto asked in a central European accent as I got settled into the spacious seat. His hand rested casually on the armrest of his chair, showing off the Hublot watch on his wrist. Older than my father, handsome and distinguished, I might have taken his question for simple friendliness if it weren't for the way I'd noticed him checking out my chest when I put my bag in the overhead bin.

"Not yet. Business first." I flashed him a friendly smile before pulling out my e-reader, a clear signal that I would prefer not to talk.

He didn't take the hint. "I'm travelling for business as well. It can get pretty monotonous after a while."

"Hmmm." I made a noncommittal noise of vague agreement, once again signalling my disinterest.

He responded by leaning closer. "Perhaps we can find a way to break the monotony together."

With an arched eyebrow, I looked back over at him. "Does that line ever work?"

He blinked at me in surprise for a second before letting out a laugh. "Quite often, actually."

"Better luck next time, then." We shared a brief smile of understanding before I turned my attention back to my tablet while he pulled out a newspaper, proceeding to ignore me for the rest of the flight. Some women would have found his forthrightness sexy, but when I contrasted it to the way Julien behaved, reading my cues perfectly and following my lead, I knew without a doubt which I found more appealing.

A concierge waited for me as I got off the plane to usher me through the immigration checks. My bags would be collected for me later, everything taken care of by my dad, who sat waiting for me in the first-class lounge. The words sat on the tip of my tongue, ready to admonish him for wasting so much money on me, but when I saw the genuine excitement in his eyes as I approached, I swallowed my complaints back down. He didn't mean to be so extravagant; he just wanted to take care of me, and there were worse things than being spoiled by my dad once in a while.

"Hey, Dad." I beamed at him as he put his drink down on the mahogany bar and got to his feet, wrapping me up in a strong, firm hug. His suit and cologne were so familiar that I could almost forget I'd only seen him once in the last year, when he and my mom came to Ecuador for a visit in the summer. "You didn't have to come all the way out here."

The airport was nowhere near the city-centre Stamer hotel where we'd be staying. One of the most prestigious hotels in the city, my mom had designed it about fifteen years earlier, and it remained just as elegant as it had been when it opened.

"Of course I came. It's so good to see you, Eve." The pride in his eyes melted my heart even further, almost making me blush. "The car's waiting, you must be exhausted."

Without waiting for me to agree, he led me to the exit, and the blast of cold air that hit me as the doors opened took my breath away. It couldn't be more of a contrast to the previous night when I'd been walking around Quito in just my dress and heels. Although I'd brought my heaviest Ecuadorian coat along, it did little to protect me from the sting of the below-zero air against my skin.

The uniformed driver of the town car sprang out of his seat as he saw us coming, hurrying to open the back door for me. Inside, the interior had been kept comfortably warm, but I still shivered as I settled into my seat. "That's going to take a bit of getting used to," I admitted while my dad chuckled.

"You'll re-acclimatize in no time."

I had a feeling he was referring to more than just the weather.

"How did the last week go?" he asked once we were on our way into the city in the darkness of the late evening. Snow lined the city streets and Christmas lights twinkled from the houses we passed, bringing up a million memories of Christmases over the years. The sunny streets of Quito seemed like a distant memory though I had just left there that morning.

Still looking out the window, not wanting to miss any of the decorations, I answered my dad's question. "Everything went well. I filed all my final reports and I met with the charity's new director today." My parents and I talked weekly while I was away, so he knew all about my work already.

"You met with Julien Labrecque?"

Hearing my dad say Julien's name out loud made my head turn sharply back to him, and I quickly tucked some stray hairs behind my ear in an attempt to cover my reaction. "That's right. Do you know him?"

My dad shook his head. "No. I read about him the other day though. He sounds pretty impressive, and very committed to the charity."

The idea of my dad researching Julien struck me as funny even as I raised my eyebrows at him in disapproval. "You're still checking up on me?"

"I'm taking an interest," he corrected me drily. "I'm proud of you and the work you've done. Once you're settled in tomorrow, we can talk more about what comes next."

That was my plan too, though I knew my ideas for the future were probably quite a bit different to his. With that ahead of me, as well as Julien's impending arrival, I would need to get a good night's sleep, so when we arrived back at the hotel, I made my excuses for an early night.

My stay in Toronto didn't seem like it would be a quiet one, so I better rest while I could.

~Julien~

The prospect of seeing Eve again kept me in a good mood through the long and cramped journey back to Toronto. My job required a lot of travel since I couldn't really get a feel for what life was like in a remote part of the world by talking through a computer, nor could I connect with people on a more personal level. Especially in my new position, it mattered to me that people saw me as a real person, not some talking head sitting in a comfortable office far removed from their world.

In the waiting area in Panama, I reread Eve's message from the day before, though I had read it so many times already, I knew it by heart. During our in-person meeting, neither of us had made any reference to the evening we'd spent together, but when I checked my phone afterwards and realized she'd entered her number as 'Madame E', my body immediately prickled with excitement. It meant she wanted more, just as I'd hoped, since I certainly did too. No one had captured my attention so firmly in a very long time.

As my flight began boarding, I slipped the phone back into my pocket and watched as the businessmen in their suits all boarded the plane first, heading for their first-class seats. Watching people throw money away always annoyed me, but first-class travel had to be one of the worst examples. The flight lasted just over five hours, and for a slightly bigger seat and a slightly better meal, people would pay more than five times what my seat in the back of the plane cost. We all ended up in the same place eventually. Was there really *nothing* better they could think of to spend that money on? Were they so blind to the needs of others? People had to travel, I understood that as much as anyone, but why they had to travel first-class, I simply couldn't wrap my head around.

After making it through the flight where I did my best to work while sandwiched between a grandmother on her way to spend Christmas with her family and a man who decided to watch porn on his phone for half the flight, I made it through the long lines at immigration, the wait at the luggage carousel, where my bag always seemed to be the last off the plane no matter when I checked in, and onto the bus to the nearest subway station. A train ran between the airport and Union Station downtown, but it cost almost four times as much as the subway fare, so I couldn't justify it, not even when the cold air blasted through the bus doors at every stop, making me glad I'd packed my winter coat, scarf and gloves. Well over an hour later, I finally made it back to my row house in the east side of Toronto's downtown, an area known as Cabbagetown.

Calling it 'my' house wouldn't be entirely accurate; I didn't own it, but I had been renting it for eight years, ever since I moved to Toronto from my native Québec City. The house belonged to an old family friend who didn't care about the fact that she could charge triple what I paid if she rented to someone else. It had provided an income for her throughout much of her life, and in her retirement, she simply wanted me to have a secure and steady place to stay. Whenever I saw her, she hinted that it would make a perfect family home, not understanding why I hadn't settled down yet. I told her my lifestyle made it difficult, and when she chose to believe that I meant the amount of travel that I had to do, I didn't correct her.

That was part of it, certainly, but not all of it. Finding a woman who didn't care about the size of my bank account, accepted the demands of my job *and* suited me sexually made things much more difficult.

The path to my front door had been cleared of snow and when I unlocked the front door, the savoury, comforting smell of a beef stew bubbling away in the slow cooker in the kitchen hit my nose. "Merci, Claire," I murmured as I dropped my bags inside the door and began removing all my winter layers. After three weeks in South America, returning to the Canadian winter came as a bit of a shock, but coming home to a warm meal certainly helped.

The long, narrow Victorian house had a typical layout for the period when it had been built. Downstairs, the front door opened into the living room, with the staircase straight ahead. At the rear of the house, overlooking the backyard, were the eat-in kitchen and a small office. In the summer, I would often sit out in the backyard with its border of shrubs and wildflowers. In winter, though, all I could see out the back window would be drifts of snow beneath the dark, starry sky.

Inside the kitchen, along with the stew, I found a garment bag hanging from the bag of one of the chairs and a note on the table.

Hope you had a good flight! This is your suit for the Stamer benefit on Sunday. I hope you don't mind that I went ahead and put your tree up too since you've been away. If you need anything else, or just want some company, give me a call. I'm available all weekend. Claire

My tree? I hadn't even noticed, but sure enough, when I returned to the living room and flipped the light on, my small artificial Christmas tree had been set up in the corner next to the fireplace. I had brought the tree and the box of decorations up from the basement before I left, intending to put it up when I returned, and Claire had taken it upon herself to do it for me.

No matter how many times I told my assistant that things like shovelling my sidewalk, making me dinner, and decorating my Christmas tree went far above and beyond her job description, she insisted that she had the time and it made her feel good to be able to help me. Since we were in the business of helping people, I took her at her word. She had a key to my house for the times like this when she needed to be able to drop off my drycleaning, and though it made me slightly uncomfortable that she spent time there without me around, I couldn't find an actual reason to complain. She certainly never made a mess; on the contrary, things were always in better shape after her visits than before. I had nothing to hide except, perhaps, the things in my basement room, which had a separate lock so she wouldn't be able to stumble upon them.

The thought of that room instantly took my thoughts away from Claire and back to Eve. I had forced myself not to message her until I got home in case there were delays on the subway or I got held up for any other reason. She was not the kind of woman to be kept waiting. Now that I'd arrived, though, I couldn't wait to get in touch and see if she would have time to see me that evening. I would need to shower and shave, but that wouldn't take long. Despite my fatigue from the day of travelling, the idea of seeing her immediately re-energized me.

Bonsoir, Madame E. As you instructed, I've been thinking of you all day. Now that I'm back in the city, I would love to make those thoughts a reality, however, whenever and wherever is convenient for you. Yours, J

Hopefully, that didn't sound too pushy. Usually, my relationships of this nature were more formal, and communication protocols would be negotiated ahead of time. Some women never allowed me to make first contact. Eve was the first domme I had come across 'in the wild', so to speak, and I didn't even know if she considered herself a domme or how much experience she had. We still had a lot to learn about each other, which I hoped we could start to do that very evening, if she agreed.

My prayers were, thankfully, answered, and in very little time at all. My phone buzzed with a reply not much more than a minute after I messaged her.

I'm having dinner with my father, but I'll be free afterwards. I'd like to see where you live. Send me your address and put on something festive. I'll be there at nine.

~Eve~

I couldn't hide my satisfied smile as I slipped my phone back into my purse and took a sip of my wine. All day, I'd been hoping that Julien would get in touch when he got back to the city, and his message had been exactly what I'd hoped for. He wanted to see me, he made that clear, and he left the nature of our encounter entirely up to me. If I'd told him I wanted to go see a movie, he would have agreed. If I'd said I wanted to go skinny-dipping in Lake Ontario, he would have said yes to that too. What made it special, though, was that he didn't act that way merely to try to have sex with me. If I told him we weren't having sex that evening, he would accept that. He let me take control simply because he enjoyed yielding his authority to me, and that filled me with an entirely different kind of satisfaction than if he had done it for a different kind of reward.

The parallels between the situation and my parents' relationship weren't lost on me. I'd asked my mom once how she and my dad knew they shared the same kink when they met, and she admitted she'd had no idea at first. "It just felt right and natural when we started. We figured it out as we went along."

That was how things felt with Julien too: right and natural, at least so far. I didn't want to jump the gun or read too much into it, but my anticipation for what the evening might bring had my whole body humming. For that reason, I'd chosen to go to his place so that we would have as much privacy as possible. Although I had my own room at the hotel, my dad was staying right next door, and the possibility, however remote, that he might come over while Julien and I were in the middle of something, discouraged me from inviting Julien to come and meet me there. On top of that, I was simply curious about where he lived and what his life looked like when he wasn't travelling the world for work.

As I raised my wine glass to my lips again, my dad came in through the doors of the restaurant, catching my eye from across the room and giving me a curt nod of apology before being immediately waylaid by someone else who wanted his attention. He was fifteen minutes late, but I had expected that. Whenever we travelled for his business, people treated him like a celebrity, everyone wanting a minute of his time. He didn't do it on purpose, and waiting with the excellent wine and the beautiful view hadn't exactly been a hardship.

The Stardust dining room on the 27th floor of the Stamer hotel had a reputation as one of the best restaurants in the city, and of course, we had the best table with an incredible view overlooking the city. Holiday lights twinkled in the distance, the CN Tower illuminated in green and red, while inside, the restaurant had been decorated in reds and golds, festive and elegant. The wine had already been waiting when I got to the table, and I didn't even want to know how expensive the bottle was. I only knew it tasted incredible.

"Are you feeling better?" He pressed his hand against my forehead as soon as he arrived at the table, as if I were still a little girl.

"I'm not sick, Dad. Just tired, but I *am* feeling better." I'd excused myself from a meeting earlier that afternoon because I needed to rest, but that had only been a half truth. Mostly, it had just been incredibly jarring to go from my office in Ecuador where we worked to help people find a few extra dollars to be able to afford food for their children, to sitting in a corporate boardroom with million-dollar sums being tossed around as if they were nothing.

My dad took a seat across from me as a waiter hurried over to pour him a glass of wine. "Good. I'm glad you're feeling more like yourself because I've asked someone to join us for dinner."

My heart immediately sank though I tried not to show it. I'd been hoping to get a chance to broach the topic of my proposal with him amongst the casual chatter of a private meal, but having someone else with us would make that almost impossible. "You're not trying to set me up, are you?" I teased to cover my disappointment, and as I expected, he smirked in amusement.

"Not romantically. I'm sure you can hold your own in that department."

He had that right, but I'd noticed he hadn't said no completely. "Professionally, then?"

"It's just an idea," he said, while I groaned internally. Not only would I not get a chance to talk about *my* ideas, he obviously had something in mind for what he thought I should be doing next. "I've asked our regional director for South America to join us. Now that you've got some insight into the region, you might be interested to know what our upcoming plans are."

I bit my tongue rather than point out how the 'insights' I had would have nothing to do with the luxury hotel market, and when the director joined us, I did my best to appear engaged and interested throughout the conversation. Once dinner had finished, though, I excused myself once again. "It's been a pleasure to meet you, but I'm still adjusting to the shorter daylight hours. It feels like it's several hours later than it actually is."

Both men smiled indulgently. "Of course," the director agreed. "Your father can pass on my contact information so we can chat more another time."

That wouldn't be happening, but of course I kept those thoughts to myself, simply saying thank you before turning to my dad. "Will I see you tomorrow?"

He gave me an apologetic grimace. "I've got a business dinner in the evening, and more meetings during the day, but you don't need to join me for them. I'm sure you'd like to just see the city and do some shopping and relax. We can have brunch on Saturday."

That sounded perfect, actually. A day off to recalibrate and maybe spend some more time with Julien, depending how our evening went, and then a leisurely brunch where I could talk to my dad one-on-one. "I'd love that. Have a good night."

The clock had just ticked past eight by the time I got back to my room, which suited me perfectly since it gave me time to change into something a little less formal for my evening with Julien. He'd seen me in the black dress I wore to the club in Quito and in the business casual suit I wore to our meeting the following day, but he hadn't seen me in my everyday clothes. I'd told him to wear something festive that evening and I intended to follow suit. My mom had sent a suitcase full of clothes for me with my dad, things I might need for the winter climate, and from that selection, I pulled on a form-fitting red sweater that complemented my hair, a checked red, white and black skirt and knee-high high-heeled black boots. Leaving my hair down, I put on a white coat, scarf and hat to make the black boots stand out even more.

I knew the look worked when I walked through the hotel lobby and felt the eyes of half the men in the room on me. As flattering as that might be, I only had one man on my mind that evening that I wanted to impress.

The taxi pulled up outside the address that Julien had sent me just before nine. His house sat on a quiet residential street full of Victorian row houses, most of them decorated with Christmas lights with glowing trees visible through their front windows. Julien's was no exception, the lights of his tree twinkling through the glass as I made my way to the front door.

The door opened before I even reached it, letting me know that he'd been waiting and watching for me, and his reaction as he took in the sight of me was all I could have hoped for. Swallowing hard as his eyes scanned me from head to toe, he looked like someone about to jump out of a plane: up for an adventure but also slightly terrified.

"Bonsoir, Eve." He kissed my cheek as he ushered me inside his house. A fire crackled in the fireplace next to the decorated tree I had seen from the window, and soft music played in the background, a mellow jazz version of a Christmas carol. It felt warm and comfortable and utterly inviting. "Somehow, you look even better than I remembered. May I take your coat?"

He looked wonderful too, I noticed, as he took my outer garments from me. He'd shaved his face, the stubble of the previous days gone, and it showed off the strong line of his jaw and his full lips even better than before. Jeans and a Christmas sweater had never looked as good as they did on his lean, firm body. He wore only socks on his feet, but when I went to remove my boots, he let out a stifled groan of disappointment.

"You can leave those on, if you like. It's up to you, of course."

So, he liked the boots. I had intended to take them off since they still dripped with melting snow, but if he didn't mind, then I wouldn't let it bother me either. Walking into the centre of the room, my heels clicking on the hardwood floor just as they had in his hotel room a few nights earlier and half a world away, I turned back to him and raised my eyebrows, getting straight to the point.

"You said you've been thinking about me, so tell me: what exactly did you have in mind for tonight?"

Chapter Four

CHECKLIST

~Julien~

The sight of Eve standing in my living room with her flaming red hair, effortlessly stylish clothes and those black boots that hugged her calves so perfectly would have brought any man to his knees. I could only thank my lucky stars for whatever good fortune had brought her into my life and especially to my house that night. When she asked me what I had in mind, the possibilities were so vast and varied that I barely knew where to begin.

However, before we got to any kind of intimate situation, I wanted to know more about her sexual background. Not who she'd slept with or how many people or anything like what, but what kind of experience she had with the dynamic that we'd fallen into so naturally in Quito. Talking things over first would help to avoid any awkward or uncomfortable situations later, no matter how much I would prefer to dive right in.

"I have a checklist that we could fill in before we begin, if you're interested in continuing what we started in Ecuador."

Her eyebrows raised curiously, her dark eyes watching me closely. "A checklist? I didn't realize there was paperwork involved."

Since her tone was teasing, I smiled. "I find it's a good way to set limits ahead of time. You haven't filled one out before?"

For the first time since I met her, Eve looked the tiniest bit unsure. "No, I haven't, but I'm happy to." As quickly as it came on, her uncertainty vanished, and with a nod of determination, she took control again. "Explain to me how it works."

"Please, have a seat." I gestured towards the sofa in front of the fire, and while she walked over to it, I grabbed the papers and pens I had set out earlier, along with a book to make it easier to write on. Sitting down next to her, close but not too close, I handed one of the papers to her. "It's very simple. On the left is a list of sexual practices and you check off if you've done them or not and if you like them or not. If there's anything either of us don't like, we won't do it. If there's something one or both of us haven't tried, we can talk about whether we're interested in trying it. And obviously, if there's something we both like, that moves to the top of the list, especially while we're getting to know each other."

Eve glanced down the list quickly before looking over at me. "Can we just fill it out together?"

With my natural desire to please, that had caused problems for me in the past. "I've found it's better to do it separately. That way, no one feels pressured to say they like something if they really don't. The more honest we are, the better the results."

She nodded in understanding before giving the list another quick glance. "I'm not sure I know what all of these mean."

As I'd suspected, her experience didn't quite match up to her confidence, but that was fine. No one started out knowing everything. Technique could be taught but chemistry couldn't, and Eve and I already had that to spare. "The first time I did one of these lists, I had to ask my partner to tell me what half of them meant. Ask me if you don't know, I would be happy to answer."

Nodding again, she started at the top and began to work her way down while I started to fill out my own list. Though my preferences were pretty well defined by that point, I always liked to complete the form fresh with each new partner. Sometimes, different women inspired different feelings in me, and with Eve, my limits seemed more fluid than ever.

"Is anal for you or me?" she asked bluntly, pointing to the question that she'd stopped at.

"In that section, it means for you. There are plugs and pegging for me further down here." On her form, I pointed to the applicable questions, trying not to look at her other answers until we had both finished.

"Fire play?" was her next question.

"That one's pretty advanced, but essentially, you would set me on fire."

Her eyes widened in surprise. "Have you done that before?"

"Once, yes."

She looked at me as if seeing me again for the first time, full of curiosity but no judgement. "Did you like it?"

"I'll tell you when we compare the forms," I reminded her with a smile. "Keep going."

For another minute or two, we both worked on the forms until Eve had another question. "Corset? For me or you?"

"Me. I have one I can wear under my clothes if you'd like me to. No one would know except the two of us, but it's a way for you to maintain control over me even when we're apart."

Nodding slowly, she looked back down at the list. She had filled out most of it but some of the fields remained empty. "I didn't realize there was so much to this."

Merde. It seemed like she might be getting overwhelmed and the last thing I wanted to do was scare her off. "It's as much or as little as we choose to make it. If you want to leave some questions blank, that's okay too. The whole point of this is to help us find our comfort zone, and then push it only in the ways that will be fun for both of us. It helps ease the uncertainty when you're not sure how far to take things."

That seemed to make her feel better, but she didn't go back to the form just yet. "How long have you known that you found this kind of thing fun?"

It flattered me that she asked, and I wanted to be as open with her as possible, especially since I had the same questions for her. "I think I had a vague awareness of it from very early on. Even in school, I was drawn to the 'bossy' girls who told me what to do. In university, I had a 'normal' girlfriend but even though she was a wonderful person, our sex life always felt a bit flat. I didn't fully understand why until I went to a strip club with some friends for a night out and one of the women gave a dominatrix performance. That night opened my eyes, and when I started dipping my toe into the club scene, I soon found what I'd been missing. Unfortunately, my girlfriend wasn't interested, and we parted ways."

Eve folded her hands in her lap over the piece of paper. "So, you go to clubs?"

"I have. At the start, almost exclusively. More recently, I've had private partners that I found online. Even *more* recently, I haven't had anything because I've been busy with work and travel. That night in Quito was the first time I'd indulged in months."

She soaked in every word, paying careful attention. "And do you love these women or is this simply sex to you?"

She didn't pull any punches, just as I expected. I wouldn't want her to, and again, I answered truthfully. "It's more than sex but probably not what you mean by love. The fulfillment I get from serving a domme goes beyond the bedroom, but I've never been in a real relationship with someone that also included a submissive element."

"Intentionally?"

Although her question only consisted of one word, I understood the meaning behind it perfectly well: did I purposefully separate sex and my 'real' life? "No, not intentionally. It just hasn't worked out that any of the women I serve are compatible with the rest of my life, or vice versa."

When she looked down again at the list in her lap, I added one more thing.

"We're not signing a contract here tonight, Eve. It doesn't have to be more than tonight if you don't want it to. It doesn't even have to be tonight if you're not feeling it. I just want to be as up front with you as possible about what I'd like, because what happened between us the other night was electric. It ticked every one of my boxes, and if there's a chance we could enjoy that again, I would love to. However, I know that we have a working relationship outside of this as well that we need to consider. More than that, I'd simply like to get to know you as a person. It's a lot of things, all at once, and maybe I've come on too strong. Tell me if I have, but I want to make it completely clear that I am interested in a lot more, as long as you are too."

~Eve~

I'd only just arrived, and already the night had taken a turn I hadn't expected. As I went through Julien's list, part of me felt I'd gotten in over my head, but another part got progressively more excited as I read through each of the items. What happened between me and Julien in Ecuador clearly hadn't been a one-time thing. He hadn't been pretending to be submissive. He knew exactly what he wanted and didn't want to waste any time. By giving me the list, he made that completely clear. The question, then, was simply whether I wanted to jump into it fully. After all my fantasizing, and the amazing evening we shared in Quito, was I ready to take the plunge and really find out if dominating someone like him appealed to me for more than just a night?

Instinctively, I knew that I couldn't ask for a better guide to explore with. Kind, patient, and open, Julien answered each of my questions thoughtfully and thoroughly, never making me feel uncomfortable or ignorant for asking. As much as our situation was about sex and attraction, it was about trust and respect too. He trusted and respected me enough to tell me exactly what he wanted, and when he said that he wouldn't be upset if I took a step back, I believed that he meant it.

I didn't want to step back, though, if I was completely honest with myself. I wanted to know more, and I wanted to get to know him too, just as he said he wanted to know me. It might be a little complicated, but no one ever said life was simple. The best things were worth figuring out.

"I'm still interested, don't worry." I gave him a confident smile, even if I still felt a little out of my depth. "Why don't we look through the list together now?"

The first items would have featured on even the most vanilla of lists, so unsurprisingly, we both said yes to them all. Oral sex: of course. We'd already done that together. Vaginal sex: absolutely. Anal: I told him truthfully it hadn't been my favourite when I tried it in the past, but if he really enjoyed it, I would be willing to try again.

"You didn't answer the one about double penetration," he pointed out when we got to that section.

I hadn't, since I didn't think it applied. "Don't we need another cock to make that happen? Or have you got a second one you've hidden from me?"

He always seemed to know when I was joking, which not everyone did, and he chuckled again at my reply. "I don't like to share, so I have no intention of bringing another man in. I do, however, have a supply of toys that can achieve the same effect. Better, even, if we also get the vibrator involved."

A shiver of excitement traveled down my spine and lower, settling between my legs. I'd never been with a man who owned his own toys before, never met anyone so completely focused on his partner's pleasure. "In that case, I'll put it as 'haven't tried but would like to'."

"Excellent."

The anticipation in his eyes matched my mood exactly as we went through a few more items. Bondage was a yes for both of us, as were edging and orgasm denial, at least on his part. We discussed a safeword for him to use in those situations and he chose Quito in remembrance of our time together there.

Before we reached the more advanced items, Julien took the list from my hands. "I know there is more, but that should be enough to get us started with tonight. First, though, I hope you don't mind if I ask you a question like the one you asked me. When did you realize this is what you like?"

I could have pretended to have more experience than I truly did, but that seemed counterproductive. He had been open and frank with me, so I answered in kind. "I would say Tuesday evening when I met a handsome stranger in a bar in Quito." He laughed again, thinking I was joking, but I actually meant it seriously, so I elaborated a little more. "I had a feeling before that about what I might enjoy, but I hadn't ever taken on the role quite like that in reality. In a way, you were my first, Julien."

Julien's eyes registered his surprise and also a good amount of appreciation. "You are a natural, then."

"You seem to bring it out in me." We shared a smile of understanding before I slipped into that role again. We'd talked long enough, and after reading and thinking about so many different kinds of situations, I felt ready for some action. "Now that we're clear, I want you to carry me to the bedroom. My boots are still wet and I don't want to get water all over your floor."

"Of course, Madame E." By using the name we'd used in Quito, he made it clear we were both entirely on the same page, the one where I was calling the shots. On that sofa, he had been the teacher and me the student, but in his room, he would defer to me.

I could have made it easier for him by standing up first, but he didn't want to be easy, I understood that much from the answers he'd given on his form. He liked being pushed and challenged and if that brought him pleasure, I would do it.

After getting to his feet, Julien reached down and lifted me off the sofa with what felt like very little effort at all, his lean body deceptively strong. The stairs creaked beneath our combined weight as he carried me up to the second floor and to a large, masculine-looking bedroom. Decorated in shades of brown and beige, it looked neat and ordered but with no extraneous decoration. No pictures hung on the walls, though he must have had some amazing ones from all his travels. No decorative items graced the shelves or bedside tables. It almost looked like a monk's room, like it belonged to someone with very few material possessions of their own, and it offered very little insight into the man who slept there.

He obviously didn't have sleeping on his mind at that moment though, and neither did I. After we were interrupted by the fire alarm in Quito before we could go as far as I would have liked, I'd been daydreaming about what it would feel like to have his cock inside me, and how I would go about it. In the list that we'd just reviewed, he confirmed that all of the things I'd imagined in my dirty thoughts were things that he enjoyed too, and there in his room, nothing stood in my way from making those thoughts very, very real.

By the foot of the bed, Julien gently placed me down on my feet. "What do you need, Madame?"

I needed him naked and ready for me, but I had one other request too. "Something to hold you down."

Excitement immediately sparked in his brown eyes as he took a few steps towards his closet. "Oui, Madame. Will these suffice?"

He pulled out a pair of fabric restraints so quickly that I suspected he had got them ready in advance of my arrival, and the thought that he might have had the very same fantasies that I did made me even more excited to get started. "Those will be fine. And a condom?"

Again, he found one immediately, placing it on the bedside table.

"Good. Now, strip."

Standing there fully clothed and in control gave me a rush of power and pleasure as Julien pulled his sweater up over his head and undid the button of his jeans. As I expected, he was already hard, his cock standing at full attention as he pulled off the rest of his clothes and stood there silently, awaiting my next instruction. His body looked just as good as I remembered it; better, even, since I'd been picturing it so many times since then, and I couldn't resist stepping closer to him and wrapping my hand around his shaft, firmly and possessively. His sharp intake of breath sent another dizzying wave of power and desire racing through me.

"Tell me, Julien: after I left you that night, did you go back to your room and finish what we started? Did you make yourself come, thinking of me?"

My hand moved slowly along the length of his cock as he tried to catch his breath. "Non, madame. I knew it wouldn't be as good as what you would have given me, so I waited."

I gave him a warning squeeze, making it clear I only wanted the truth. "You waited? But you didn't even know if you would see me again."

"C'est vrai, but I waited anyway."

The way he stuttered out 'that's true' in French made my thighs clench. His accent sounded sexy all the time, but when he actually spoke in French, it took it to another level. Would he swear in French when I made him come? I couldn't wait to find out.

"On the bed."

My voice sounded huskier than usual as I gave the order, and obediently, Julien lay down and offered his arms to me as I looped one end of the fabric restraint around his wrist and the other around the bedpost. Repeating the process on the other side, I took a step back to survey him, his arms spread wide, his cock hard and ready, already leaking a tiny bit of precum. I wanted to lick it up but I also wanted to make him wait. I wanted a million things at once when it came to him, but more than anything, I wanted that cock inside me to ease the aching emptiness that grew stronger with each passing second.

"You look wonderful like that," I told him truthfully. "And now, I'm going to let you see me too. You're going to watch me while I undress, and you'll watch as I use your cock as my own personal toy. The whole time, you're not going to move a muscle or say a word. Any last questions before we begin?"

Julien smiled, his hands clenching in anticipation within his restraints. "Non, Madame. I'm at your service."

~Julien~

With Eve standing at the foot of my bed, her eyes devouring and owning every inch of me while I lay tied to the bed by my wrists, it seemed almost impossible that she could be as new to this dynamic as she claimed. The way she held herself, the cool control and confidence in her bearing and her expression, the words she used, and most of all, the way she made me feel, suggested a wealth of experience. However, since I didn't think she'd lied to me, I had to accept she simply must be a natural at it. Some kind of prodigy, maybe, and I got to be the lucky one she chose to experiment with. Rarely had I ever felt so blessed.

As soon as I gave my agreement to what Eve suggested, she mimed zipping her lips shut, letting me know that I could no longer say a word. Unless I chose to use my safeword, I had to do my best to follow her orders precisely. Some submissives liked to push their domme in order to receive a punishment which would be pleasurable for both the giver and receiver. They would speak on purpose after being ordered not to, simply to get a reaction. That had never been my style, though. If I disobeyed, I did it by accident, because I couldn't control myself in the heat of the moment, and though I would take the punishment that came with it, and enjoy it, I didn't seek it out specifically.

My cock lay flat and heavy across my stomach, its head brushing against my belly button, and every time Eve looked at it, it seemed to take on a life of its own, twitching and jumping towards her. The self-denial I'd practiced since our interrupted night in Quito had paid off: I couldn't remember the last time I felt as ready and eager for a release as I did then, and knowing that Eve would choose the method and timing of my satisfaction only made the anticipation sweeter.

Each nerve ending tingled, each part of my body primed and on edge as I watched her slowly begin to remove her clothes.

I'd seen her gorgeous pussy the other night when she let me eat her out, but I hadn't had a glimpse of the rest of her yet, and I couldn't tear my eyes away when she pulled her red sweater up and over her head, revealing a tantalizingly sexy red bra that matched the shade of her hair almost exactly. That couldn't be an accident. Everything Eve did felt deliberately designed to inspire desire and drive me crazy.

Within my restraints, my hands clenched, my fingers itching to touch her. Her pale skin looked flawless, her breasts swelled perfectly against the fabric of her bra, and the curve of her waist called to me. I could almost feel it beneath my fingertips, though my hands remained firmly tied to the bedposts. Giving me a wink, Eve turned around and undid the zipper of her skirt, pulling it down to reveal a pair of red panties that matched her bra. As she bent down to remove her skirt, she gave me a perfect view of the thin piece of fabric between her legs, just barely covering her pussy that I remembered so well. I'd been dreaming about the taste of her, and I couldn't wait to taste her again, and hopefully, if she allowed it, to get my cock in there as well.

A low, strangled groan came out of me at the mere thought of it as Eve stepped out of her skirt, and she immediately turned back to me, her expression stern. "What was that?"

As much as I wanted to apologize and promise I wouldn't do it again, I forced myself to remain silent, knowing that uttering those words would be a worse breach of her order than I'd already made. Lowering my eyes, I held my breath to await her verdict. When I had disobeyed Eve in Quito, she forced me to wait and watch her touch herself. As sexy as I found that, I also wanted to touch her myself. My whole body cried out for it, and so, I kept silent.

Several seconds ticked past as Eve judged my compliance, but finally, she let me off with a warning. "That's the only exception I'll make."

Raising my eyes back to her, I nodded in confirmation, letting her know I understood and accepted her decision gratefully.

The expectation set, she reached behind her back and undid her bra, letting it fall away to reveal her beautiful breasts. Her pale pink nipples had already stiffened to a firm peak, as clear a sign as my stiff cock that she was enjoying herself just as much as I was. When she ran her fingers across those nipples, closing her eyes and letting out a soft sigh of pleasure as she did, it took every ounce of self-control I had not to remain still and quiet, but somehow, I managed it.

Eve's panties came off next, and when she tossed them aside, standing there looking utterly gorgeous in nothing but those fucking irresistible black boots, I could hardly believe my eyes. She was absolutely, completely flawless. My hands clenched again, my muscles straining against the fabric that held me firmly in place, but I kept my mouth closed other than to allow my tongue out to wet my lips that had gone dry with desire.

Moving slowly and deliberately, she walked up the side of the bed, easily within arm's reach of me if I could move my arms, but since I couldn't, I could only watch as she ripped the condom wrapper open and pulled it out. Expertly, she rolled it down my cock, the brief contact sending a wave of pleasure through me and heightening my anticipation even further. She wouldn't be putting it on if she didn't intend to take me inside her, to use my cock as her 'personal toy' as she'd put it, and just the idea nearly made me weak as my eyes followed each movement eagerly.

Sure enough, as soon as my cock was wrapped, she climbed up onto the bed and straddled me, pressing her pussy down against my cock as I bit my lip hard to hold in my groan of satisfaction. The contact of her body against mine and the sight of her on top of me, still wearing her boots, was almost more than I could take.

Eve rocked back and forth a couple of times, watching me carefully, testing me to see how I'd react. My teeth dug into my lip deeper, almost hard enough to break the skin. In every possible way, she had me right on the edge.

And when she decided I'd earned it, when she lifted my cock to her entrance and sank down onto it, I nearly had an out-of-body experience. The sight of my cock disappearing inside her coupled with the warmth of her body wrapped around me felt so good I almost couldn't take it. In my mind, I swore in satisfaction, but in reality, not a sound came from me, just as she'd ordered.

"Such a good boy," she murmured, sending another shiver of pleasure through me, my whole body contracting with fulfillment. Even though she was younger than me, hearing her call me a boy affected me in ways I couldn't fully explain. "And such a nice, thick cock for me to ride. You're a perfect toy."

Tabarnak. Once again, her instincts were spot on. She knew exactly what would turn me on, and as she began to ride me just as she'd promised, my need rose higher, and after only a few strokes, completely against my will, my hips bucked up towards her, driving my cock even deeper into her as she came back down onto it.

Instantly, Eve stopped and the heat in my body turned to ice. The fear I felt over having failed her and what she might do to punish me paralyzed me, but in an entirely pleasurable way. That fear was a powerful aphrodisiac, and I'd long since given up trying to figure out why. Sometimes, things simply were the way they were.

"You promised me you could behave," she reminded me as she pulled herself off of me, letting my cock fall back to my stomach with a devastating thud. The wetness I could feel on the condom as it rested against my skin, *her* wetness, turned me on even more as I held my breath to see what she would do next. "Was that a lie?"

Not wanting to get myself in more trouble, I didn't speak, even though she'd asked me a direct question. I shook my head instead, but my denial didn't fully satisfy Eve. I didn't expect it to.

"For that, you can wait a little longer for your orgasm. First, you're going to get me off." With that pronouncement, she crawled further up the bed towards me, grabbing onto the headboard as she crawled onto my arms, her calves in her boots pressing down on my biceps as she lowered herself onto my face. "When you make me come, I'll decide if you've redeemed yourself."

That was more than fair, and I eagerly set out to earn my redemption. Without my hands to aid me, I had to rely on my tongue more than ever, but luckily, I remembered perfectly well what had worked for her back in my hotel room in Quito. Breathing in her delicious scent, unable to breathe anything else, I set to work fucking her with my mouth. Her arousal was already high, another point in my favour, and I didn't waste a lot of time with foreplay. I dove right in, focusing on her clit most of all as I kissed and licked my way across the beautiful landscape of her body. Her hips rocked gently against my face, coating my lips with her moisture, and when her thighs started to tighten around my head, I clamped down on her clit to help take her over the edge.

Pride and satisfaction flowed through me as she came, my cock twitching in excitement, and Eve seemed to be satisfied too. She returned to my cock, sighing happily as she impaled herself on it again, and that time, I managed to keep utterly quiet and immobile. Even as she began to ride me again, her body rising and falling on me, her hands roaming across her breasts and down to her clit, all the parts of her that I desperately wanted to touch myself, I managed to hold it all in and simply watch her and enjoy the show.

"You're close, aren't you?" she finally asked, her voice low and content.

I could only nod. I'd been close ever since we got to my room, but I waited for her to give me permission, and at last, she did, with one condition.

"I'll get you there if you say my name again in that ridiculously sexy accent of yours."

That, I could certainly do. "Eve." My voice came out growled and strained from the effort of holding everything else back. I sounded like a man possessed, but Eve doesn't seem to mind.

Instead, with a gleam of satisfaction in her eyes, she leaned forward onto her hands, her breasts hanging over my chest as she increased her pace, pumping her hips against me with new urgency.

"Calisse, Eve, j'adore te baiser. Tu es parfait."

The words flowed out of me with my restriction lifted, and it seemed to work for Eve, though I didn't know if she understood me or not. Did she know I'd just told her I loved fucking her, or that I found her perfect? Whether she did or not, her body contracted above me again, and that gave me the final push I needed.

Days of denial ended in one of the most intense orgasms of my entire life as I submitted to her in the most basic way, giving her the orgasm that I'd saved for her. She'd claimed it from me, and at that moment, in the heat and closeness of my room, I would have found it very difficult to deny her anything at all.

Chapter Five

AFTERCARE

~Eve~

As the last shudders of my orgasm worked their way through my body, a deep satisfaction flowed through me on the heels of sexual pleasure, and another, newer sensation too: a strong tenderness towards the man beneath me who had just given me exactly what I wanted.

Even though I'd never experienced it before to this extent, I knew exactly what the feeling was: a need to care for him and make sure he knew just how much I appreciated the way he just submitted to me.

My mom had explained the importance of aftercare to me when she told me about her relationship with my dad. Scenes could be intense and both partners could suffer from an adrenaline drop afterwards. Transitioning into a situation where the dominant partner looked after the needs of the submissive one helped to provide an outlet for both of them. She had explained it all to me, but only when I looked down into Julien's trusting, handsome face did I fully understand it. I didn't take anything about what just happened between us for granted and I wanted him to know that.

Gingerly, I lifted myself off of him, his cock sliding out of me and landing back on his stomach, slick with the proof of my own fulfillment. To make him comfortable, the first thing I could do was remove the condom, and as I pulled it off, my mind flashed back to the list Julien had me fill out. One of the items on it had been cum drinking, and though I didn't mind swallowing it during a blow job, it didn't particularly turn me on. Julien, however, had checked it off as a yes, I noticed when I snuck a peek at his list, even though we hadn't gone through that part of the form together yet.

Although I didn't know if it would turn me on to see him do it, the only way I would know for sure would be to try, and so, holding the used condom up in front of him so he could see my actions, I dipped my finger into it. Julien's brown eyes tracked my finger as I brought it to his mouth, and without hesitation, he opened his lips, his tongue darting out to draw my finger in where he sucked on it hard, his eyes on me in that sweet, submissive way of his, sending a small zing of excitement rippling through my body.

Alright: apparently, I did find that sexy. At least when Julien was the one doing it, still tied to his bed. Who knew?

Tossing the condom in his trash can, I returned to the bed and removed his restraints, gently rubbing his wrists and his shoulders to ease any discomfort he might have experienced while tied up. The smile of appreciation on his face made it more than worthwhile.

"Do you need some water?" I asked him while rubbing his arms. "Wine? Hot chocolate?"

Julien's smile widened, showing off his white teeth and sending another small shiver through me, despite how perfectly satisfied he'd just made me. He really was breathtakingly good-looking. How on earth was he still single? Was it just what he'd told me earlier about not being able to find someone who satisfied his kink and complemented him in daily life too?

It didn't seem that impossible when we were together.

"Water would be perfect, thank you. There's a jug in the fridge."

That sexy accent of his did nothing to quell my feelings of attraction. I hadn't understood exactly what he said to me in French just before I came, but it sounded amazing. He could have been listing off STDs for all I knew, but it didn't really matter. Every word out of his mouth sounded incredible.

Still naked, the heels of my boots clicking on the hardwood stairs, I made my way downstairs, through the living room with the Christmas tree still lit up, to a small, functional kitchen, just as devoid of decoration as Julien's bedroom. He clearly didn't grow up with an architect for a mom and an interior decorator as a surrogate aunt as I had. The cupboards were well organized, though, and I quickly found a tall glass that I could fill with the filtered water from the jug in the fridge.

Just as I finished pouring, I heard a soft knock at the front door. Obviously, I couldn't answer it in my present state, still completely naked, so I returned the jug to the fridge and headed back to the staircase, intending to let Julien know about the knock in case it might be important. However, just as I got to the bottom of the stairs, the front door opened on its own and a woman walked straight in, accompanied by a blast of cold air until she closed the door behind her.

"Oh!" Her face froze with her mouth in a perfect 'o' shape as she noticed me standing there. The main lights weren't on, but in the multi-coloured light emanating from the Christmas tree, she would still clearly be able to see my nudity, other than the knee-high black boots I still wore. In contrast, she was wrapped up in her winter coat and scarf, blonde hair peeking out from beneath the hood of her coat. She looked to be around my age, and clearly not expecting to walk in on a naked woman with a glass of water in Julien's living room.

Why was she just walking in, though? He didn't mention a roommate, and he'd made it pretty clear he didn't have a girlfriend since he mentioned not having had sex at all in months. Unless he'd lied, but I didn't think so. My dad taught me signs to look for to judge when a person was being truthful or not, and everything about Julien told me he spoke the truth. Not to mention that she'd knocked first, so it didn't seem like she lived here.

Since I could do nothing to hide my current state, I didn't bother trying to. "Can I help you?" I asked instead, making it clear that I had every reason to be there while her presence required an explanation.

"I... uh, I just forgot to leave Julien's... Mr Labrecque's... tie earlier." In her hand, she held a small paper shopping bag, which she held up to show me, her eyes focusing on the bag rather than on me. "I didn't know he had company."

Obviously. "And you are?"

"C-Claire. His assistant."

Oh, shit. I'd actually had a conversation with her over email earlier that day to try to schedule a meeting with the charity's board, but she didn't know that. She would, though, as soon as I turned up at her office the following week. Pretending not to know her might make things more awkward then, since she would obviously know I had fucked her boss anyway, so in a split second, I decided not to hide it. Instead, I walked over to the sofa where Julien and I sat earlier, where a throw blanket lay draped over the back of it. Placing the glass of water down, I wrapped the blanket around myself, went back over to her and held out my hand.

"I'm Eve Sudlow. We emailed earlier today. It's nice to meet you, even this way."

Her eyes still wide and startled-looking, full of confusion, she tentatively took my hand and shook it. "Oh. Yes. Ms Sudlow. I didn't realize that you and Mr Labrecque... uh... knew each other so well."

Telling her that we'd only met two days earlier might not help matters, so I kept that to myself. Both of us wanted to get out of this situation as soon as possible, so I did my best to give her an opening. "I'll let him know that you brought the tie over. Thank you."

Taking the bag from her, I took a step back, and she took the hint. "Thanks. Have a good... uh, I mean, goodbye."

With that, she practically ran back out the door, the air hitting me again and making me shiver as she closed the door behind her. Since I could do nothing but laugh about it, I chuckled as I turned the deadbolt on the door, ensuring no one else could simply walk in, threw the blanket back over the sofa, and headed back up the stairs with the tie and the glass of water.

Julien was still on the bed and naked, but sitting up, and he gave me a curious look when I walked back in. "Did you turn the TV on? I thought I heard voices."

"You did, but that was me and your assistant, Claire. She stopped by to bring you a tie and I had to introduce myself." I lifted the bag in my hand as proof, and Julien's face turned pale, the blood slowly draining from it.

"She saw you? Like that?" He looked down at my naked body in dismay, as if it were something to be ashamed of, and indignation immediately stirred inside me.

"You seemed to like the look of it well enough a few minutes ago."

He winced at my sharp words. "I didn't mean it like that. You're gorgeous, Eve. It's just that I usually try to keep my personal and pro-fessional lives separate."

Placing the bag with the tie on his dresser, I walked back over to the bed and handed him the glass of water. This wasn't the aftercare I'd imagined, but I couldn't ignore what he'd just said either. "Are you expecting an apology from me? She walked straight in, I couldn't exactly avoid it. And if you really want to keep your business and private life separate, fucking me isn't exactly the best way to do that."

Julien's expression immediately clouded over with regret. "I'm sorry, I didn't mean it to sound like I was accusing you of anything. Of course it's not your fault. It's just bad luck, but I'll deal with it. Thank you for the water."

He offered me an apologetic smile, and with a sigh, I accepted it, taking a seat next to him. "Does your assistant always have free rein of your house, even when you're here?"

He shrugged, looking a little sheepish. "She usually just comes in when I'm away, but maybe she thought I'd be asleep because of the long flight. I don't really like it, but she means well."

Of course he didn't like it. Julien's natural inclination was to help people, not to have them serving him. I could tell that about him almost from the first moment we met. His submissive nature also would have prevented him from simply telling her to stop. Instead of pointing any of that out, though, I picked up on the other thing he said, about how she thought he might be asleep. "You do look a bit tired. How are you feeling?"

"Exhausted," he admitted with a self-deprecating smile. "In the very best way. I should probably sleep, but you're welcome to spend the night if you like."

Although I appreciated the invitation, I should get back to the hotel in case anyone noticed my absence. "You need to rest, not worry about me. I'll go back to my hotel, but I enjoyed tonight very much, Julien."

With those words, I wanted to make it clear that I would be happy to see him again, and he picked up on that immediately. "I enjoyed it too. If you're free tomorrow, I can show you around the city, or take you to dinner, or you can come back here. Whatever you like, as much or as little as you want. I have no other plans."

Well, that worked out well since I had no plans either. "I'd like to see some of the city. Maybe you could choose something Christmasy for us to do and we'll see how it goes from there? I can meet you at ten o'clock at City Hall."

After his comment in Quito about large corporate hotels, meeting him in the Stamer Hotel lobby didn't seem like the best way to start our day. City Hall would be much more neutral.

Julien quickly agreed, his smile showing his pleasure. "That sounds perfect. Can I call you a taxi?"

"There's no need. I have an app on my phone. You've done enough for tonight, Julien. Thank you for everything, and I'll see you tomorrow."

It only took me a moment to put my clothes back on, Julien watching me appreciatively the whole time, and I leaned down to give him a kiss before taking my leave.

"Good night."

With his cologne still lingering in my nose and the sight of his naked body still firm in my mind, I returned to my hotel, feeling much more worldly than I had when I left and excited about all the new things I might still learn with Julien as my guide.

~Julien~

When I woke in the morning, it didn't take long for the memories of the night before to come back to me. The strain in my arm muscles from having been tied up certainly helped, and as I stretched them out, a smile of satisfaction spread across my face.

The night had been very nearly perfect. Despite being new to the scene, Eve had confidence and charisma to spare, and we clicked sexually in a way I'd very rarely encountered before. Never with someone who I also wanted to spend time with outside the bedroom. The prospect of spending the day with her, and hopefully the night as well, already had my heart racing in anticipation.

The only slight mar on the whole evening had been Claire's unexpected arrival, and as I thought back over that part of the evening, I realized I probably could have handled it better when Eve told me. In the moment, my surprise got the better of me. Rather than imagining how disconcerting the whole encounter must have been for Eve, I fretted over my own reputation instead. I would have to apologize to her for that properly now that I could see the whole situation a little more clearly.

I should also get in touch with Claire and make sure she felt okay and that she didn't suspect anything inappropriate going on between me and

Eve. In a way, she only had herself to blame for letting herself into my house uninvited, but even so, it must have shocked her. At least she only knew that Eve and I had slept together and nothing about the specifics of how that encounter went. All things considered, it could have been worse.

Good morning, I texted Claire while still lying in my bed. *I understand you met Eve last night. I'm aware of the potential conflict of interest that arises from seeing her personally while working with her professionally. I intend to declare that conflict to the board, so you don't need to worry about keeping it a secret, but I would appreciate if you could be discreet about it. Obviously, I didn't know that you would come over last night or I wouldn't have put any of us in that position.*

A frown pulled at my lips as I typed the last sentence. Why *had* she come over, anyway? She told Eve she'd forgotten to leave the tie with my suit, but I had other ties. I could have made do. It seemed awfully far out of her way to come to simply bring me another one.

In any case, I reread the message a couple of times before sending it. Hopefully, it struck the right tone. I didn't apologize because it really hadn't been my fault, but I acknowledged that she might be feeling awkward about it, and I addressed the biggest concern from a work perspective. It should do the trick.

With that out of the way, I also sent an email to the head of the board to advise him of the potential conflict of interest before any rumours could get started. I didn't think Claire would spread it around, but I intended to take Eve out that day as she'd asked me to, and although the city was big, we could still run into someone I knew. It seemed better to declare my relationship now, even though calling it a relationship seemed premature. At that point, we'd only really had two evenings together, and though they were spectacular, there certainly hadn't been any kind of commitment made on either side.

I still had several hours before Eve and I were scheduled to meet, so I got up and went for a run around my neighbourhood. The cleats on my winter running shoes gave me good traction on the snowy sidewalks. As long as no ice had formed over top of the snow, I felt safe from slipping, and my body quickly warmed up from the exertion even in the freezing temperatures. With my breath puffing out like a smokestack in the chilly air, I weaved my way through the streets of Cabbagetown, waving hello to everyone else out and about, on their way to work or simply getting some exercise like me.

The air inside the house felt almost too warm by the time I returned, and I had a quick shower to restore my equilibrium. A casual sweater and jeans with warm boots and a coat should be perfect for what I had in mind, and Eve seemed to like the look the night before. A dash of cologne and I was ready to go.

Just before I left the house, I checked my phone. Nothing had come in from Eve, so it seemed we were still on, but I did have a reply from Claire.

I'm sorry for interrupting your evening. It's none of my business. Claire

The message sounded stiff and uncomfortable, but what she said was true: it really *wasn't* her business, so I didn't bother to reply.

The blue sky outside the front door was deceiving, making it look warmer than it actually felt. For December, though, it could have been worse, and I tucked my gloved hands into my pockets as I rounded the corner of Nathan Phillips' Square. The curved edges of the distinctive City Hall rose up into the blue sky at the far end of the square, beyond the ice rink with skaters gliding around the ice. Despite being mid-morning on a work day, the square bustled with people visiting the stalls of the Christmas market, and the enticing smells of coffee and fried dough beckoned me in.

What I hungered for was neither food nor drink, though, and despite the crowd, it didn't take me long to spot Eve standing at the edge of the ice rink, watching the skaters. She might as well have had a spotlight on her, she stood out so much to me. Her distinctive red hair beneath her white winter hat and the effortlessly stylish clothes she wore made her look like a model, and I was far from the only one who noticed. Both men and women turned to look at her as they went by, but she seemed oblivious to it all, not paying any attention to anyone at all until I got into her line of vision and her face immediately brightened, sending a wave of warmth through me that immediately chased away the external cold.

How in the world did I get lucky enough to be the one she looked at like that?

"Good morning." I kissed her on the cheek as I got close, inhaling her elegant perfume. "Did you sleep well?"

"Very well." Her dark eyes twinkled, letting me know she gave me at least part of the credit for that. "You?"

"Exceptionally well." I returned the compliment sincerely. "Before we do anything today, though, I want to apologize for my reaction last night when you told me about Claire. I'm so sorry that my initial response was so callous."

Eve brushed my concern away with an elegant wave of her hand. "No harm done. I figured you were caught off guard."

"I was, but that's no excuse. I should have put your feelings first."

"You're allowed to have your own feelings too," she pointed out. "I understand why you felt the way you did, and I accept your apology. Now, I don't want to hear another word about it today, understood?"

I couldn't resist a direct order, and she knew it. "Oui, Madame."

The twinkle in Eve's eyes grew stronger, letting me know my submission affected her just as much as it did me. "So, what's your plan for today? Are we staying here?"

She had instructed me to choose something Christmasy for us to do, and the market and skating rink in Nathan Phillips' Square would certainly qualify, but I didn't want to do anything quite so predictable. "I thought I would take you to see a more historical Christmas. We'll have to take the subway and a bus to get there, I hope that's okay."

Curiosity filled Eve's smile. "That sounds intriguing. We could get a taxi if you prefer, as my treat."

Since she'd just spent a year volunteering, I wouldn't want her to waste that much money on me. Truthfully, I wouldn't want her to spend any money on me, but I understood that many dommes naturally enjoyed spoiling their subs. It enhanced their feelings of power in the relationship and gave them a rush, so although monetary gifts had never been my particular kink, I could compromise with her if it brought her pleasure. "Next time, perhaps. You can pay for the subway fare today, though."

"Deal." With a smile, Eve linked her arm through mine and we headed out to begin our first real date.

~Eve~

Julien's apology was appreciated but unnecessary from my perspective. I understood that private and public lives didn't always mix. The people that worked at Stamer Hotels didn't know that my dad had a BDSM dungeon in his house or that my brother frequented voyeur clubs. They had no right to know, and though my family members weren't ashamed of their kinks, they didn't necessarily want them broadcast to the world either. That seemed to be where Julien's reaction came from, the more I thought about it. That, and the fact that he wouldn't want anyone to think he might be backing my project proposal simply because we were sleeping together.

I understood completely, so even though he could have been a little more sympathetic at the time, I didn't bear a grudge. I'd never been one to manufacture drama; my life had enough excitement in it without creating additional angst where there didn't need to be any.

When we reached the entrance to Osgoode station, Julien let me walk in front of him down to the subway platform, following my lead as usual. He pointed me towards the northbound trains, but otherwise, he seemed content to stay behind me, and I noticed several women throwing envious looks in my direction. They found him handsome, since he looked incredible in his fitted black winter coat, jeans and boots, but their appreciation was only skin deep. They had no idea how perfect he really was; perfect for someone like me, anyway.

As most commuters were at work on a Friday morning and the train headed away from downtown, there were plenty of seats, and we found an empty pair next to each other. Puddles of melted snow dotted the floor where people had been sitting or standing, reminding me of my boots on Julien's floors the night before.

His eyes lingered on them too as a soft smile crossed his face, leading me to believe we were on the same train of thought. He pretty much confirmed it in the next breath. "How do you feel after last night?"

As usual, I understood his question perfectly. He wanted to know if I regretted anything about the evening or if I'd experienced any kind of drop afterwards. I'd rarely met anyone who seemed so tuned in to my emotional level, but from my point of view, everything had gone very well indeed. "I feel great. In fact, I've been thinking a lot about your list."

Curiosity sparked in his eyes. "Really? About anything in particular?"

"A few different things." I gave him my best mysterious smile, fully intending to keep him guessing, building the anticipation for later. I really had been thinking about it, even in my dreams. I'd had one in particular that left me in a wet, throbbing mess when I woke up. "I did have a few more questions for you too, though."

As I expected, Julien immediately agreed. "Of course. Please, ask away."

Before I did, I cast a quick glance around the carriage to make sure we couldn't be overheard. Everyone else seemed to have their eyes on a book or their phone, and no one sat right beside us, but even so, I leaned a little closer to him. "I understand what you enjoy in the bedroom, but I'm a little less certain about what you want today, when we're just spending time together. How do you expect me to behave?"

"That's a great question, Eve." His words were full of so much appreciation that they didn't sound patronizing at all, though they very easily could have in a different tone. "And the answer is: I don't really know. As I told you yesterday, I've never been in a relationship with my domme outside of the bedroom, and so I've never spent time with them like this either. But the way that you behaved in the club in Quito, and in my office there too, seems perfect to me. You don't need to put on an act or feel like you need to be firm all the time. Just be yourself."

Somehow, he'd hit on exactly what had me worried. Although I enjoyed being in charge, I didn't want to feel pressured to do it every waking moment or feel like I couldn't let my guard down. Sometimes, I just wanted to get excited about things, especially when Christmas was involved. He definitely had me curious about where we were going and what he'd planned for us to do that day.

"I can do that," I assured him, relaxing back into my seat. "How long is the subway ride?"

"About forty minutes."

That should be a perfect amount of time for us to get to know a little more about each other. Although I had sucked his cock back in Quito and had sex with him the night before, I still knew very little about the man in front of me. "In that case, tell me about yourself. Where did you grow up?"

Julien leaned back too, his body angled towards me in an open and inviting way. "Québec City. French is my first language, as you must have guessed." I nodded in confirmation, encouraging him to continue. "My mother actually disliked me speaking English at home, but I learned it at school and from TV and music. The other languages came later, through travel and university studies."

His talented tongue awed me, in more ways than one. "Why didn't your mother want you to speak English?"

The muscles around his mouth tightened just a fraction; if I hadn't been watching him so closely, I might have missed it. "It reminds her of my father. He was American and only spoke English. To this day, she doesn't like to hear me speak it."

His use of the past tense when it came to his father seemed significant. "They split up, I assume?"

Julien nodded in confirmation. "They were barely even together. I never met him."

"That must have been challenging," I sympathized. I knew very well how fortunate I'd been to grow up with a loving, supportive family. Many people weren't so lucky. "Did your mom fall in love again?"

"No. It was just the two of us, always." That answered my next question, about whether he had any siblings, and he changed the subject before I could ask anything else. "What about you? Did you grow up in New York?"

I always appreciated when a man truly listened to the things I said, and Julien's question showed he paid attention. I had only mentioned New York once, briefly, but he'd picked up on it. "That's right. Right in the city. My parents work together, and I have an older brother. I also have a best friend who's almost like a sister. We'd hardly gone more than a few days without seeing each other before I disappeared to South America for a year."

"And she didn't want to spend a year volunteering with you?" he asked, his tone gently teasing. The work we did wasn't for everyone, and he seemed to recognize that.

"She's in love. She would have been miserable being away from her fiancé." Noelle messaged me almost every day, like always, but Aaron had taken my place as the one she turned to first, which I completely understood. They had their own lives and ambitions now, but it didn't change how much we loved each other. I couldn't wait to see her when I got back to New York.

Julien nodded thoughtfully. "And you had no one special to miss?"

He was digging for info about my relationship status, obviously, but I didn't mind. He'd been open enough with me about his situation. "I've dated before, but never seriously. I definitely haven't found 'the one' yet."

"And you believe in 'the one'?" Nothing in his tone or body language suggested he disagreed; he just wanted to know what I thought.

"I'm not sure if I believe there's only one person out there for us, but I definitely think there are some people you just click with, where things feel easy in a way they don't with others. I've seen it happen: my parents are a great example, and my brother and best friend both found their perfect match too. I won't settle for anything less."

"I didn't imagine you would." Julien's warm brown eyes stayed locked on mine as he leaned even closer. "I don't believe you settle for anything, Eve."

"You know me pretty well already."

As the subway rumbled on towards its destination, we swapped more stories of our childhood and our friends, and it all felt just as easy as I'd always imagined. Though I tried to keep my expectations in check, I couldn't help thinking that maybe when it came to 'the one', I wouldn't have to wait much longer at all.

Chapter Six

CHRISTMAS IN THE CITY

~Julien~

"Black Creek Pioneer Village?" Eve peered up at the sign above the visitor centre entrance curiously, her expression as open and interested as it had been the whole time we'd been talking on the trip there. She had a way of giving things her full attention that made them seem like the most interesting thing in the world. "Is that pretty much what it sounds like?"

"Pretty much. Black Creek is the name of the area, named after the river that flows through here, and the village is an open-air museum that looks at life here back in the 1800s. At Christmas, they do special displays about how Christmas was celebrated. You said you wanted something Christmasy, so I thought it would be a good fit."

"It sounds perfect. You did well." Her smile of approval filled my whole body with warmth, which would come in handy as we walked through the chilly, snow-covered village. "I'll get the tickets."

That sounded like a direction, not a suggestion, so I stood back and let her pay for our admission. She'd asked me how she should behave on our date and I told her to be herself, so I had to honour that and let her do what made her comfortable. Despite the fact that we'd already slept together, this was still technically a first date, and we could see what worked and didn't work for both of us if we decided to extend this relationship beyond a day-by-day basis.

Once inside, I asked Eve if she wanted to take one of the guided tours.

"I prefer to explore at my own pace," she replied with a wink that immediately had blood rushing to my cock. I'd never been with anyone I felt so comfortable with yet who could also turn me on in the literal blink of an eye. The combination of the kind and giving woman on the subway ride and back in the office in Quito, and the demanding and controlling woman I'd seen in the hotel and in my bedroom absolutely fascinated me.

Inside the museum, Eve's interest and curiosity continued. Historic houses from around the province had been moved to the site to make up the village we wandered through that day. We watched a demonstration in the tinsmith's shop and visited the farm and piggery which were original to the site, learning about how the family would often have been snowed in at Christmas. In one of the more upscale homes, we chatted with a woman in period costume about the Christmas baking that the servants would have done at the time.

"I'm quite glad I don't have to spend the whole day in the kitchen," Eve said with a laugh as we left the house and continued down the snow-covered street to the next house. The crisp snow crunched beneath our feet as our breath puffed out above us, rising in the still air until it disappeared entirely. "The women in Ecuador were always polite when I tried to cook for them, but I think they were just humouring me."

"You didn't learn growing up?" That surprised me since she seemed so competent in every way.

She gave an elegant shrug. "Oh, my mom taught me the basics, but she never mastered the more complex techniques herself. She was too busy working. Our meals growing up were fairly basic unless we ordered out."

"What kind of work does your mom do?"

Eve's eyes lit up, making it clear she enjoyed speaking about her mother. "She's an architect. She loves visiting places like this." She gestured around us to the historic buildings lining the street. "She could talk your ear off about different architectural styles throughout history and why buildings are designed the way they are."

"I think I would find that very interesting." As the words came out of my mouth, I hoped they didn't sound too much like trying to invite myself into her life more than she'd already invited me in, but Eve didn't seem put off by it.

"What about your mom?" she asked me instead. "What does she do?"

"She works in a dépanneur."

"A what?" Eve's confused look made me laugh, since I had suspected she wouldn't be familiar with the word.

"It's like a corner store in Québec. A convenience store. She left university to have me so she didn't get to finish her education and there weren't a lot of options for employment that would be flexible with a young child."

"That sounds a lot like many of the women I worked with in Ecuador," Eve pointed out, completely accurately. "Does she enjoy her work?"

"Sometimes yes, sometimes no. Like most jobs, I think."

We reached the next building, a church from the 1850s, and I held the door open for Eve. The tour group had just left, leaving the building empty except for us, so we sat down to continue our conversation. Sprigs of evergreen leaves brightened up the interior, but nothing heat-ed the space around us, making it only slightly less cold inside than outside.

"Is that how you feel about your job?" Eve asked with a smile as we settled down on the cold wooden pew. "Sometimes you like it and sometimes you don't?"

"Of course. That's true of everyone. Anyone who says otherwise is lying." I smiled back at her to let her know my answer was partly in jest. "As long as I like it more than I dislike it, I'll count myself lucky. We can't expect to enjoy ourselves all the time. Life doesn't work that way."

"No, it doesn't, for most people." She sighed lightly as she looked around at the starkness of the Protestant church, the white walls and the plain windows so different from the French Catholic basilica of my youth. "What did you do while your mother worked?"

"She had a group of women who all supported each other. They watched me while she worked and she looked after their children when they needed it. A lot like the women you worked with in Ecuador." I consciously echoed her earlier words and she smiled in acknowledgement.

"So, you had a group of strong women watching out for you? Were they often strict with you?"

Her dark eyes took on a twinkle that I already recognized, one that meant her mind had drifted to more carnal territory, and I would readily follow down that path whenever she asked me to. "Are you trying to discover the origin of my kink?"

"Maybe. It could be useful information," she teased, and I loved that she felt comfortable enough to speak so openly about it, and that she obviously took a genuine interest in wanting to know more about me and what turned me on.

"Well, I can assure you it has nothing to do with my mother."

Eve's bright laugh soared up to the church rafters.

"Did you inherit your dominance?"

I was trying to tease her back, but she surprised me by nodding. "I think I might have. Not from my mother, though. From my father. He's the one in control."

Before I could ask her anything about her father, the door blew open as another small group entered, bringing an icy blast of air with them. Eve shivered as it hit us, and I immediately put my arm around her to give her some of my body heat. "Let's keep going and get somewhere warmer."

Outside, more people milled around, making it impossible to pick up our earlier conversation, so we headed to the next building down the road: an old schoolhouse. Another couple came out as we went in, but once inside, we again had the building to ourselves.

Eve strode up to the front of the classroom and picked up a wooden paddle that lay across the teacher's desk. "They took their discipline seriously, didn't they?"

The sight of her standing there, as gorgeous as always, with the paddle in her hand sent a shot of arousal through me so strong that I had to reach out to steady myself on the back of one of the desks.

Missing nothing, Eve broke into a mischievous smile. "This works for you, doesn't it? Maybe *this* is your origin story?"

I answered her truthfully, as I always tried to. "I don't remember any crushes on teachers, but it definitely works for me. In fact, it's one of my favourite scenes to play. I even have some props at my house."

"Really?" Eve's raised eyebrows let me know she found the idea intriguing. "Well, maybe if you're a good boy for the rest of the day, you can show them to me later."

"Avec plaisir." *With pleasure,* I replied, and the pleasure would definitely be mine.

We were interrupted yet again as more people came in, and Eve immediately fell back into a light conversational mode, putting the paddle down as we talked about what it would have been like to be in school two centuries earlier. The promise she'd made lingered in my mind, though, leaving my body in a state of anticipation that I knew would last the whole day long, until she decided to satisfy it.

~Eve~

Julien truly took me by surprise with the trip to the pioneer village, in a very good way. Most men I'd dated before would have taken me somewhere fancy or expensive to try to impress me, especially on a first date. There would have been private dining rooms or private concerts or over-the-top gifts. Once, a guy gave me diamond earrings on a first date, as though he needed to prove to me that his interest in me extended beyond my money.

Of course, Julien still had no idea that I came from money or who my family were, though I suspected that his choice of activity wouldn't have been any different even if he *had* known. As we walked around the village, pointing things out to each other, swapping stories from our lives and making each other laugh, nothing about the way he behaved seemed the least bit artificial. He brought me there because he found it interesting and he thought I would too, and though that sounded simple, in my experience, it really hadn't been all that common. And that didn't even take into account the conversation we'd had in the schoolhouse, which had my imagination racing and my anticipation building, looking forward to the moment we could return to his house and put his fantasies into action.

Eventually, I would have to tell him about my family, since I knew that honesty was the basis of any good relationship, but first, I wanted to enjoy the day with him as Eve Sudlow, charity volunteer and domme-in-training. Those were parts of me too, parts that I liked, and it seemed that Julien did too.

"Are you getting hungry?" he asked as we completed our loop of the village.

I hadn't really thought about it until he mentioned it, but when I glanced down at my watch, I was surprised to see we'd been there for two hours. Noon had come and gone, and breakfast with my dad seemed like a long time ago. "Yes, actually. Where can I take you for lunch?"

With my question, I wanted to make two things clear: he could choose the restaurant, but I intended to pay for it. Julien didn't argue with me but neither did he choose an upscale restaurant like some men would have. After a short walk down the snowy sidewalks once we left the village, he opened the door for me to a fast-food restaurant.

"This is the Pita Pit. They're all over the place now, but they started here in Ontario," he explained with a smile. "I survived on them when I first moved here. You can build your own pita and I think they have Christmas drinks."

"I did ask for Christmas things today," I had to agree, thinking once again how different our day was from my usual dates, in a good way.

Inside, we placed our order at the counter, including an eggnog smoothie for me since he'd suggested it. As we sat and ate at the laminate table, we chatted more about the pioneer village and about the women the charity helped around the world, and how going to a place like the restaurant we were in and ordering food the way we just had was a luxury that neither the early settlers nor many of the women we supported could imagine.

"The place I have in mind for this afternoon is also something almost beyond imagining," he told me as we finished eating. "It's excessive, but beautiful."

Slurping up the bottom of my smoothie, I licked my lips, and his eyes immediately moved to them, making me smile. I loved that no matter how gentlemanly he behaved, he didn't hide the fact that I turned him on either. "You have me intrigued, Julien. What do you consider excessive?"

That word didn't seem to apply to anything in his life from what I'd seen to that point.

He looked down, away from my lips, as if the sight of them tempted him too much. "It's another historic house, but one that was owned by a very wealthy family. They spent an obscene amount of money on it, but these days, it's a museum, open to the public, so I suppose it had some worth in the end."

His choice of words jolted me from our comfortable, casual flirting. "Obscene?" I repeated curiously, wondering if I'd misheard him. The word sounded different with his accent.

Julien nodded firmly to confirm I'd understood him correctly. "The house cost over three million dollars to build in 1910. That's more than a hundred million dollars today. The idea of any one person having that much money is obscene, don't you think?"

Suddenly, I wished I hadn't finished my entire smoothie already, since my mouth went dry as I scrambled for a response. My family had much more than a hundred million dollars, but of course Julien didn't know that. He didn't mean it as a personal insult, no matter how much it might have felt like one at that moment.

In fact, in some ways, I agreed with him. I had decided to spend the year after graduation volunteering rather than going to work for Stamer Hotels like my father wanted me to because I didn't simply want to cater to the rich. There *was* too much wealth concentrated in the hands of too few, so I didn't disagree in principle. My concern stemmed instead from his choice of word, as though being rich was some kind of moral flaw, or as if simply possessing that much money made someone a bad person.

"I suppose it depends how they earned the money and what they do with it," was the answer I finally decided on. "Nothing is black and white."

Julien's smile almost distracted me again. He really was damned handsome when he smiled. "I suppose I shouldn't be surprised that someone as empathetic as you are can even empathize with the rich."

That gave me a perfect opening to explain exactly why I could identify with the rich and come clean about my background, but the words seemed to stick in my throat, held there by a new fear that the truth about my family might change the way he viewed me. We were having such a nice day getting to know each other, and we still had the evening to look forward to, including his school teacher fantasy that I definitely wanted to know more about. It seemed a shame to ruin it by blurting out my net worth in the middle of the Pita Pit.

Before I got a chance to say anything at all, Julien got to his feet. "Anyway, the house is rather wonderful as a museum, and they always decorate it specially for Christmas. I think it will meet your criteria for something Christmasy for us to do."

He looked so eager for my approval that I slipped back into my dominant role to give it to him. "It sounds very promising. I have faith in you, Julien, so lead the way."

The flush of pleasure on his face at having my praise sent an answering wave of heat through me, and as we walked back out into the snowy streets, heading back to the subway, I tried to put our conversation to the back of my mind. There would be time for us to talk about my family later. For a little while longer, I could just be Eve.

~Julien~

I couldn't help smiling as Eve got her first glimpse of our second destination of the day and an expression of delight spread across her face.

"I didn't know Toronto had a castle!" she exclaimed as she looked up at the crenellated roofline and the towers. Her dark eyes had gone so wide, I could see the house reflected in them. "And the tree is gorgeous. My mom would love this."

The tree in front of the house *was* impressive but she hadn't seen the one inside yet, and I felt like a kid on Christmas morning as I took her by the hand to lead her through the door. "Does your mom like Christmas?"

Eve laughed in that light, magical way of hers. "That's an under-statement. It's by far her favourite time of year, and she always made it incredible for me and my brother growing up. I'm pretty sure she's never been here before, though, so I'll have to tell her about it. It's rare that I get to share something with her about Christmas that she doesn't already know."

Once again, Eve paid for our entry. When I tried to offer my card instead, she gave me a stern look of disapproval that made my heart beat faster and my cock twitch.

"What were your Christmases like as a kid?" she asked me when we'd stepped inside. "Did your mom...oh!"

Whatever she'd been about to ask trailed off into the air as she caught sight of the forty-foot-tall tree in the Great Hall and her mouth dropped open in astonishment. Cinnamon sticks and oranges with cloves hung from the tree, filling the air with a spicy, festive fragrance as a string quartet played carols in the background. The central room of the house had a soaring wooden hammerbeam ceiling, more than three stories up, with windows and balconies from the upper floors overlooking the ground level view we had. Octagonal chandeliers hung from the ceiling, fitted with lights that looked like candles, and a large fireplace was built into the wall on the left. The tree itself stood in front of a large bay window, stretching up to the ceiling, and the lights from the tree shone down on us both, reflecting across Eve's beautiful face and making her look even more enchanting, if such a thing were possible.

"What is this place?"

Her breathless wonder was so endearing that for a moment, I could almost forget she was the same woman who'd made me crawl to her on our first night together in Quito. How she could be both of those women was a mystery I very much looked forward to solving.

"This is Casa Loma. As I mentioned before, a very rich man built it back in the 1910s as his family home. It has almost a hundred rooms, and at the time, it was the largest home in Canada. It cost an exorbitant amount to build, but within ten years, the owner had gone broke and had to sell it to the city."

I couldn't quite keep the satisfaction out of my voice at the way things had turned out, and Eve turned to me, her excitement fading a little as her brow furrowed. "Why is that a good thing?"

Since she seemed concerned, I tried to make a joke to bring back her beautiful smile instead. "Well, if he hadn't, it wouldn't be a museum and we wouldn't be here now."

The smile I'd hoped for did come, but it looked far less genuine than before. "You seem to take the idea of anyone being rich quite personally," she commented, her eyes moving back to the tree, but it didn't really seem like she even saw it, staring blankly ahead. "Is that because of working with the charity?"

She had picked up on my feelings precisely, but my reasons were a little more complicated than that. "That's part of it, certainly. When I spend my days trying to help people who could feed their family for a year off what that vase costs, it's hard not to find this kind of wealth ostentatious."

Eve looked over at the vase I pointed to before looking back at the tree. "I understand that. What's the rest of it, then?"

"Pardon?" She'd lost me with her question, especially with her gaze focused on the tree. I couldn't be sure if she'd moved on to talking about something else, but she clarified that she hadn't.

"You said the charity work was part of the reason you're anti-wealth. What's the other part?"

The other reason was more personal, and something I had only shared with a handful of people in my entire life, but Eve had been nothing less than open with me. I didn't want to dodge her question, and I certainly didn't intend to lie to her, so that only left me with the option of telling her the truth. "It has to do with my father."

At last, Eve's eyes returned to me, surprised and curious beneath the lights of the tree. "What do you mean? I thought you never met him."

Once again, it pleased me that she had been paying such close attention, even if the subject wasn't a happy one. "I didn't meet him. As I said before, he was American, but I didn't mention that he was very rich. He came to Québec for the summer with his family's business and my mother fell in love. She thought he loved her too until she got pregnant. He and his father both accused her of planning the whole thing to try to 'trap' him, though how she could plan to get pregnant without him taking part, I don't quite understand."

The corner of Eve's lips turned upwards, taking my sarcasm as I meant it, but the look in her eyes remained sympathetic. "What happened next?"

"They told her to get rid of the baby, and when she refused, they wrote her a cheque, said that would cover the child support, and told her not to name the baby after him if she had a boy. That was the last time she saw him."

Eve exhaled slowly, her natural empathy shining through. "And he never made any effort to get in touch with you?"

"Never. He must know I exist, but it doesn't seem to trouble him." My voice sounded flat, as it always did when the topic of my father came up. I'd learned that trick a long time ago, to not let myself feel the betrayal and abandonment. Numbness was preferable to pain, I learned that lesson as a little boy when all the other kids had fathers and I didn't.

"He behaved terribly," Eve agreed, stating the obvious. "But I don't see how that's directly related to his wealth."

I didn't see how she could miss it. "He literally paid her off to disappear. He saw her, and me by extension, as something that could be bought and sold as he needed. That's the way so many wealthy people view the world, forgetting that the people around them are people too. It's like an infection that comes with a large bank account. It's the only way someone could justify building a place like this when people were starving on the streets outside."

I gestured around at the house around us once again, and Eve turned to look too, biting on her lip almost nervously. "Well, I suppose it's good that he gave her some money, at least. It must have helped the two of you."

She seemed determined to find a bright side where there wasn't one. "My mother never cashed the cheque."

Once again, Eve's mouth dropped open as she turned back to me. "Why not?"

"She didn't want to be someone who could be bought, no matter what he thought of her. There were times when she first told me the whole story that I thought she must be crazy, times when we really could have used the money, but the older I get, the more I understood why she made that choice. I respect it. She taught me that money truly is the root of all evil, and I haven't seen much to convince me otherwise."

I could see Eve's pretty throat contracting as she swallowed almost painfully hard. "This man... your father... he wasn't a Stamer, was he?"

Where on earth did that question come from? "The family who owns all the hotels? No. Why do you ask?"

She shrugged, looking both relieved and slightly nervous. "It's the first rich family that came to mind."

It seemed strange that she should mention the Stamer name since I had the upcoming benefit dinner at their hotel in two days, a dinner that I hoped, if all went well between Eve and I until then, she might accompany me to. However, that wasn't something I wanted to put on her just yet, so I changed the subject instead. "That's my mother's story. I don't usually share it because it's her story to tell and not mine, but I hope that explains a little bit why I sometimes come off as a bit harsh towards the rich. I don't wish them any ill, honestly, I just know that that kind of lifestyle would never be for me. Now, why don't we go and see the rest of the house? This is just one of the ninety-eight rooms."

"Yes. Of course." Eve smiled at me again, but her eyes still seemed uncharacteristically dull and I didn't quite understand why. Hopefully, with the rest of what I had planned for the day, we could recapture her earlier enthusiasm and end the evening back at my house as I'd hoped.

There were still many more things I wanted to do with her before the day ended.

Chapter Seven

CAGED

As gorgeous and interesting as Casa Loma was, I could hardly concentrate as we walked through the period rooms, each decorated for the season. Beneath the coloured lights of the trees, my stomach churned with uncertainty as I weighed everything Julien told me and tried to figure out what I should do.

He must have thought it strange when I asked if his father was a Stamer, especially since I provided no good explanation for my question. I couldn't really imagine my dad behaving the way Julien's father had behaved, but everyone made mistakes. If he *had* done something like that, I wouldn't expect him to go around bragging about it. Just the thought that we might be blood relatives had given me a major ick that I needed to dispel, no matter how out of left field the question must have seemed to him.

At least his answer had reassured me on that point, but only that one.

On some level, I could understand Julien's feelings. There *were* rich people who viewed other people as commodities to be bought and sold. Some rich people *did* waste money on frivolous things when others had to get by with nothing. I couldn't argue with either of those things. Where I disagreed and where I took his viewpoints more personally was in the generalization of those attitudes and behaviours to *all* wealthy people. Judging someone by the size of their bank account, whether big or small, seemed no better to me than judging them on any other superficial measure. As someone who dedicated his life to helping others, it puzzled me how Julien felt justified in painting a whole segment of the population with such a wide, unflattering brush.

If I told him the truth about my background, would that change his opinion? Or would it only change his opinion of me, making him regret the time we'd spent together? Maybe I would have a better chance of changing his mind if I approached it as the 'normal' girl he saw me as, and only revealed my own wealth once I'd got him to address his prejudice?

Honestly, I couldn't tell if I was being clever or cowardly by keeping silent. He'd only told me the things he had because he didn't know my background. By staying silent as long as I had, I'd already made it more awkward for when the truth eventually came out, and it *would* come out sooner or later, I had no illusions about that. Wouldn't it be better, then, to rip the bandaid off and get it over with? Would he feel betrayed if I kept it from him just a little longer?

"Eve?" Julien's hand gently brushed against my back as I headed for the door of the small study we were in. "It's this way, up the stairs."

He gestured towards a once-hidden staircase, concealed next to the fireplace, as I forced my attention back to our surroundings. My parents had a secret room in our home too, although it served a different purpose than simply getting around. Was that another thing that all rich people did? I'd never really thought about it that way before. I'd never been ashamed of my family before either, but given the turmoil that my thoughts were in, I found myself second-guessing everything.

"If you're not interested, we don't have to stay," Julien added, concern lining his brow. "I thought you would like it, but if I'm wrong..."

"No." I cut him off firmly in a tone of voice I knew he wouldn't be able to resist. Uncertainty wasn't a good look on me. I had to stop wallowing in indecision and form a plan of action, and my plan, at least for the rest of the visit, would be to stop worrying. The conversation we needed to have wasn't one that could be had in public anyway, especially not in the middle of a tourist attraction. It could wait until we were alone together again, and until then, I would put it out of my mind. "I'm enjoying myself very much, I promise. Let's go upstairs. I'm assuming that's where the bedrooms are?"

I raised one eyebrow just a touch, just enough to be provocative, and Julien immediately relaxed. "Yes. Would you like to visit them?"

"Always."

With the balance between us restored, we visited the rest of the house, exclaiming over the things that were considered cutting edge a hundred years earlier and remarking on the beauty of the house itself. The conservatory was Julien's favourite room, the stained-glass dome soaring above another beautiful Christmas tree, while I chose the Oak Room with its intricately carved wooden panels and yet another elegantly decorated tree in the large bay window.

"I could imagine sitting in here while you waited on me," I teased him, keeping my voice low so the others in the room couldn't hear. The more I thought about it, the more defined the image became in my mind, and I shared all the details with him, suspecting he would find it just as enticing as I did. "Wearing only a bow tie and a cock cage. That was one of your checkmarks on the list, wasn't it?"

We hadn't gotten that far when reviewing our lists together the night before, but I noticed that he'd checked it off along with the corset. I'd never seen a cock cage in person before, but I understood the basic principle: it restricted his cock so he couldn't get an erection, not until the person holding the key set him free. I'd looked them up when I got back to my hotel room the night before to educate myself a little further.

That kind of control appealed to me, and I knew it did to him too, especially from the way his eyes gleamed when I said the words out loud.

"If that's something you would like, we can try it tonight. I was going to offer to cook you supper anyway, so if you'd like it served to you that way..."

I certainly would like that, but he seemed to be forgetting something. "I thought you were going to show me your teaching props tonight." That thought hadn't entirely left my mind all afternoon either.

Julien shrugged, trying to look unbothered, but the light in his eyes betrayed his excitement. "There's no reason we can't do both. The day is still young."

He had that right, and maybe it wouldn't hurt to put off the conversation we needed to have just a tiny bit longer. Long enough for us to satisfy our mutual curiosity, and to satisfy each other mutually too.

Afterwards, we would still have the whole weekend to talk before the meeting with his board the following week, by which point I would have to reveal exactly who I was. As long as I told him before that, it would be okay, and until then, the more he got to know me, the more he could see that I didn't fit the stereotype he had in his head.

As we left Casa Loma together, heading towards his house and the pleasures that awaited us there, I had almost convinced myself that I'd made that decision based on what was best for both of us and not just for me.

~Julien~

The afternoon sky had already started to darken as Eve and I left Casa Loma. Whatever had been bothering her after our arrival there seemed to have been resolved, and in her eyes, I could see the same anticipation for the night ahead that I felt. Not only was she beautiful, confident and dominant, she had a sense of adventure that I found incredibly attractive in a woman, and when she brought up the idea of me wearing the cock cage for her, I knew right then, if I hadn't already guessed it before, that we were going to have another incredible evening.

The only problem was that the thought of it had me so turned on, I would need to cool down in order to be able to fit into the cage in the first place. Luckily, I knew just how to do that, so when we reached my house, I checked to make sure we were still on the same page.

"I would like to cook for you, Madame E, in the uniform you were imagining for me. Would you like to help me put it on?"

Eve's dark eyes filled with heat as she looked up at me. "Absolutely."

"Good. I'll just need to grab some ice."

Eve followed me curiously to the kitchen, watching as I filled a small glass with a handful of ice cubes. I'd learned the trick from my first domme, the first one to fit a cage on me, and it pleased me that I could share my knowledge with Eve who was proving to be an eager student.

Back up in my room, I placed the glass of ice down on top of my dresser, grabbed a bottle of lube from inside one of the drawers, and went into my closet to find my favourite cage. It had been a gift to me from a previous domme, the one I'd had my most intense domme/sub relationship with, and though that relationship hadn't ended well, I could still appreciate and remember the things I'd enjoyed about it. As for the cage, I hadn't worn it in quite some time since there seemed little point in wearing it without a domme to hold the key for me. The thing I found enjoyable about it was giving up the control over my own arousal to my mistress by quite literally handing her the key to it.

Different kinds of chastity devices existed, usually made of plastic or silicone, or, in the case of the one in my hands, metal. It had been specially sized to fit me so that it wouldn't be too tight or chafe too much. A hole at the end of the metal enclosure made it possible to urinate without removing it, meaning I could keep it on as long as my domme deemed necessary. With Eve, I suspected we would just try it for that night, but perhaps in the future, if she wanted me to wear it longer, I could. As I'd explained to her about the corset, it acted as a secret reminder of my domme's control even when we were apart, something the two of us knew about but no one else did.

However, the key thing to putting it on was that my cock had to be completely flaccid, and with Eve around, that had hardly ever been the case. As I turned back to her and held out the device for her inspection, my cock already strained against my pants, and the situation didn't get any better when Eve took the cage from me and turned it over in her hands, examining it thoroughly. Seeing her slender, manicured fingers on it and watching her eyes move across it gave me almost as much of a thrill as if she had touched me herself.

"And this doesn't hurt you?" she asked once she'd looked at it from every angle.

"No, not at all. It simply prevents me from getting hard. It puts the keyholder in control of my arousal. I enjoy it, as long as my partner does too."

Eve nodded in understanding, her eyes moving between the cage and the front of my pants. "Well, let's get it on, then. Clothes off, all of them."

With those words, her voice took on the commanding edge that I found impossible to resist. Unfortunately, it also made my cock throb even more, so by the time I got undressed and stood naked before her, I was nearly at full-mast.

Eve's eyebrows raised as she looked between the cage in her hand and my stiff cock. "I don't think this is going to work with you in that state."

"It won't," I agreed, letting out a choked laugh. "That's what the ice is for. You need to cool me down."

Understanding dawned in her eyes and, placing the cage down on the bed, she stepped over to the dresser to grab an ice cube from the glass. Holding it between her thumb and index finger, she placed it down directly on cock while I drew in a hissed breath between my teeth at the sudden cold.

"Think unsexy thoughts," she whispered in a far-too-seductive way, but I did my best to follow her instructions anyway. While she continued to rub the ice cube slowly up and down my shaft, I tried to recall all the random Montréal Canadiens hockey stats from when I was a teenager. The combination soon worked, leaving me both limp and shivering as Eve placed the ice cube back in the glass.

Eager to move on while the situation was in my favour, I explained the procedure to her. "The ring goes on first, over my balls and then my cock goes through it afterwards. You can use a good amount of lube to help."

I left her to actually put it on if she wanted to, and as I expected, Eve eagerly took up the challenge, squeezing a generous dollop of lube into her hand and coating me with it. The cold metal helped to keep me grounded as she pulled one testicle gently through the ring and then the other. At that point, she stopped, looking uncertain. "I'm going to have to bend you a little to make it fit."

Another strained laugh left my lips as I tried my best not to find her bluntness attractive. "Yes, that's fine. I'll tell you if it hurts."

As gently as she could, she bent my cock downwards to slide through the ring along with my balls, until I was all the way in and the ring sat firmly against my pelvis.

"Perfect," I assured her. "That was the hard part. No pun intended."

My reward for that joke was a twinkle in her dark eyes that sent a shot of arousal through me so strong that we would need to act fast to complete the caging before it became impossible again.

"Now, fit the cage over the rest of me. It locks into the ring with the key."

With her light but firm touch, Eve slid the cage over my cock, ensuring the head was properly positioned against the hole in the end, and with only a couple of tries, she got it secure, turning the key and taking a step back to assess her work. "Does that feel alright?"

"It's perfect," I promised her again, and with a smile of satisfaction, she slid the key into her pocket and reached back over to the glass. As I watched, she grabbed the ice cube she had previously used on my cock and popped it into her mouth, licking her lips as she did.

Once again, blood rushed to my cock, but that time, it had no noticeable effect. With no room to grow, I remained unerect, unfulfilled, and completely at her mercy.

Just the way we both wanted it.

~**Eve**~

My day with Julien was turning out to be one new revelation after another. I'd learned things about his past, about his views, and things about myself too, the latest of which had everything to do with the way it made me feel to see him under lock and key.

I couldn't say that the cage on its own struck me as particularly sexy. When he took his pants off and his cock sprung out, eager and ready, I found the sight of it and the memory of how it had felt inside me the night before incredibly appealing. Working with him to get the cage on had felt far more clinical than sexy, and now that he'd been firmly locked away, his cock looked rather defeated and deflated within its metal prison.

However, while the physical reality of it didn't turn me on, what I *did* like, and where I knew his enjoyment came from too, was in the surrender of control. When he handed me the key, placing his ability to orgasm directly and literally within my grasp, *that* might have been the sexiest thing I'd ever seen, and the accompanying rush of power it sent through my body had me primed and ready for him once again.

Julien went to his closet and began to rummage around again. "You said you wanted me in a bow tie," he reminded me, having taken my teasing back at Casa Loma quite seriously. When I said I wanted him to serve me in a cock cage and a bow tie, I hadn't thought he would take it so literally. "I'm not sure I have one, though."

"That's okay. This one will do." Reaching past him, I pulled out a tie that hung on the rack, and grabbing Julien's hand, I tugged him back out into the centre of the room where I tied it not around his neck but over his eyes like a blindfold.

"It will be hard to cook like this," he joked, but I wasn't joking around. I wanted to come, and I wanted him to work for it.

"That's enough talking. Time to put that mouth to better use."

A grimace crossed his face just for a second, not because of my words but because of the effect of the cage on his arousal. Obviously, he'd found the idea sexy, but his physical reaction to it was being inhibited, and I left him standing there while I quickly shimmied out of my pants. The cooler air against my bare skin made me shiver, or maybe it came from the anticipation. Julien waited silently and patiently, naked, caged and blindfolded in the middle of the room while I lay myself down on the bed.

"Come and find me," I invited when I'd made myself comfortable. "You can have an appetizer before supper if you can find it."

A smile of delight lit up his face as he stepped forward tentatively, his hands out in front of him. I could have helped him by speaking again, letting him follow the sound of my voice, but I didn't. Instead, I simply watched him as he felt around for the bed, all the while running my hands over my body to get a bit of relief from the aching need building up inside me.

At last, his knees hit the mattress and immediately, he bent down, reaching out to try to locate me. His fingers brushed against my foot, and with a hum of satisfaction, he grabbed onto it to keep himself oriented while he climbed onto the bed between my legs. His hands journeyed slowly up my calves, over my knees to my thighs, his touch getting closer and closer to where I wanted it most. Only inches away, he paused, frustratingly, and just as I was about to remind him of his duty, he lowered his head instead, sniffing deeply before his tongue connected with my wet, ready pussy.

Fuck. He looked incredible and he felt even better as his tongue dipped inside me, getting a proper taste just as I'd invited him too.

"You spoil me, Madame," he murmured, his tongue flicking upwards, closer to my clit. "Nothing I make you will taste half as good."

"Then you better give me what I need in return," I suggested, half commanding and half begging. Though I was technically the one in control, at that moment, he had me in the palm of his hand.

With that hand, he slid two fingers inside me, the third and fourth fingers on his hand, and as he pushed them all the way in, his index finger rubbed against my clit. For someone who couldn't see what he was doing, he had a very good grasp on the situation, and when he lowered his head again, adding his tongue to the work his fingers were doing, my eyes closed too. The sensations overwhelmed me as he fucked me with his fingers and sucked my clit, and given how turned on I already was, it didn't take long for him to push me over the edge.

"Don't stop," I managed to moan as my orgasm shuddered through me. Greedy for more, I needed him to keep going. I craved overstimulation while knowing that he suffered from a lack of it, and he readily obliged. His fingers moved even faster, coated in my wetness, his lips on my clit got rougher, and no matter how much he might have needed a break, or to come up for air, he didn't stop for a second.

My second orgasm built slower than the first one, but when it finally arrived, it hit me hard, my whole body convulsing as my thighs clenched around him.

"Holy fuck," I panted as I tried to catch my breath afterwards. "I should blindfold you more often."

Julien smiled up at me, his lips glistening. "Pour le plaisir de ton goût, je me jaugerais les yeux."

If I needed any further reason to think him sexy, he had to go and start speaking French too. "What does that mean?"

He pulled his body up the bed, his face moving closer to mine, his eyes still covered. "For the pleasure of your taste, I would cut out my own eyes."

A startled, breathless laugh burst out of me. "I think I liked it better in French. It sounded less gory."

As he grinned, I could imagine how his warm brown eyes would be twinkling, if I could see them. "Things often sound sexier when we don't understand them."

I had to agree, and while we were on the subject, I had a few more questions about his native tongue. "How do you say 'pussy' in French?"

"Plotte." He wrinkled his nose. "It's quite vulgar though. More like cunt."

"What about cock?"

"Graine. At least, that's what we call it in Québec. In France, they say bitte."

"Are there a lot of differences between Quebec French and France French?"

"Yes, quite a few. We use a lot more English words than they do. For example, we use the verb faker, like the English fake, if someone is faking an orgasm."

The example he'd chosen made me laugh again. "I wouldn't think you knew anything about that. I'm sure no one has ever had to fake one with you."

Julien's cheeks flushed with pleasure at the compliment. "I'm very flattered that you have such a good opinion of me."

His happiness sent a warm affection spreading through my body in return. It seemed so strange to me that this eager-to-please, almost meek man could be the same as the man who spoke so forcefully against the excesses of wealth.

As soon as that thought crossed my mind, my own blissful mood began to dim, remembering that I still had to reveal my true self to him. But not right that minute.

First, he'd promised to cook for me, so I stood him back up and removed the tie from his eyes, tying it around his neck instead. Wearing only that and his cage, just as I'd requested, Julien went to the kitchen and began to make us supper while I sat back on his sofa next to the soft lights of his Christmas tree, with the glass of red wine he'd poured for me, wondering if something this good could truly be meant to last, or whether the secret that still lay between us would blow it all up before it ever really had a chance to start.

Chapter Eight

A LESSON

~Julien~

If Eve could be any more perfect, I really didn't see how. The more comfortable she got with me and the more she let her true self come out, the more blown away I was by her. From the competent businesswoman in the charity office in Quito to the excited tourist at the pioneer village, to the sexy, confident dominatrix in my bedroom, each and every facet of her appealed to me. Although I'd only known her a matter of days and I'd never been one to lose my head before, as I stood in the kitchen making supper for us both, I couldn't help wondering if this could be something real. Had I finally found someone who fit into every part of my life, no matter how contradictory those parts might seem from the outside?

The tiles on the kitchen floor felt cool against my bare feet, and when I opened the freezer to pull out some frozen shrimp, the rush of cold air on my naked skin sent a shiver through my whole body, making the metal of the cage clank against the ring holding it, giving me another reminder, if I needed it, that I still wore it. Part of me had wondered if Eve would remove it quickly out of concern for me, but she seemed to trust me when I told her that it didn't hurt. The weight of it took some getting used to, especially since I hadn't worn it for a while, but that heaviness only made its symbolism more potent to me.

The balance of power and control in a domme/sub relationship was a very delicate thing. Although Eve held the key to the cage, at any time, I could use my safeword and request it back. By handing it over to her, we both acknowledged that I trusted her to do that. If that balance got thrown off, if that trust got misplaced, that was when a relationship fell apart, as it had between me and the woman who had gifted me with the cage in the first place.

But so far, Eve had done nothing to suggest to me that I couldn't trust her. In fact, as I snuck a look at her out in the living room, sitting on the couch next to the Christmas tree and looking out the window at the falling snow, I was reminded of a Christmas tradition my mom and I used to have, back when I was a moody teenager who didn't always appreciate her. The more I thought about it, the more I thought the tradition might work equally well for two people who were just getting to really know each other.

So, after I invited her to sit down at the dining table and served her the pad thai I'd made, still wearing the 'uniform' she'd chosen for me, I brought up my idea.

"Did you do gifts in Christmas stockings when you were growing up?"

Eve laughed as she dug her fork into the food in front of her. "I told you: my mom is *crazy* for Christmas. When it comes to Christmas stuff, you name it and we did it." She put the fork into her mouth as she finished eating and let out a happy moan of satisfaction. "Julien, this is amazing!"

As usual, her compliment filled me with pride. "I'm glad you like it. I was taught how to make it when I volunteered in Thailand several years ago. It's better with fresh seafood, but in the middle of winter in Canada, we have to make do."

"It's perfect," she assured me, digging back in for another mouthful. "What about you? Did you have stockings growing up?"

"Yes, but when I was eleven or twelve, we started doing it a bit differently."

"What did you do?"

Eve had a way of asking a question that made me feel like she'd never found anything more interesting than she would find the answer to it. The rush it gave me at being the focus of that attention was almost intoxicating.

"My mother and I would fight quite a lot in those days. I would be angry with her and she would be frustrated with me, just in the way that all parents and children are, I think. But each day in December, we would put something small into a stocking for the other person. It didn't have to cost anything. It could be something we saw that made us think of the other person or just something we thought they might like. It might be something we made. The items themselves weren't really that important. Then, on Christmas Eve, she would ask me: do you like me enough today to give me my stocking?"

Eve smiled, appreciating my mom's bluntness as I thought she might. They might actually like each other, if my mom could get over her aversion to speaking in English.

"Sometimes, there was no question because we were having a good day. Other years, I would be angry with her on that day, for whatever reason, or just sad or bitter about not having the kind of Christmas that others did, people with more disposable income than we had and a father too. But no matter how I felt, when I would look at the things in the stocking and remember why I had put them all in there, it would remind me that love wasn't only about loving someone when it's easy. It was about going through the ups and downs together, and sticking by each other through it. And every year, in the end, we would open up our stockings together."

"That's really lovely." Eve's smile radiated warmth and understanding. "She sounds like a great mom."

"She always tried her best," I agreed. "But the reason I mentioned it is that I wondered if you might want to try it with me this year. Not because I think we'll be angry with each other, but just to see how much can change in just a few days as we get to know each other better. The thing I choose for you today might be very different from what I choose in a week's time."

She definitely hadn't anticipated that, and Eve's eyes widened in surprise. "For Christmas?"

Merde, I hadn't explained myself properly. Of course we wouldn't be spending Christmas together. "I just meant over the next week, while you're here in Toronto. You said you're here all of next week, right?"

"Yes, that's right. We leave next Friday."

"So, maybe we could exchange stockings on Wednesday or Thursday, after your meeting with the charity board, before you leave. If you want to."

The more I had to elaborate, the more foolish I felt. We barely knew each other, all things considered, and I'd just asked her to get me a weeks' worth of gifts. It sounded ridiculous the longer I thought about it from her point of view, and I had my mouth open to take it all back when Eve spoke again.

"I'd love to, Julien. In fact, I already know the perfect thing for today."

~Eve~

The more Julien explained about the stockings, the more I liked the idea. My gut reaction, based on all my past experience, had been to worry that he would use it as an excuse to try to impress me with expensive gifts, but as soon as I thought about it for more than a moment, I realized that fear was completely unfounded. He didn't believe in wasting money; he'd made that *very* clear, so whatever things he put in the stocking for me would be more symbolic than extravagant. They would show me how he perceived me and how he felt about this connection between us. And the simple fact that he suggested the idea of exchanging the gifts just before I returned to New York showed me that he saw us spending the next week together at the very least.

It would also give me a chance to examine how I felt about what was happening between us and about him, and to try to put those feelings into physical form. I relished the challenge.

The first thing that immediately sprang to mind from the day we'd spent together had to do with the key that sat in my pocket. Growing up, my best friend's parents always hung a key on their Christmas tree, and I remembered the explanation when I asked them why.

"I gave it to Holly the night I asked her to marry me," Jackson told me. "Although it opened my apartment door, it also meant that I gave her free access to every part of my life. To my heart. I trusted her with all of it, to come and go as she pleased, and she's never let me down."

Noelle rolled her eyes in that way kids always do about their parents' love stories, but I'd always remembered that, and thinking of the way Julien had entrusted me with his key, I could see some similarities. Yes, it provided access to his cock rather than his house, but the underlying sentiment felt the same: it all had to do with trust.

As we finished eating, him still wearing the tie and the cage and nothing else, the key sat even heavier in my pocket, calling to me. He'd shown me his trust in me, more than proven it, and I wanted to reward him for it.

"You mentioned props," I reminded him bluntly as he cleared the dishes away. "Is that still on the table for tonight?"

The plates clattered as they hit the counter, as if his hands had shaken while putting them down. "Oui. If you like."

When we were in this dynamic, everything we did was only if I liked it, and we both knew it. "Show me."

Wordlessly, he offered me his hand. We must have made an interesting visual with him mostly naked and me still fully clothed, him taller and stronger than me but making himself subservient to me, but to me, being there in that moment, it felt completely natural as I let him lead me to a door under the stairs, a door that opened to another staircase, going down.

"The basement is unfinished," he warned me. "We don't have to stay down there if you don't want to, but you can at least come and see what I've got."

With each step, my curiosity grew stronger. At the bottom of the staircase was a large, mostly empty room with a concrete floor, unfinished walls and a hanging lightbulb above our heads. It looked disconcertingly like the kind of place they showed on serial killer documentaries, the kind of barren, bleak environment that would make the viewers shout at their TVs, wondering what woman would have been stupid enough to walk into a place like that in the first place.

Had he brought me there just to kill me? I really didn't think so. It seemed like quite a lot of effort to go to, but it didn't change the fact that my heart beat a little faster as Julien let go of my hand and reached behind a jar on a shelf to retrieve a key to open the only door on the lower level. Every choice I'd made since we met started to feel rash and reckless, beginning with leaving the bar with a total stranger back in Quito. Not a soul in the world knew where I was. I hadn't even told my dad about Julien. No one would ever think to look for me there.

Just before my thoughts could spin completely out of control, Julien opened the door and pushed it open, flicking on the light as he stepped inside and asked me to follow. "Come and take a look."

Tentatively, I stepped forward until I could see into the room, ready to turn and run back up the stairs if I had to, but as the room came into view, I breathed a sigh of relief, laughing at myself for my wild imaginings.

Inside, the room bore a lot of similarities to the dungeon my parents had, though smaller and less elaborate. There were some BDSM apparatus that I recognized and a few restraint and impact items that looked familiar too. There were also quite a few things I didn't recognize. One item in particular, a bright pink strap-on dildo, caught my attention, but I focused my attention where Julien was pointing: a small bookshelf with a few items tucked away on it.

"Most of the women I've played with have their own costumes," he explained, looking sheepish about the small selection. "These are just a few accessories I keep on hand for some of my favourite scenes."

Curiously, I stepped close to get a better look. The first item I picked up was a lacy black mask like something from an 18th century masquerade ball, covering only the top half of the face. Almost instinctively, I placed it over my face to see how it felt. "So, this works for you?"

When I turned to face him, wearing the mask, Julien let out a grunt of discomfort, his body bending slightly at the waist, reminding me that his cage was still very much in place. It seemed he *did* like it, but perhaps I shouldn't tease him *too* much before I removed the cage.

Putting the mask back down, I picked up a leather riding crop next. I'd used one on a horse before, in my younger days when I learned show jumping at my aunt's farm in upstate New York, but I didn't think mentioning that would be appropriate. Instead, I turned the crop over in my hand, wondering how it would feel on the skin. If Julien owned it, he must like it, but I'd never hit another person before, not with *any* kind of instrument.

"It doesn't have to be used forcefully," he said, as if he were tuned into my thoughts. "It can simply be for aesthetic, for intimidation, or for a lighter sensation. It's up to the domme how she wants to use it."

My hand brushed over several of the other props, Julien offering an explanation where necessary, before landing on a pair of thick-framed black glasses with no lenses. "Are these for the teacher?"

"Yes." His voice sounded tight, as if even the thought of me wearing them turned him on. "And the belt."

A wide leather belt sat next to the glasses and I picked them both up. "Anything else?"

"Shoes." The word sounded almost painful as he pointed down to a pair of stiletto heels. "The rest is up to you."

I got the picture. "Okay, here's what we're going to do. First, I'm going to take the cage off. Second, you're going to go upstairs and get dressed again. When ten minutes have passed, you'll come back to the kitchen, which is now our classroom. Any questions?"

Tongue-tied with arousal, he simply shook his head as I reached into my pocket to pull out the key. As soon as the cage was removed, he pulled the ring off himself, moving quickly before his cock could start to swell. "I'll be there on time, Madame," he promised before making his way upstairs, leaving me alone in his supply room to figure out how I wanted to play this and exactly how to make the rest of the scene as pleasurable as possible for both of us.

~Julien~

I'd never taken anyone down to the supply room in my basement before. Usually, my dommes preferred to play in their space where they had all their own equipment and props. On the rare occasions that I had someone over at my house, I went down alone to get what we needed, or had it set up before she arrived. It felt significant to me to visit the room with Eve, like it would help her to understand me even more than she already did, and although she seemed a little overwhelmed when we first walked in, she soon rose to the occasion, as usual.

Like I certainly had since she took my cage off.

Tucking my stiff cock back into my pants as I got redressed couldn't be called comfortable, but I didn't mind a bit of discomfort when I anticipated getting such a wonderful reward. The ease and willingness with which she entered into the roleplay floored me once again. She was like a fish taking to water, finding her comfort zone and her element, and I felt privileged just to be able to witness it, let alone participate in it.

With a close eye on the clock, I waited until the ten minutes she'd requested were up before I headed back down the stairs. I'd chosen a t-shirt and jeans, trying to look like a typical college student, but I'd left my feet bare. Socks would be one less thing to take off when the time came.

Speaking of time, Eve hadn't wasted any. My dining room table had been pulled out to serve as a desk with a chair in front of it that she must want me to sit in, when she instructed me to do so. The dishes from dinner had all been moved into the sink, clearing the counter off in case we needed to make use of that too. I honestly couldn't guess what she might have in mind.

Then, there was Eve herself. My gaze fell first on the high black stiletto shoes, giving her an extra four inches of height that only increased her commanding presence. Around her waist, she'd secured the belt from my supply room. Wider than a usual belt, it didn't cause quite as much sting when being struck with it, but there was something about seeing the domme take it off to use it on me that did crazy things to my body. And finally, she had the thick glasses on her face, looking down at a book she'd picked off my bookshelf, and she'd also pulled her hair up into a stern, sexy bun.

She looked absolutely fucking perfect.

My arrival seemed to go unnoticed as she didn't look up from her book, but I knew better. As soon as she licked her finger, slowly and dramatically, before turning the next page, I knew she had already started the scene. I simply had to wait and see what she wanted me to do.

At last, she glanced up at me over the rim of her glasses, her expression cool and unimpressed. "You're late, Julien. Do you *want* to fail my class?"

"Non, Madame E. Je m'excuse."

One critical eyebrow raised, her look of disapproval growing stronger. "What have I told you about only speaking in English?"

Crisse. That would be difficult, since my brain reverted to French every time she made me dizzy with lust, but if she wanted me to try, I would do my best.

"I'm sorry. Why did you want to see me, Professor?"

"Sit down."

Her eyes moved to the chair, just the tiniest movement, and my body immediately obeyed. I had taken a seat almost before I consciously decided to move. My hands folded across my lap, partly to look penitent and partly to try to hide my growing erection.

Eve snapped her book shut, the sound making me jump. "Your last term paper was a big disappointment. I know you're capable of better work. What's holding you back?"

"Nothing, Professor. I'll try harder next time."

"Julien." With a sigh, Eve placed the book down on the table and walked around to my side of the 'desk'. Leaning down, she hooked a finger under my chin to raise my head, forcing me to look at her. "If you can't give me a good reason for your shoddy work, then I'm afraid I'll have to punish you."

Oui, calisse. Even through my lust and arousal, I tried to make note of everything she did. It all came so naturally to her, and just the thought of her in this persona could fuel my fantasies for a long time to come.

"So, let's try this again." Her voice got dangerously quiet as she leaned even closer to me. "What would make your work better?"

"I... I don't know, Professor." Playing clueless, I hoped she hadn't been kidding about the punishment, and when she pushed me back with a disappointed huff, I got my answer.

"If the promise of success won't motivate you, then maybe the fear of failure will. Stand up and pull down your pants."

I gave her my best startled expression, as if the command had come out of nowhere. "Professor?"

"You heard me. Pull them down and put your hands flat on the table. Now. Every second you waste will be another lash."

Quickly, I got to my feet, fumbling with the buttons as my hands trembled, not in fear but in anticipation.

"One." Eve counted the seconds as I hurried to pull my jeans down, leaving my underwear on as she hadn't mentioned it. "Two."

My hands hit the table as I leaned forward, my legs spread to help keep my balance, my jeans around my knees.

"Better. But not quite good enough." With her eyes locked on mine, she slowly undid the belt around her waist. "This should help you move a little faster next time."

Her small hand could barely wrap around the width of the belt, but she didn't let that stop her. Stepping behind me, out of my line of vision, she took her time, leaving me waiting in limbo, not knowing when the strike would come.

When it did, I jumped in surprise. She put some force into it, not playing around, and my cock immediately jumped inside my briefs.

"Count them off as I give them to you," she ordered, and I did, counting each strike on the back of my legs until she got to five. The sting wasn't insignificant, but it didn't truly hurt either. Just enough that I could feel it. "Have you learned your lesson now?"

"Oui, Madame."

I didn't mean to do it. Through my haze of arousal, the words dropped from my lips in French, and she struck me once more.

"Yes. Yes, Professor," I tried again, and satisfied, she laid the belt down on the table next to me.

"Stand up," she commanded, and when I did, her eyes dropped to my crotch. "Is that for me, Julien? Did it make you hard when I hit you?"

I forced myself to meet her eyes, her dark, inscrutable eyes behind the thick black glasses. "Yes, Professor. It's all because of you."

"Show me."

Not wanting to disobey her, I pulled down my underwear, revealing my cock that somehow looked even bigger and harder after seeing it locked away in the cage. From the way Eve's lips parted, I felt certain she noticed it too.

"Is this the real reason your work has been so mediocre? You're too turned on to concentrate?"

That certainly seemed like a possibility. "That might be it, Professor."

Eve smirked, pleased with my agreement. "Well, I always do anything I can to help my students. If I let you fuck me, will you promise to get an A on the next paper?"

"Yes. I promise."

My eager tone made her laugh as she instructed me to get fully undressed. I had thrown a condom in the pocket of my jeans, so I put it on once I had my clothes off, and Eve somehow managed to get her pants off without removing the shoes, which truly impressed me.

When we were both ready, she climbed up on my dining room table, lay on her back, grabbed her book again, and spread her legs. "See if you can make me lose my place."

Grinning at the challenge, I grabbed hold of her heels and placed them beneath my arms where I would feel them but they wouldn't accidentally puncture anything I didn't want punctured. She leaned back on one elbow, the other arm holding her book, turning her attention back to it while I guided my stiff cock to her entrance.

The wetness that greeted me there was the first real proof I had of just how much she was enjoying the scene too. She looked so cool and controlled on the outside, I appreciated seeing the proof from her body that inside, she must have been feeling it just as I was.

I started off slow, pushing into her inch by inch, the table steady beneath us. Eve stifled a yawn, even as her thigh muscles clenched.

The pace got faster, fast enough that she had to reach down and grab onto the table with her spare hand to steady herself, but still, she didn't look up from her book.

I went for her clit next, rubbing it with my fingers as I continued to thrust into her, even harder than before. Eve's teeth dragged across her lower lip and her eyelids began to close, but still she fought me, trying to keep reading. With an uncharacteristic show of dominance that surprised us both, I pulled the book from her hand and tossed it across the room.

Eve's eyes went wide. "I'll have to punish you again for that."

"I hope you will, Professor. But first, I'm going to finish my current assignment."

With nothing left to distract her, Eve gave in. As I thrust into her again, she let out a moan, one of the many she must have been holding in, and as my fingers rubbed over her clit again, she gasped.

"This is... top... quality work, Julien." She tried her best to stay in character, but at the last second, she broke. "Fuck, yes, right there."

I followed her instructions, giving her exactly what she asked for, and when she came on top of my dining room table, I immediately followed. Knowing I'd pleased her gave me the greatest pleasure of all, and my body seemed to melt into a fully satisfied pool of warmth and fulfilment as I gazed down at her.

We'd only just begun to explore, and already, I couldn't imagine how it could get any better.

Chapter Nine

MARKET

~Eve~

The gentle chime of my phone woke me up in the morning. In my flannel Christmas pajamas, tucked into the warm, comfortable bed in my hotel room, feeling both satisfied and hopeful, I took a moment for a long, luxurious stretch as the world came back into focus around me.

The evening with Julien couldn't have gone any better. Although I took control in our sexual encounters, he pushed my boundaries in all kinds of ways, and though not everything we tried would end up being for me, I loved that he was willing to introduce me to things and let me make up my own mind. His confidence about his own sexual preferences turned me on immensely. He knew what he liked and he didn't hide it or apologize for it, and the fact that we fit so well together just made it even better.

That didn't even begin to cover his charm, good looks, intelligence and passion.

Only one thing stood between me and total contentment with the whole situation, and that had to do with the confession I still had to make to him. After I returned to the hotel last night and looked around at my expensive room in the hotel that bore my name, doubts began to creep in about my decision to keep quiet about my family. Yes, I wanted him to like me for me, to give me a chance before he judged me based on something out of my control, but how could he truly know me if he didn't know the truth of my circumstances? How long did it take before withholding information became outright dishonesty?

I hadn't been able to come up with an answer to that before I fell asleep, and I felt no closer to one that morning as I reached over to grab my phone off the bedside table. The text that woke me came from my dad.

I've made a reservation for brunch at the restaurant for 11. See you there.

Groggily, I glanced over at the clock and started in surprise as I realized it said 10:07. The day with Julien must have worn me out more than I realized, and I didn't have a lot of time to waste, but I couldn't resist taking a peek out the window once I got out of bed, on my way to the bathroom.

The morning sky was a light china blue, pale and delicate above the snow-covered city. The previous night's snowfall still rested on the rooftops and the branches of the trees, covering everything in a blanket of white as far as I could see. With no clouds, the temperature would be colder, but I decided to go ahead with my plan to wear a skirt for the day anyway. I had some thick tights that would help keep my legs warm, and Julien might appreciate seeing me in it.

We didn't have any firm plans yet. I told him I had some other commitments but that I would let him know as soon as they were complete. He told me he'd be staying home to catch up on work, despite it being Saturday, and to text him as soon as I knew more. The implication seemed clear on both sides: we would make spending more time together a priority, as much as we could.

Having showered and dressed in my white sweater and red-and-white checked skirt with red tights and white boots, I found my dad at the window table in the restaurant where we'd eaten the other night. He had his nose in some papers as I walked up, but as soon as he caught sight of me from the corner of his eye, he looked up and smiled, immediately brushing the papers aside.

"You look rather festive. Your mother would approve."

"But you don't?" I teased him. We all knew my dad liked Christmas too, he just liked to pretend he didn't get as excited about it as my mom did.

"Of course I do." He stood up to kiss my cheek. "You look beautiful, especially with that smile on your face. I take it you had a good day yesterday?"

I nearly stumbled as he pulled out my chair for me. Obviously, I couldn't tell him *everything* I'd done with Julien, but I could share the safe-for-work content. "Yes, actually. I met up with a new friend and visited some interesting places around the city." As we looked over the menu, I told him about the pioneer village and Casa Loma. "If you're ever looking for a date idea for Mom, she'd love it."

One eyebrow raised at me. "What makes you think I need dating advice?"

I raised mine right back at him. "What makes you think I don't have advice worth listening to?"

His answering smirk was all the answer I got, but it was enough. We'd always gotten each other, me and my dad, except when it came to what I wanted to do with my life, and that was the thing I really wanted to talk to him about that morning. So, once our orders were placed and I had his full attention, I bit the bullet.

"Dad, I appreciate you setting up the dinner with the director the other night, but I have to be honest: I'm not interested in working with him."

That part, I didn't expect him to have a problem with, and he didn't. "Alright. Honestly, your mom wasn't too thrilled about that idea anyway since it would have you travelling quite a lot. I'll talk to a few other people and see what other opportunities might be of interest."

That was where the problem was going to be. As difficult as it would be for him to hear it, I had to be completely honest with him, and thinking of the passion Julien had for helping people helped me to find the courage to say it outright, without any further delay. "Dad, stop. I'm not interested in working for Stamer Hotels in *any* capacity. However, I would like to work *with* the business."

His brows furrowed at me from over the table as he leaned forward, the sun through the window glinting off the silver strands in his dark hair. "What do you mean?"

Forcing myself to hold his piercing gaze, I shared my vision. "I've had an idea for a charitable program that would match up charities, young people, and corporate recruitment. It would see young people just out of college, just like me, volunteering abroad through charity programs, funded by corporations who are interested in hiring those young people upon their return. It's a social responsibility windfall for the companies, the charities get free skilled labour, the participants get invaluable experience, and people around the world get to benefit from it. I think it could be amazing, and I'm really excited about it."

The clattering of silverware from the other diners in the room suddenly seemed almost deafening as I stopped talking and my father made no reply. My heart pounded in anticipation of his response, yet I also felt a new lightness at having finally gotten it off my chest. There was no going back now; he knew exactly how I felt.

"So... you wouldn't be working for Stamer Hotels?" he finally asked, speaking slowly as if it didn't entirely make sense to him.

"No."

"Who would you be working for, then?"

"At first, I'm hoping to run a pilot project with one particular charity. Eventually, I would create a separate foundation to run it so that more charities could be involved. It would be a charity of its own, essentially." He still looked so confused that I reached across the table and put my hand on his. "Dad, it's not the end of the world. You knew when I did this charity placement that I wanted to explore other things."

"I did, but I always thought you'd come back to us in the end. You're a Stamer, Eve. You're more like me than anyone, and this business is our legacy."

"It's *your* legacy," I corrected gently. "Being a Stamer has nothing to do with the hotels. I'll always be a part of this family, no matter what I do. It doesn't mean I love you any less."

As he inhaled, his nostrils flaring slightly, I thought perhaps I'd just hit the nail on the head without even realizing it. He loved me and he loved his business, so he wanted me to love the business too. Me rejecting the business felt to him like I had rejected him in some way, but that had never been my intention. Loving someone didn't necessarily mean sharing the same feelings about every single part of their lives. In fact, sometimes, loving someone meant accepting that you didn't always agree.

Clearing his throat, my dad gave my hand a squeeze before reaching for his wine glass. "Alright, let's hear the numbers. I assume you've got a business plan? Convince me that it's going to work."

That was exactly what I needed. "I've actually got a meeting set up next week with a charity board. Can I practice my presentation on you?"

"At least three times, if you want to nail it. We can start with the first run-through now."

The smile he gave me wouldn't be considered big by anyone's standards, but it said so much to me: in that smile was understanding, respect, support, and love, and I honestly couldn't remember why I'd been so worried to open up to him about it in the first place.

Maybe it really was better just to get things out in the open, as soon as possible. Maybe that applied to Julien as well. It would definitely give me something to think about before I saw him again later that day.

After finishing our brunch together, my dad suggested that we visit one of the city's Christmas markets. "I still need to buy a few gifts before we get back to New York. Having you there would make it much more bearable."

His tortured tone made me laugh. My dad hated shopping, but luckily for him, his personal assistant usually took care of anything my mom didn't. Only when it came to personal gifts did he bite the bullet and do it himself.

After how supportive he'd just been in reviewing my presentation with me and giving me a ton of useful notes and suggestions, helping him pick out a few gifts was the least I could do, not to mention I had a few I wanted to get myself. "Sure. That sounds like fun."

"I wouldn't go that far." His dry reply had me laughing again, and I excused myself to use the restroom while he called a car for us. While on my own, I sent Julien a quick update.

It looks like I'll be busy this afternoon, but I'm still hoping to see you later.

His simple reply filled my heart with warmth. *Have fun. I'll be waiting.*

The market my dad chose was located in the Distillery District, a complex of industrial Victorian buildings, once a distillery and now a popular shopping and entertainment district. For the Christmas season, the whole place had been transformed into a 'winter village', full of market stalls selling handmade, artisanal goods and delicious-smelling food, with an enormous decorated Christmas tree at the entrance. Lights were strung above our heads as we entered the pedestrian-only, cobblestone streets, and I could imagine it would look even more magical at night. Even during the day, it felt pretty special.

After posing for a selfie in front of the Christmas tree that my dad immediately texted to my mom, he offered me his arm to walk through the market itself. The gesture, so ingrained for him, reminded me of the first time he'd done it, the first time I was old enough to be able to take his arm comfortably as we walked side-by-side. We'd been going to a movie in New York, just me and him since neither my mom nor Noah had been interested in it, and it had made me feel almost impossibly grown-up. Years later, the exact same gesture left me feeling nostalgic.

Wasn't it funny how a little time could alter a person's perspective so much?

We took our time looking through all the booths. Although I already had a gift for Noah, I picked him up a Christmas ornament from a hockey-themed stall. He and his father-in-law often went to hockey games together, and since he and Olivia had just started putting up their own tree the year before, it still needed more personalized decorations to fill it out. The one I chose felt like a good fit.

At another stall, I found a hand-knit stocking that came from a fair-trade collective in Asia. It would be perfect for my stocking exchange with Julien, so I immediately bought it while my dad watched curiously. "Who's that for?"

"Just a friend." I didn't want to say anything more until Julien and I had discussed whether we were going to continue with a relationship beyond next week. I certainly hoped we would, but I didn't want to jump the gun by assuming.

At a jewellery booth, we found a necklace with hanging miniature Christmas lights pendants, each made of a different semi-precious stone. With the price set at a few hundred dollars, it sat further back in the stall, out of reach, but my dad zeroed in on it immediately. "It's perfect," he told me with that soft look in his eyes reserved just for my mom. Immediately switching to negotiating mode, he turned to the woman in the booth. "How many of these have you made?"

"About ten so far. They're all one-of-a-kind," she assured him. "Each one is handmade and takes several days to make."

"And how many have you sold?"

His businesslike tone, or perhaps the cut of his suit and his well-groomed appearance seemed to convince the woman he had a genuine reason for asking. "To be honest? None yet. They're a little expensive because of the materials and time taken."

"Good. I'll take all ten. How much would you need to stop making them?"

"Dad!" I knew exactly what he was doing. Just getting the necklace for my mom wasn't enough; he wanted to make sure she was the only one who had one. While the thought had a certain romanticism to it, it seemed a bit selfish as well. What if the woman *wanted* to keep making them? And what about the cost? Weren't they better things he could spend the money on?

The jewellery-maker didn't seem to share my concerns. "A thousand dollars on top of the cost of the ten necklaces?" she suggested, trying not to look too excited. Mostly, she seemed a bit stunned.

"Done." He pulled out his credit card and nodded at her to start packaging everything up. "Did you want to say something, Eve?"

"Never mind." He looked so pleased with himself that I didn't want to lecture him. With the best of intentions, he honestly didn't have a clue what he'd done wrong.

"Is there anything you like?" he asked, gesturing to the other items in the stall.

They were all beautiful, but the handmade jewellery I'd received from a woman in Ecuador that I helped to find a new home for her and her baby meant far to me. "No, thank you. Don't tell me you're still shopping for *my* present?"

He gave an almost sheepish shrug. "Okay, I won't, but if you see something you love, I might send you away to look at something else for a minute, for completely unrelated reasons." When I rolled my eyes, he grinned, a rare sight from my dad, as he reached over to put his arm around me, pulling me close and giving me a kiss on the forehead. "I've missed you, Eve."

As the stall owner held out her card machine to take his payment, I took a step back, and another voice said my name, one coming from behind me. "Well, hello, Eve."

Besides Julien, I didn't think I knew anyone else in Toronto, and the voice certainly didn't belong to Julien. Feminine and a little cool, I had no idea who it belonged to until I turned around. Even then, it took a moment for me to make the connection since the circumstances of our first meeting had been so unusual, but eventually, I put it together.

"Hi. It's Claire, right?" It helped that Julien's assistant was dressed almost the same as she had been the night she'd walked in on me in Julien's living room, in her winter coat, hat and scarf, just a hint of blonde hair peeking out from underneath. In the daylight, I could see her pale blue eyes much better, though I wouldn't say they looked much more friendly than they had that night.

"That's right." She glanced between me and my dad, who was still paying for his purchase, and my stomach immediately constricted. Did she recognize my dad? What if she said something to Julien about seeing me there with him before I had a chance to? Guilt and worry immediately began to gnaw away at me, as her expression seemed to grow even colder. "You're making the most of your time in town, I see."

Assuming she meant the market, I glanced around and nodded. "It's a beautiful city and the people are so friendly. I'm enjoying my stay very much. Are you getting some shopping done too?"

Since she had a bag in her hand, I hoped we could find some common ground by talking about something completely innocent. However, she tightened her grip on the bag as my gaze fell on it, making her look even less friendly than before. "Yes. Just a few things for people at work."

"That's nice. I'm really looking forward to meeting the rest of the team there on Wednesday." My heart was still pounding, trying to guess what might be going through her head from her expression, but she didn't give me much to work with other than vague disapproval. Was that residual disapproval from finding me at Julien's or did it mean something else? Honestly, I couldn't guess.

"Well, we'll see you then. Enjoy the rest of your day." With one more glance at the back of my dad's head, she turned and left, just as my dad finished paying.

"Who was that?" he asked, having heard me speaking to someone but too busy with his transaction to pay full attention.

"Someone from the charity I worked with. Pretty random to run into her here." I kept my voice bright to try to avoid any further questions, and it worked. Satisfied with that answer, my dad and I moved on to the rest of the stalls, but my thoughts remained with Julien and the sword I could feel dangling over my head. Hopefully, I would still have a chance to tell him the truth before he found out from Claire or someone else.

Hopefully, I hadn't already waited too long.

~Julien~

Although I'd taken Friday off, spending the whole of Saturday in my home office wasn't an unusual situation. More work could always be done, and since I had nowhere else I had to be and Eve had other obligations for the day, I took advantage of the time to try to get caught up on anything I'd missed the day before. Aside from a quick break to run some errands and pick up a couple of things for the stocking I'd already started assembling for Eve, I barely left my desk all day until someone knocked at my door mid-afternoon.

Immediately, my heart beat a little faster in anticipation. I hadn't expected Eve to simply turn up without making arrangements with me in advance, but it would thrill me if she had. Running a hand through my hair to make sure it looked alright, I made my way quickly to the front door, a smile already on my face.

However, when I opened the door, Claire stood there instead, her hands shoved in her pockets, looking even more unsure of herself than usual. "Hi, Julien. Can we talk?"

I hadn't heard from her since the short text she'd sent me the day before, and I hadn't been looking forward to the awkwardness of Monday morning. Though it surprised me to see her there, I appreciated that she'd taken the initiative to come over and talk things out in person. It would be better for both of us in the long run. "Of course. Come in."

As soon as I stepped aside, she walked in, stomping her boots on the welcome mat to remove the loose snow before taking them off. Taking her hat, scarf and coat, I hung them all on the coat rack before gesturing to the couch in the living room, next to the tree that she'd decorated for me.

"Do you want something to drink?"

"White wine?" she suggested, and though I hadn't really meant something alcoholic, I didn't refuse her either. We weren't at work so there was no reason we couldn't.

Returning to the living room with two glasses of wine, I handed one to her before taking a seat in the chair across from her.

"You've got everything you need for the benefit tomorrow, right?" she asked. "I'm still available if you want some backup."

I still intended to ask Eve to attend it with me, so that wouldn't be necessary, but I didn't bother saying that to her. I wanted to get to the point. "You didn't come here to talk about the benefit, did you? I assume you want to talk about Eve."

Claire nodded, taking a long sip from her glass as if it would help her to speak. Lowering it again, she licked her lips. That gesture from Eve would have driven me crazy, but when Claire did it, I felt nothing at all. Funny how much the sexiness of an action depended on the person doing it.

When she finally did speak, her words were blunt and to the point. "In all the time we've worked together, you've always been completely professional, so it worries me you'd be getting involved with a volunteer, especially one who wants to work more closely with you in the future."

I assumed that had been her concern, and it seemed my suspicions were correct. "As I told you in the text, my personal feelings have nothing to do with the program that Eve is proposing. I've declared my conflict to the board, they're aware of it and we've agreed that although they'll take my opinion into account, I won't have any direct say into whether they approve the program or not. Everything is above board, Claire, so you don't need to worry."

"I'm not worried about the charity," she confirmed, to my relief. "I know you wouldn't do anything to endanger everyone's hard work or the charity's reputation. I'm worried about you, though."

Me? That statement took me completely by surprise, and though I couldn't quite imagine what she meant by it, I tried to guess. "You think my position is compromised?"

Claire quickly shook her head. "No. I'm not worried about you professionally. When you told me you understood the implications and were doing all the right things, you put my mind at ease about that."

"Then, what are you worried about?"

Taking another gulp from her wine glass, Claire looked me in the eye. "I'm worried that you're going to get hurt. By Eve, I mean."

How she had jumped to that conclusion, I had no idea, and my initial reaction was defensiveness. "First of all, it's not really any of your business, Claire. And second, you don't know Eve at all. Why would you assume anything about her?"

Claire's startled, hurt expression immediately made me feel guilty for snapping at her, and her words didn't help. "I thought we were friends."

Tabarnak. I hadn't meant to offend her. "We are." *Work* friends, I added in my head, but she had done plenty of more personal favours for me too. Maybe it shouldn't surprise me that she felt she knew me better than she actually did.

"And don't friends look out for each other?" she asked next.

I couldn't deny that. "They do. I'm sorry, I appreciate your concern, but I don't understand it. As I said, you don't know Eve."

"I got a pretty thorough introduction to her the other night," she argued back, and my eyebrows raised in surprise. Claire wasn't usually so direct, so it must have really upset her. "Most people in her situation would have been at least a little flustered, but she didn't seem bothered by it at all."

What did that have to do with anything? "So… she's going to hurt me because she's confident? I'm not following."

"Confidence is one thing, but a lack of embarrassment can be a sign of a lack of empathy." She sounded like she was quoting something, like she'd looked it up. "It can show selfishness."

"That seems like quite a leap to make based on one interaction." With each new word out of her mouth, I found myself questioning not only Claire's decision to come to my house, but also my faith in her judgement in general.

"I thought so too," she quickly agreed. "It was just a gut feeling, and I wasn't going to say anything to you about it until what happened today."

Once again, I felt I'd missed something. "What happened today?"

"I went to the Christmas market in the Distillery District, and I ran into Eve there."

A smile crossed my face at the thought; Eve would love it there. I could almost picture how excited she'd be by the architectural details and the Christmas decorations, and it made me glad to know she was enjoying herself, even if I wished I could have been there with her.

"She wasn't alone," Claire added. "She was with another man."

She clearly wanted a reaction out of me, but I didn't plan to give her one. Eve told me she had plans and though she hadn't said specifically with whom, I hadn't asked either. She didn't owe me any explanation.

"Men and women are allowed to spend time together without it being romantic," I pointed out to Claire mildly. "Just like we're doing now."

"He kissed her." Claire blurted the words out almost too forcefully, as if the volume of them would convince me to take her seriously. "He bought her jewellery and he kissed her."

Against my will, my stomach twisted. Strangely, the kissing part didn't even bother me as much as the jewellery part did. Eve wasn't the kind of woman to be swayed by gifts like that.

At least, I thought she wasn't. "You actually saw that happen?"

Claire nodded vigorously. "With my own eyes. She saw me a minute later, and she looked incredibly guilty, probably wondering how much I'd seen. She must not have wanted it to get back to you. Because why else would someone who wasn't in the least bit bothered about me walking in on her naked suddenly be worried about me seeing her with another man, unless she had something to hide?"

That was a good question, and one that only Eve could answer. When I saw Eve that evening, I would ask her myself.

Chapter Ten

CONFESSION

~Eve~

On the way back to the hotel with our purchases from the market, my dad's phone rang. From his clipped responses, I couldn't tell what was going on, but when he hung up, he turned to me with a sigh. "I'm sorry, Eve, I've been called into another meeting this evening. I'd been planning on taking you to see the Nutcracker as a surprise, but I'm afraid I won't be able to."

For someone who claimed to be indifferent towards Christmas, he sure seemed to have a lot of nostalgia about it. He and my mom always used to take me and Noah to see the Nutcracker in New York every December when we were young, and that must be why he'd thought about taking me to it that evening.

"That's okay, Dad. It's a sweet idea, but I'll be fine on my own. You know you *could* delegate some of this work to other people though, right?"

Despite his seeming invincibility, my dad was getting older. His 60th birthday wasn't *that* many years away, and with Noah already in place to take over for him, he could start to step back a little if he wanted to. No one would blame him.

He knew exactly what I was getting at, and an unimpressed look was my reward for my concern. "I'm not ready to shuffle off to the retirement home just yet."

I pursed my lips at him across the backseat. "No one's saying that. I only meant that it's a Saturday evening in December. You shouldn't have to drop your own plans to deal with company business."

"I wouldn't if it wasn't important. It'd be a shame to let the ballet tickets go to waste, though. Do you want them? Maybe you could take your friend that you went sightseeing with yesterday?"

That idea made me smile. Julien struck me as the kind of man who would appreciate a cultural evening, and if I made it clear the tickets had been donated to us, that I hadn't paid for them, he shouldn't mind the cost of them. "Sure. I can see if they're available."

He transferred the tickets to my phone before pulling up his calendar to look at his plans for the next day. "We're definitely having dinner together tomorrow evening, though. Five o'clock. Dress up."

That sounded intriguing. "What's the occasion?"

"You'll see." His smirk let me know I wouldn't be getting any further information on the subject out of him.

When we returned to the hotel, he went to his meeting while I went up to my room to drop off my purchases and to send a text to Julien. I had no idea if Claire would have said anything to him yet about running into me, so I decided to keep my tone light, testing the waters.

This is a little random, but I have free tickets to the Nutcracker tonight. Would you like to go? Dinner first, my treat.

His reply made me laugh when it came in a moment later. *Ballerinas have never been my thing, but those hard-assed ballet teachers in the movies? Yes, please.*

He didn't seem angry with me, so that must mean Claire hadn't spoken to him yet, thankfully.

Is that a yes on the ballet, then? I responded.

Yes. I know a quiet restaurant near the Four Seasons Centre where we can go for dinner and talk.

We did need to talk, but it surprised me to hear him say it. Maybe he just meant the restaurant wasn't too loud, and good for conversation? Although his English was excellent, he did occasionally phrase things in a way that I wouldn't have.

It didn't take me long to freshen up and make my way down to Queen Street, where both the performing arts centre and restaurant were located. On my way, I passed a key cutting store, which I took as some kind of sign. The man working there thought it a bit strange that I simply wanted a key, not cut to any specific pattern, but he sold me one anyway. Just before I left the store, I noticed that they also sold smoke detectors, and I bought one of those for Julien's stocking too. It reminded me of our evening together in his hotel in Quito and how we'd been interrupted by the fire alarm. Hopefully, it would make him smile.

Tucking both purchases into my purse, I found Julien waiting for me, as promised, in front of the Korean restaurant he'd chosen. Inside, dark walls made the candlelit booths appear even cozier. Lined up around the edge of the room, each bench had high backs separating the booths from each other, making each one as close to a private room as possible. Each table had a built-in grill in the table itself, so we could cook all the meat to our own liking, and once Julien had placed the order and the waiter had brought our drinks, we were finally left alone.

"Did you have a good day?" Julien asked, his fingers resting lightly around his drink glass. Unlike his flirty texts earlier, he seemed a little subdued, but perhaps I had just gotten too used to how unrestrained he was in private.

I gave him a warm smile to try to set him more at ease. "I did, thank you. What about you? Did you get a lot of work done?"

"Quite a lot, yes." He returned my smile, but his brown eyes had a distance in them that hadn't been there before. Or was I just imagining it, worried about how he might react when I told him the truth I'd been concealing? "What did you do?"

I could answer that honestly, since it led into what I wanted to talk to him about anyway. "I went to the Christmas market at the Distillery District. It's beautiful there."

"It is." He nodded in agreement. "Did you go alone?"

The way he asked the question and his general uneasiness made sense to me in only one context: Claire *had* talked to him. She must have. Why else would he be acting so strangely?

In that case, I was going to have to come clean, ready or not. "No, I didn't go alone, but I did run into someone there, someone you know. I'm guessing you already know that."

His lips tightened, making him look even more uncomfortable than before. "Claire told me she spoke to you and she told me what she saw. I'm not jumping to any conclusions, Eve, or at least, I'm trying not to. I understand we haven't made any kind of commitment to each other, and I'd prefer if we were honest with each other."

Commitment to each other? What did that have to do with my dad? My brow furrowed deeply as I tried to figure out what he meant. "Wait. What did Claire tell you?"

Julien swallowed, his fingers gently spinning the glass around on the table to give him something to focus on. "She said she saw you with another man. She said he kissed you and bought you jewellery."

She said *what?* The whole time, I'd been worried that she'd discovered my secret, but obviously, she hadn't recognized my dad at all. She thought...

She thought...

The ridiculousness of what she thought and the relief I felt over not having been unintentionally outed combined to draw a long, deep laugh out of me, which both startled and confused Julien.

"Why is that so funny?" he asked curiously, his eyes a little brighter as he realized I wasn't upset.

"The man she saw me with was my father!" As handsome as my dad might be, he was *not* my type, not to mention he was more than thirty years older than me. Claire might have those kinds of daddy issues but I definitely did not.

Relief flashed in Julien's eyes, along with more confusion. "You were kissing your father?"

"Not like that!" I shook my head in disbelief. Had Claire really mistaken the innocent affection my father showed me for something else, or had she been trying to drive a wedge between me and Julien? She certainly hadn't wasted any time in telling him about it. "He kissed me on the forehead. And the jewellery he bought wasn't for me; he bought it for my mom, for Christmas."

"Oh." Julien's expression cleared entirely, his face breaking into a relieved smile that looked much more characteristic on his face. "I'm sorry. Obviously, she misunderstood."

I wasn't sure about that. It felt to me to be almost a willful misconstruction rather than a simple error. Thankfully, Julien took the initiative to ask me about it rather than simply taking her word for it. It stung a little bit that he would have even harboured doubts about whether I would be spending time with someone else behind his back after I told him I wasn't seeing anyone, but I couldn't entirely blame him. After all, in the grand scheme of things, we hadn't known each other very long.

And besides, there was *something* I'd hidden from him, just not that. Maybe this was the time to get that out in the open too, once and for all.

~Julien~

I couldn't have felt any more relieved or more foolish after Eve explained she'd spent the day with her father.

I'd tried to steel myself for whatever her response might be. I hoped she wouldn't deny it or try to hide it, but equally, I feared her saying that I'd assumed too much and that she'd never been interested in being exclusive with me. On the walk over to the restaurant, I'd imagined a thousand different ways she might react, but I had never expected her to start laughing.

When she told me why, that the man she'd been with had been her father, I felt a million times lighter all at once, but also embarrassed about putting her on the spot in the first place. She didn't seem put out by the accusation, but I felt terrible; I should have trusted her more than that. She hadn't done anything at all to make me think I couldn't trust her.

Eve leaned towards me across the table, her dark eyes catching the light from the candles between us. "There *is* something I want to tell you, though, Julien. Something about my father."

For a moment, I almost thought I could see guilt on her face, and it reminded me of what Claire had said: she thought Eve looked guilty that afternoon, and that had been part of the reason Claire assumed Eve had done something that might hurt me.

Maybe Claire had it wrong, just like she'd misunderstood the whole situation, because Eve shouldn't have looked guilty about being there with her father. What else would she have to feel guilty about?

I tried my best to set her at ease, especially since she'd taken the whole mix-up so well. "Of course. You can tell me anything. What..."

My question was interrupted as a shadow fell across the table. "Julien? I thought that was you."

Looking up at the smiling man with the greying hair who had just approached us, I did my best to return his smile sincerely. "Mr Measner. This is a nice surprise."

I both meant that and didn't mean it at the nice time. The head of the charity's board was a charming, friendly man, and we got along very well. Normally, I would have been happy to see him unexpectedly, but I'd been waiting all day to spend some time with Eve and I didn't want to waste any of the time we had.

However, since Eve would be meeting him later in the week at the meeting about her proposal, speaking to him that evening might be a chance to erase any awkwardness caused by my disclosure to him that Eve and I were seeing each other socially. With all that in mind, I quickly introduced her. "Eve, this is Mr Measner, the chairman of the charity's board. Mr Measner, this is Eve Sudlow, the young woman I told you about who will be sharing her proposal with the board next week."

"A pleasure to meet you." With a friendly smile, he held out his hand to Eve, who shook it firmly and confidently. "This is my wife, Patricia. We're here to grab a quick supper before the ballet tonight."

"So are we," Eve told them, also shaking hands with Mrs Measner and gracing them with one of her beautiful, elegant smiles. "It's a Christmas tradition for me, it's not fully Christmas without the Nutcracker."

"We're just the same," Mrs Measner agreed. "We always took our children, and now, we usually take the grandchildren, but this year, it's just the two of us. It'll be a bit strange."

She sounded a bit sad about it, but Eve had a perfect response. "I bet there will be a little less pressure without having to worry about entertaining someone else. You can just enjoy it."

"I think you're right." The two women shared a smile of understanding, and pride swelled inside me at Eve's natural charm and ability to put everyone at ease.

Unfortunately, she seemed to put Mr Measner *too* much at ease. "Well, if we're all on the same timeline, why don't we join you?" he suggested. "You can tell me a little about your proposal before the meeting."

"Harold, they're on a date," his wife admonished him quietly, trying to pull him away, but he simply scoffed.

"Nonsense, they just said it was a quick meal. I'm sure Julien doesn't mind?"

Actually, I did mind, but I also didn't want to rob Eve of the chance to make a good first impression on someone whose vote would be vital to secure approval for her project. My own feelings would have to come second. "Not at all. We were just talking about it ourselves."

That was a lie, but one that paved the way for them to join us. Mrs Measner slid into the booth next to Eve while Mr Measner took a seat next to me while I gave Eve a small shrug of apology.

As we cooked our food on the grill in the centre of the table, ate and drank, Eve told the Measners all about her time as a volunteer in Ecuador. There were several stories I hadn't heard yet, and she had us all eating out of the palm of her hand, gasping and laughing where appropriate, and even drawing some tears from Mrs Measner at one point. Only when she'd fully established that she knew exactly what it was like to do the work on the ground did she move on to a vague outline of the program she wanted to propose.

"It sounds amazing," Mrs Measner declared, and though her husband remained a little more tight-lipped, I could see Eve had impressed him too. How could she not? Everything about her was impressive.

By the time she'd finished, the time had come to head over to the ballet, and we walked over as a foursome. The tickets Eve had were excellent and so was the production, but sitting next to her for hours without being able to touch or kiss her was its own kind of torture. She looked absolutely incredible in her red and white outfit, and the sight of her legs in her tights and skirt next to me successfully distracted me from what was happening on stage for most of the performance.

At last, the show ended, and Eve and I stepped out into the winter's night. Snow had begun to fall again and although it was late, in my mind, the evening had just begun. I couldn't wait to see where it took us.

~Eve~

With each new situation I saw Julien in, he impressed me even more. At supper with the Measners, he was charming and persuasive, offering support and validation for my ideas in a subtle but effective way. At the ballet, he fit in perfectly, enjoying himself without being pretentious about it. He made me laugh and he made my stomach flutter whenever he looked at me with that expression that suggested he couldn't wait until we were alone again.

With each passing day, it became clearer just how easily I could fall in love with him. In fact, I felt pretty certain I'd already begun to. Maybe I had even started to on that very first night in Quito.

And I still hadn't told him exactly who I was.

I'd started to tell him at supper, before the Measners arrived, but I didn't have a chance to finish. I didn't get out anything at all except that there was something about my father he should know. If Julien found that odd, he didn't seem to be dwelling on it as we walked through the downtown streets back to his house, the snow falling all around us like we were in a giant snow globe. We walked with our arms linked, pointing out the light displays at the houses we passed by and the trees in the windows. Everything felt light and easy, and not at all the right time to bring up something difficult or heavy.

As soon as we were in the door of his house and had removed our outer layers, wet with the falling snow, Julien brought me over to the couch, inviting me to sit down while he knelt at my feet.

"Let me please you tonight, Eve," he requested, as if I would be doing him a favour by saying yes. "Please let me make you come right here on this couch."

His hands slid up my tights as he said the words, tentatively and eagerly at the same time. The desire that shot through my body no longer took me by surprise when it came to him, but it did play havoc with my emotions. As much as I wanted to give in to it, and to him, I also wanted to tell him the truth. I didn't want it to sit between us a moment longer. "Wait, Julien."

Immediately, he stopped, those warm brown eyes of his looking up at me, open and trusting. "Yes?"

"I... I need to confess something to you first." My mouth felt dry as my heart thudded heavily. What if, after I told him, he never looked at me that way again?

"Confess?" Excitement sparked in his eyes, excitement that seemed completely at odds with the nature of what I needed to tell him. "*Mon Dieu*, sometimes I think you can honestly read my mind. First, you stepped into the role of the teacher at the pioneer village, and now, you've just hit upon another of my favourite role plays."

"Role play?" I repeated in confusion. I hadn't been talking about a role play. I simply wanted to tell him the truth.

Unaware of my train of thought, Julien nodded enthusiastically. "Probably because I was raised a Catholic, it seems particularly taboo for me, which makes it even more appealing."

He had completely lost me, which was unusual. Normally, we were on the same page. "What are you talking about?"

Julien chuckled, getting back to his feet. "Wait here. I'll be right back."

Wasting no time, he left the room, heading down to the basement and, I assumed, his supply room there. It didn't take him long, as he'd promised, and when he returned, he wore a full priest costume; not simply the white collar with a black shirt, but a full set of vestments.

"Where on earth did you get that?" I asked in surprise.

Julien blushed as he shyly laughed. "I told you: it's a particular fantasy of mine. For a brief time, I did consider becoming a priest myself. I like to help people and I wanted to make a difference. Unfortunately, the lack of sex turned out to be a dealbreaker."

Imagining Julien as celibate certainly didn't seem natural, but on the other hand, I could see how it would have appealed to him too. Through his charity work, he *did* help others, and a lot of his sexual turn-ons included self-denial. In a way, it made perfect sense. "So, what's your fantasy?"

"It's quite simple. I'm a young priest, newly ordained, and taking confession. A woman comes to my confessional, whispering details of all the dirty thoughts she's had about me, and I'm unable to resist her."

At last, I understood the connection. I'd just told him I wanted to confess something to him, and he must have thought I meant it in a light-hearted way, so he wanted to make a game of it. I *loved* that idea, and his fantasy turned me on too, in a way I never would have expected. He continued to teach me new things about myself every day.

If I actually did confess the truth to him, would it kill the mood? Or, in the spirit of forgiveness, would he give me a penance to perform and a chance to make it up to him? Would telling him, not during sex but during the foreplay to it, be a cheat? Or would it make the whole scenario a little more real?

Looking up at his handsome, eager face, I made up my mind. What-ever the outcome, I needed to get it off my chest. I'd waited far too long already. "I'm ready to make my confession now."

Immediately, he set the scene, clearly having anticipated my agree-ment. "Since we don't have a confessional, we'll use two chairs, back-to-back." It only took him a moment to go into the kitchen and come back with two chairs which he set up side-by-side, their backs in alignment, facing away from each other. "Please, take a seat."

As he sat down on one of the chairs, facing the back of the house, I lowered myself onto the one facing the front window. The curtains were drawn so no one could see in and Julien had left the lights low, only the soft glow of the Christmas tree lights and the light coming from the kitchen helping to brighten the room.

"You said you have something to tell me," Julien began. "Something to confess. What is it?"

Taking a deep breath, I spoke the words I'd been about to say at supper, before we were interrupted. "I come from a very wealthy family."

I couldn't see Julien's reaction, which made it both better and worse at the same time. The disappointment and confusion in his eyes would have nearly killed me. Even imagining it made my heart hurt.

As he didn't say anything, as the silence stretched out around us, the whole room began to feel colder. When Julien finally answered me, his voice sounded cooler than before too. "Do you think that's a sin?"

That was the crux of the issue, wasn't it? I answered him as truthfully as I could. "Not really, but I know that you do. You've made that pretty clear over the past few days. It's why I didn't tell you earlier. I didn't want you to judge me because of who my family is."

In the stillness of the room, I could hear the desperation in my voice, begging him to tell me I was wrong and that he wouldn't hold it against me.

"How wealthy?" he asked, his voice still cool and detached.

"I don't have the exact figures," I joked weakly before answering his question honestly. "It's in the billions, though."

His huffed exhale chilled me even further. "There aren't a lot of people in the world with that much money."

"No, there aren't, and I know you believe there shouldn't be any. I'm not going to argue that with you. But I know all kinds of people, rich and poor, and there are good and bad people out there no matter what the size of their bank account is. Having money doesn't make people bad, Julien. It doesn't make *me* a bad person."

"And what about lying to me?" A bit of heat had started to edge back into his voice, but not in a good way. Anger pushed the words out more forcefully. "Does *that* make you a bad person?"

I winced as my hands gripped the edge of my chair, forcing myself to stay in place and not turn around. The current set-up was working, allowing us to talk things out in a calm and rational manner. If I looked at him and saw the disappointment in his eyes, it would only make it harder. "I'm sorry for not telling you before, and I agree it wasn't right to keep it from you, but no, I don't think it makes me a bad person."

"So, you think you can make up for it?" The hardness in his voice made him sound far more dominant than usual. It made for a complete reversal of our usual dynamic, with him demanding my submission.

In the current situation, I gave it willingly, bowing my head in penitence. "I'd like to try. I still want to give us a chance, Julien."

"Then let me see you. Take off the tights and spread your legs for me."

His unexpected words sent arousal and confusion rushing through my body at the same time. Was that really it? He wanted to move on, just like that? I had expected him to be furious and question everything he felt for me, but maybe, in the end, it hadn't been as big a deal as I'd let myself believe. Maybe it was just like what happened with my dad, where I'd built the problem up in my head into something bigger than it needed to be. Although he might not agree with my choices, he cared enough about me to move past it, and maybe Julien was the same.

The relief that washed over me nearly made me weak as I tugged off my tights and panties, leaving them on the floor. Getting to my feet, I walked around the chairs until I stood in front of Julien, and the look on his face, disapproval mixed with need, sent my own arousal even higher. Combined with the relief I felt, it almost made me giddy as I tried my best to follow the parameters of the fantasy he'd laid out earlier, wanting to make his dreams come true since he'd agreed to give me another chance.

With all that in mind, I slipped fully into the role of the penitent parishioner. "I thought you weren't supposed to want me, Father. Aren't *you* the one sinning now?"

His clenched jaw let me know just how much that worked for him. "I only want to look. Nothing more."

We'd see about that. Lifting my skirt to give him a glimpse of my pussy from the front, I turned around and bent over to give him the full effect, and Julien's hissed inhale sent another spike of desire through me.

"Calisse, you're fucking perfect."

"What does that mean?" I asked, still bent over, but with my head turned to the side so I could see him. "You say it quite often."

"Calisse? It's like... holy fuck."

I liked the sound of it in his native tongue better. "Are you sure you only want to look, Father? You could touch if you want to. Or even taste."

His groan seemed to rumble straight through my body. "I can't."

"I'm pretty sure you can. All you need to do is get on your knees."

With another groan, Julien slid off the chair, onto his knees, as if powerless to resist.

"There. It's almost like praying, isn't it? Now, just come a little closer."

He muttered something in French, something that had the cadence of a prayer as he gradually inched his way forward. Maybe he prayed for the strength to resist me? We both knew that was a lost cause.

At last, when he was just a few inches from me, he stopped. "Good," I praised him. "Now, close your eyes and stick out your tongue."

"Eve." My name came out of him like a growl, like a man possessed.

"There's nothing unholy about that, is there, Father?" I asked as innocently as I could. "Close your eyes."

With a shuddering breath, he followed my instructions. His eyes closed and his tongue came out, hesitantly, and I took a step back so that his tongue connected directly with my pussy. "God, help me," I heard him mutter before he gave up all pretense of resistance.

With all the enthusiasm of a man starved of pleasure, he began to explore me, licking, kissing and sucking on my pussy from behind. My head dropped down between my knees as pleasure raced through my body, surrendering to the need he created in me and all the other emotions he stirred up inside me. When I came, he didn't stop, carrying on as if he couldn't get enough, until I was right on the edge again.

Finally, he stood up and pulled me over to the couch, almost roughly. There, he bent me over again, and lifting his robes, he revealed his stiff and ready cock beneath it, already in a condom. He must have put it on when he got changed.

With both of us still fully dressed besides our missing underwear, he drove into me from behind as I gripped the back of the sofa to keep my balance. "You feel like heaven, Eve," he panted from behind me.

"Worth going to hell for?" I teased him back, which only made him thrust harder, until I couldn't speak at all, other than moaning his name. The sofa rocked beneath me with each powerful thrust, his firm cock taking possession of me as he gave me exactly what I needed.

Soon, I came again, and he followed shortly after, muttering in French once again. Once he pulled out of me, I collapsed down onto the couch, sated and satisfied, and feeling at peace again at last. At last, everything was out in the open.

"I enjoyed that more than I expected to," I admitted once he'd removed the condom and come back to sit beside me, his robes back in place.

"Me too, and I expected to like it very much." Julien's eyes twinkled in contentment. "Your confession was a nice touch."

A nice... touch? The corners of my mouth pulled down as I looked over at him. "What do you mean?"

"Finding something I could be angry at you with. I hadn't imagined that scenario before, but it worked perfectly. You couldn't have come up with a better excuse."

As his words sank in, my stomach sank with them, all the happiness I'd been feeling immediately evaporating into the air around me, making my body feel like lead.

Did he... did he think that had been part of the role play? I thought my tone and the fact that I'd referred to him by name had made it clear. Besides, I told him before we began that I wanted to tell him something. From his responses, I thought we'd been on the same page.

Did that mean he didn't really forgive me after all?

His next words made it clear I had it exactly right, to my utter horror. "Billionaires, though?" he teased. "That might be pushing it."

Fuck. He honestly thought I'd been joking. What was I supposed to do now? If I told him it hadn't been a joke, that I'd used the scenario he'd suggested to make my true confession, would he be even angrier? Had I screwed this up once and for all?

"I... I should go."

"Eve?" Julien's brow furrowed as he watched me get up and grab my tights, pulling them back on as fast as I could. "What's wrong?"

Since I was already in over my head, I lied some more. "I just... I didn't realize how late it is. I have plans tomorrow, I need to get back to my hotel."

"Okay." He didn't argue, but I could see the concern still in his eyes. "Can I do anything to help?"

"No. Thank you. I'm fine." With my tights on, I went to the door to grab my boots and my coat.

"Are you busy all day tomorrow?" he asked, still sitting on the couch, his warm, compassionate eyes on me. "I have a party to attend in the evening for the charity. I was wondering if..."

"I'm busy," I blurted out. "Sorry. I'll... I'll text you when I can. Good night, Julien."

With that, I yanked his front door open, stepping back out into the snowy night before he could say anything else at all.

Chapter Eleven

EXPOSED

~Julien~

The silence that fell once Eve closed the door behind her felt different than the silence I'd worked in all day. In both cases, I was alone, but before, I'd had the anticipation of seeing her and the pleasure of her company to look forward to. As I sat on the couch in my priest's robes after she'd gone, I only felt confusion.

What happened to make her run off the way she did? I'd never seen her behave that way, so nervous and uncertain. She could barely even look at me, and when she did, her dark eyes seemed distant and cool. The role play I'd suggested had been a little bit outside our usual dynamic, but not enough that it should have made her uncomfortable. If it had, why wouldn't she have just told me so? Eve didn't usually have any trouble telling me what she wanted.

As I returned the chairs we'd been using to the kitchen and went back to the basement to retrieve the clothing I'd left down there earlier, I reviewed the whole evening in my head, trying to figure out what went wrong. The sex had been wonderful, as usual. She drove me absolutely crazy, in the best possible way, and I felt pretty certain she'd enjoyed it too, based on the strength and frequency of her orgasms.

Although she seemed surprised by the role play when I first brought it up, she quickly jumped in, as willing to try new things as always. The only thing that made me cringe when I thought back over it had to do with the *way* I had suggested the role play in the first place. She said she had something to tell me, and I never gave her the chance. Caught up in my own fantasies and how eager I'd been to please her, I didn't give her the space to tell me whatever she'd wanted to say.

The more I thought about it, the more convinced I became that it had been the problem, and looking at it from her point of view, I could only feel ashamed of myself. I put my needs ahead of hers, which a good sub should never do. By submitting to her, I trusted that she would fulfill my needs, and she hadn't let me down. That night, though, I'd treated Eve as if she'd only come to my house for sex, rather than as a partner I respected and whose ideas and thoughts I valued.

No wonder she got upset.

When I finished cleaning up, I headed straight up to my room and sent her a text to apologize.

Eve, I'm sorry I didn't give you a chance to talk tonight. Whatever you want to tell me, I want to hear it. I know you're busy tomorrow, but if any time opens up, no matter how short, please let me know and I can come to you.

With that sent, I composed one more message, that one a lot cooler and to the point.

The man you saw Eve with is her father.

I left it at that, and a moment later, my phone rang. With hope filling my chest, I snatched it back up, anticipating it would be Eve, but Claire's number showed on my screen instead. With a sigh, I answered it.

"It's late, Claire."

"I know, but I had to apologize. I'm so sorry, Julien. I didn't want you to think I'd lied to you on purpose. I honestly thought it looked like..."

"I understand," I cut her off, wanting to forget the whole thing. I only sent her that message in the first place because she and Eve would be seeing each other at the office later that week and I didn't want her to give Eve the cold shoulder. "And I appreciate your concern, but I think it's best if we keep our work and private lives separate going forward. We're still friends, Claire, but professional friends only."

The pause on the other end of the phone was so long that I almost began to wonder if the connection had been lost. Finally, she spoke again. "Are you taking Eve to the benefit tomorrow?"

Seriously? What had I just said? "That's none of your..."

"I need to let them know if you're bringing a guest," she snapped before I could finish. "When I RSVP'd for you, they asked if you'd be bringing a guest. I said no. Do I need to change that?"

Looking at it that way, I supposed it did count as a work-related question after all. "I see. In that case: no, I'm not taking her. I'll be going alone."

It truly disappointed me that Eve wouldn't be available to attend with me. Not only would I have had a lot more fun with her there, she would have been a great asset for the charity. She seemed to be able to talk to anyone, and from the school that she attended, she would have at least some experience of dealing with the type of donors that would be there.

"And you're sure you don't want me to come rather than going alone?" Claire asked next. "I can help you keep track of people's names and businesses, and all the other stuff you hate doing."

Again, she had a point. Talking up the charity, I could do in my sleep, but chatting about other peoples' businesses and remembering who did what and who was connected to whom had never been my forte. I didn't particularly want to spend time with Claire, but the event was still a business occasion, first and foremost. "Alright. Since no one else is coming, you might as well."

We made arrangements to meet in the lobby of the Stamer Hotel, where the event would take place, just before the benefit was scheduled to begin. As soon as I hung up with her, I immediately checked to see if I had a reply from Eve, but she hadn't sent anything yet. It didn't even show that she'd read the message. I hoped she hadn't had any trouble getting back to her hotel, but I had no way of knowing other than messaging her. She hadn't even told me what hotel she was staying at.

Eventually, I had to give up waiting for a response and go to sleep. Hopefully, she could find a bit of time for me the next day and we could talk over whatever she'd wanted to talk to me about in the first place. If by any chance she changed her mind about accompanying me to the benefit, I would happily inform Claire that she had been replaced.

Whatever happened the next day, it felt like it would be important for us and our fledgling relationship. Being able to communicate with each other and work things out when something upset one of us would be vital if we were to have any future at all. We complemented each other so well in every other aspect that I had to believe we could work that out too.

Hopefully, by the time I went to bed the following night, everything would be settled between us, and I'd be feeling a lot better than I did right then.

~Eve~

Julien's text only made me feel worse. His regret came through in every word as he apologized for not giving me a chance to talk, not understanding that I *had* told him what I wanted to say. He just didn't realize it.

Even though it had passed midnight when I got back to the hotel, I sent a text of my own, but not to Julien. I needed to talk to someone else, someone who could help me figure out how to dig myself out of the hole I'd wound up in.

Hey, I know it's late, but if you're up, can you call me, please?

I'd just started my bedtime routine when my phone rang, and relief flooded through my body as the face of my best friend, Noelle, appeared on the screen, barely illuminated in a dimly-lit room. "What's going on?" she asked in concern, understanding without me having to tell her that I wouldn't be in touch so late if it weren't important.

"I just need to talk, if that's okay. Wait, is that... are you in bed?"

I caught a glimpse of a hand on her shoulder, and she immediately turned the camera to include her fiancé in the conversation. "We are, and Aaron's right here. Is it something private? I can kick him out."

"You can, can you?" he demanded in mock offense before turning to me. "Honestly, though, if it's anything *too* personal, I'll go."

"Actually, I don't mind if you stay. I could use a man's perspective."

"Ooh, is it about a man?" Noelle squealed in excitement, making Aaron wince next to her, the sound going right into his ear. "I was starting to think you were on a chastity strike."

"Is that even a thing?" I had to wonder. "That makes it sound intentional. I didn't think people did it on purpose."

With a sigh, Aaron steered us back on course. "I'm happy to offer an opinion, but it's the middle of the night. Maybe we could just get started?"

With that in mind, I gave them both a quick overview of my relationship with Julien to that point, starting with meeting at the bar in Quito right up to the events of that evening. Going into the finer details of our sexual encounters seemed unnecessary with Aaron right there, but I did explain that we had complementary tastes. Most importantly, I explained how he only knew me by my professional name, and about the comments he'd made about rich people, how I'd almost been outed by his assistant, and finally, ending with what happened at his house that night, when I thought I had told him the truth and he thought I'd been joking.

"What do I do now?" I asked them both plaintively once I'd finished the whole story. Hearing it out loud only made me more uncertain about how we could move past his hangup and my unintentional deception in a healthy, constructive way.

Aaron seemed to agree. "If he's going to judge you or your family based on something as superficial as that, maybe you're better off without him. There must be other guys out there who share your kink and aren't prejudiced jerks."

"Aaron!" Noelle nudged him in the ribs with her elbow. "She can't just 'find another guy'. She's in love with him."

"Well, she didn't say that!" he argued back, rubbing his chest defensively.

"She didn't have to. It's obvious."

As usual, Noelle saw straight to my heart, foolish as it might be. "Leave it to me to fall for the one guy on this earth who *doesn't* want to marry into a rich family."

"There's nothing you can do about your family," Aaron pointed out. "So, he's going to have to decide whether he can deal with it or not. You haven't done anything wrong."

"Other than not telling him the truth as soon as I realized it would be an issue," I countered. "If I'd just sucked it up and told him then, I wouldn't be so screwed right now."

"I don't think you can fully blame yourself for that, Eve." Noelle was firmly on my side, as always. "He made you feel uncomfortable about telling him. He made you feel it wasn't safe. That's on him."

"So, what do I do?" I repeated. As much as I appreciated the pep talk, they still hadn't given me any actionable advice.

Noelle and Aaron exchanged glances in that unspoken way that couples often did. "You're not seeing him tomorrow, right?" she asked me.

"He's asked to see me, but at the moment, no. We haven't arranged anything. My dad's got something planned for the evening."

Noelle nodded in determination. "Okay. Here's what you do: take a break. You've been thinking about this guy non-stop since you got there, right?"

"Pretty much, yeah," I had to admit.

"Reply to his text, make it clear you're not angry with him, but say you're not available. You can take the whole day to think about it and he can too. Maybe he'll realize on his own that you already told him. If he doesn't, you can explain it to him calmly once you've both had a chance to reflect on how much you miss each other after a day apart."

"And don't take all the responsibility," Aaron added. "Make sure he understands that he screwed up too. If he doesn't, revert to Plan A: find someone else who deserves you."

"Thanks, guys." It still wouldn't be easy, but at least I had a plan. After letting them go back to sleep, I sent one more text before crawling into my own bed.

I'm afraid tomorrow really is busy for me, but I could come and meet you at your office for lunch on Monday. We can talk then. Let me know if that works. E

After a lazy morning the next day, I went out into the city on my own to do a bit more shopping. My dad had told me to dress up, but I didn't have anything formal to wear in either my own suitcases or the things my mom had sent, so I would have to buy something. The glitzy, high-end stores in Yorkville made me uncomfortable, with dresses that cost more than most peoples' monthly salaries, so I went down to Queen Street instead and browsed some of the vintage stores there.

In the fourth one, a 1950s dress immediately called to me, its red colour a near-perfect match for my hair. With a sweetheart neckline, three-quarter length sleeves and an A-line skirt with plaid accents hidden in the skirt pleats, it felt both classy and fun at the same time.

"That would be gorgeous on you!" the store assistant gushed, ushering me into the dressing room with instructions to come back out and show it to her when I had it on. By some kind of divine intervention, it fit me perfectly, and the assistant agreed. "You *need* to get that dress. If you can't afford it all right now, we have a payment plan option."

I hadn't even glanced at the price tag, and when I did, it cost far less than one night at my dad's hotel. "That's fine, I'll put it on my credit card. I love it."

Back at the hotel, I spent the afternoon in the pool and sauna, trying to enjoy my day of relaxation and not miss Julien too much. He had responded to my text, saying that he would love to see me on Monday, but he left it at that. I had a feeling he was waiting for me to take the lead, but as Noelle had suggested, I kept my distance, leaving my phone up in my room while I made the most of the hotel's facilities.

Finally, the time came to get ready for the evening, and I made a real effort, not knowing exactly what my dad was up to. My hair and makeup looked perfect with my dress, if I did say so myself, and when I went to knock on the door of his suite at the time he'd given me, he looked equally sharp in an expensive, pinstripe suit.

"That dress is beautiful," he told me in approval. "You're going to blow them all away."

"Them?" I repeated curiously. "What 'them'?"

"You'll see," he replied, enjoying the chance to drag out the suspense a little longer as he offered me his arm. Together, we headed back downstairs, but not to the lobby. Instead, we stopped on the second floor, where the hotel conference rooms and ballroom were located.

Conversation and music drifted out from the open ballroom doors as soon as we got off the elevator, and I looked up at my dad in surprise. "A Christmas party?"

"Not exactly." Still not giving anything away, he led me into the room.

Whatever was going on, no expense had been spared. Waiters in tuxedos circulated with trays of champagne and canapes while a live band played on a small stage at one end of the room. Tables were arranged for a formal dinner, and a podium stood at the far end of the room.

With my arm still linked with his, I followed my dad as he strode through the room, nodding to people in acknowledgement but not stopping for anyone until we arrived at the podium I'd spotted earlier. Stepping up to the microphone, my dad began to speak, immediately commanding everyone's attention in the room.

"Thank you all for coming tonight. As you all know, we're here to raise money for a very worthy cause."

What in the world was he talking about? Money? A good cause?

He beamed over at me, clearly enjoying my confusion. "My daughter recently returned from volunteering with the charity for a year, and she can speak personally to the good work that they do."

The charity? *Oh, no.* My stomach dropped as I recalled Julien's words the night before: he'd mentioned that he had a party to attend on behalf of the charity. Was *this* that party? Did that mean...

My dad was still talking, unaware of my internal panic. "With that in mind, I'm delighted to introduce you all to tonight's guest of honour: my daughter, Eve Stamer."

All eyes in the room moved to me, and as my heart pounded, I did my best to force a smile. Faces seemed to blur into one another as my eyes travelled around the room, until they landed on one face, one very familiar one, staring back at me in complete and utter shock.

~Julien~

My phone hadn't left my side all day. I had the ringer turned up to full volume, and even so, I kept pulling it out to check I hadn't missed a call or a text. Despite Eve saying she had no time, I hoped she would change her mind, whether just to talk or maybe even to attend the party with me that evening. Only when it came time for me to get ready for the benefit did I have to accept it probably wasn't going to happen.

Dressed in the suit and tie that Claire had got for me, I gave myself a critical look in the mirror before leaving. On my own behalf, I didn't care about fitting in at these kinds of events, but as a representative of the charity, I needed to do my best not to rock the boat. It would be a challenge for me to hold my tongue around the conspicuous wealth sure to be on display, but for the charity's sake, I would try.

The benefit involved a formal dinner and reception. At the end of dinner, I would be invited to say a few words about the charity's work to help entice potential donors, but I'd been asked to keep it brief. No need to disturb anyone's self-satisfaction too much by talking about real problems in the world.

Despite walking past it many times, I'd never been inside the Stamer Hotel before, and I had to admit to being surprised when I walked into the lobby. I'd expected something staid and formal, maybe with gilded gold on the walls, but the open and airy design actually felt quite vibrant. Even so, the clientele made up for it. Even in my best suit, I felt underdressed and out of place.

"Julien!" Looking relieved, Claire got up from a sofa next to the fireplace as she saw me walk in. "You're nearly late."

"These things never start on time." I'd been to enough of them to confidently make that statement. Claire wore a floor-length, glittering silver dress that complemented her blonde hair quite nicely. She'd obviously made an effort, so I paid her a compliment for it. "You look nice. Where did you leave your coat?"

Her cheeks flushing, she pointed me in the direction of the cloak room, and once I'd left my own outerwear behind, we headed up to the ballroom together.

Inside, the party looked almost exactly as I imagined it would. Elegant, overdressed people mingled in small groups on the edges of the room while round tables covered with white tablecloths and sparkling place settings had been set up in the centre. A live band played light versions of Christmas carols and appetizers were passed around by waiters who avoided eye contact with the guests.

"It smells amazing," Claire whispered to me, obviously seeing the event through different eyes than I did. Pasting a neutral expression on my face, I led her over to the small welcome table.

"Good evening. I'm Julien Labrecque, and this is my colleague, Claire Daniels."

The woman at the table gave us a warm smile. "Of course, we're delighted to have you here, Mr Labrecque. I'm Jennifer Ramirez with Stamer Hotels. Claire, it's a pleasure to meet you in person."

The two women had obviously spoken over email, so they exchanged pleasantries while I cast a curious glance around the room. "Where can we find Mr Stamer?"

"He hasn't arrived yet, but he'll be here shortly," Jennifer assured us. "Please, get yourselves a drink and something to eat if you like. As soon as Mr Stamer gets here, we'll get everyone seated. You'll be at his table."

"You see: I told you it wouldn't start on time," I whispered to Claire as we made our way further into the room. While she took a champagne flute from one of the waiters, I asked for sparkling water instead. I wanted to keep a clear head for the evening, especially on the off chance that Eve might get in touch later.

Luckily, we didn't have to wait too long before the party's host turned up. As he began speaking, everyone in the room turned towards him, and I took a few steps closer to get a better look at him with Claire close on my heels.

I hardly saw the man at the podium though. My attention was immediately drawn to the woman at his side, looking somehow even more stunning than I had ever seen her before in a red dress that looked like it had been made for her.

"Isn't that Eve?" Claire stage-whispered to me, loud enough that others around us glanced over at her. I didn't look at her, though; my eyes were glued to the redhead at the front of the room.

What was she doing there? Why wouldn't she have mentioned to me that she would be? Was she there with someone else? Had she lied to me when she said she wasn't seeing anyone?

What was I missing?

I was so focused on her that I missed most of what Mr Stamer said. Only his final words got through the swirling storm of questions inside my head, like a foghorn blasting through the mist. "... my daughter, Eve Stamer."

All the blood in my veins seemed to freeze in place, cold washing over me from head to toe as I stared at her, at the woman I *thought* I knew. With her polished, professional smile, she surveyed the crowd, accepting their attention with all the grace of a queen on her throne, until her eyes got to me.

Even across the distance between us, I could see her falter, and it hit me like an ice pick digging into my still-frozen heart. She hadn't known I would be there. It didn't make a lot of sense to me, given that the benefit was *for* the charity, but at that moment, I felt sure about it. She looked just as shocked to see me as I was to see her.

Eve looked away as her father continued speaking. "Eve will give us all an account of her experiences after dinner, and she'll be followed by the charity's CEO, Julien Labrecque, who will explain about the wider implications of the charity's work and how your donations can help. I hope you all came prepared to open your wallets tonight."

Some laughter and good-natured grumbling spread around the room, but I couldn't react. I still felt completely frozen in place, unable to move.

"First, though, it's time to eat. Please, take your seats."

He turned back to Eve, who leaned over to whisper something to him. He gestured at a nearby table, which didn't seem to make her happy. Whatever happened next, I couldn't see as people started walking in front of me to find their table.

"You... uh, you didn't tell me you're dating a Stamer," Claire said from beside me, looking rather stunned by the news, though not nearly as stunned as I felt.

"No, I didn't," I replied tersely. How could I have, when I didn't know?

Honestly, I didn't know which of the feelings inside me should take precedence. Betrayal? That certainly had to be a contender, since Eve had apparently lied to me right from the start. Disappointment? I felt that keenly too, as the relationship I'd imagined with Eve seemed to disappear right in front of my eyes, the future I'd begun to imagine for us vanishing as if it had never been there at all. Or what about embarrassment, when I didn't even know the most basic facts about the woman I had told people I was involved with?

In any case, I didn't want to talk about it with Claire. I didn't want to talk to anyone other than Eve. "Where are we supposed to sit?"

"Jennifer said we're at Mr Stamer's table," she reminded me, and it took all my strength to suppress my groan. Yes, I wanted to talk to Eve, but not in front of a table full of people where I couldn't ask her any of the questions I truly wanted answered. Not in front of Claire, and not in front of her father.

It didn't seem I had much choice, though. Forcing myself to move, my whole body still feeling stiff and awkward, we made our way to the table at the front of the room, where Eve and her father were already seated, and I did my best to brace myself for whatever came next.

Chapter Twelve

IMPOSSIBLE

~Eve~

"You could have warned me you expected me to speak in front of a roomful of donors tonight!" I whispered to my dad as he stepped away from the podium, looking completely satisfied with himself.

"Why? You've never had trouble speaking in front of a crowd," he pointed out, completely accurately. "I've loaded some of the pictures you sent us to be projected in the background while you're speaking. It'll be perfect. And with the charity's director here, you'll have a chance to make a good impression ahead of your pitch to them."

Unknowingly, he'd just hit upon the real reason for my panic. It had nothing to do with speaking in public at all. "Have you spoken to Mr Labrecque?"

I couldn't call him Julien, not without giving away the intimacy between us. My dad had no idea that just the night before, I'd been moaning Julien's name while he made me come.

"Not yet, but he'll be sitting with us for dinner." My dad gestured down to the table next to us at the front of the room, and my stomach sank even further. He'd just told everyone to sit down, meaning Julien would be on his way over to us at any moment. I couldn't bring myself to look over and see for myself. What would be going through his head at that moment? Would he give me a chance to explain? Would he ever look at me the same way again?

My legs feeling like lead, I sank down into one of the seats at the table as gracefully as I could, my heart thudding painfully in my chest.

How on earth was I going to face him?

My dad took the seat next to me, saying hello to people who walked by on the way to their own tables while I stared down at my plate in misery. Only when I heard a very familiar voice did I force my gaze upwards again.

"Mr Stamer? I'm Julien Labrecque."

He'd come up on the other side of my dad, focused on him and not on me, and my dad got to his feet to shake his hand. "It's good to meet you. Glad you could be here tonight. I believe you already know Eve?"

My whole body tensed before I realized what he meant; I'd told my dad that Julien and I spoke in Quito. He only knew about that, not any of the time we'd spent together over the past four days.

Julien's brown eyes moved over to me, cooler than I'd ever seen them before as he answered my dad. "Yes. We've met, though I didn't know she was your daughter."

My throat tight, I held his gaze as long as I could before my eyes dropped back to the table, shame and guilt overwhelming me. Why hadn't I just told him when I had the chance? Why didn't I stay the night before and explain to him that the things I'd said hadn't been part of the game? It all seemed so obvious, now that I couldn't do anything about it.

"This is my assistant, Claire Daniels," I heard Julien say next, and that made my head snap back up again. I hadn't even noticed Claire beside him. Julien had blocked out everything else for me.

"Ms Daniels." My dad shook her hand too before turning back to me. "Do you know Eve?"

A slightly too-smug smile flashed across Claire's face as she mimicked Julien's reply. "Yes. We've met."

Seemingly oblivious to any of the tension between us, my dad gestured at the seats next to him. "Great. Why don't you sit here so we can have a chance to chat?"

Obediently, Julien took the chair next to him while Claire sat on his other side, still looking far too pleased with the whole situation. She might not know exactly what the problem was, but she must guess from the way Julien and I were avoiding each other that something had happened, and her reaction to it told me all I needed to know.

She wanted Julien.

I didn't know how I'd missed it before. Maybe I'd hoped I'd left that kind of drama behind in college. Maybe I simply couldn't understand why anyone would secretly pine over a man and not make a move. Whatever the reason I hadn't seen it before, I saw it clearly enough then. The way she ran to tell Julien about seeing me at the market made complete sense in that context, as did her randomly turning up at his house late at night on the night she'd walked in on me naked. She must have been hoping to spend some time with him herself that night.

And Julien was completely clueless about it, even as she leaned a little closer to him, her hand brushing against his while my dad spoke to him.

"Eve has told me nothing but good things about her time with the charity, so I wanted to do what I could to support the work you're doing. I hope you get a lot of new donors tonight."

"It's very generous of you," Julien replied, his tone formal but not stilted. He was doing a far better job than I was at covering up how he felt. "We wondered why you made such a large donation, but now, I understand."

His eyes moved to me again for a split second before returning to my father.

"It was all a bit mysterious," Claire added, jumping in uninvited. "Especially since Eve gave us a different surname in all her interactions with us. We didn't know about the connection."

That little snake. She made it sound as if I had some underhanded reason for going by another name, which had never been the case.

Luckily, my dad quickly set her straight. "I'm to blame for that. I insisted that she use her mother's maiden name while abroad to ensure her safety. If people knew her connections, she might have been in danger."

He turned to me with a protective smile, trying to draw me into the conversation. He must have been wondering why I hadn't said a word yet.

"I can imagine," Claire agreed sympathetically... or at least, in a tone she meant to sound sympathetic. It sounded fake as hell to me. "Someone with billions of dollars at their disposal would be a tempting target."

At last, I had a response ready, sitting on the tip of my tongue, but Julien's reaction stopped me in my tracks. As soon as Claire said the word 'billions', the realization hit him. I could see the exact moment he made the connection.

I had told him the night before that I was worth billions and he hadn't believed me. Now, he knew I'd been telling the truth, and he knew that I *had* told him. Would that change anything about how he felt, or would the distance in his eyes remain, simply because of who I was?

~Julien~

Mr Stamer was just as I expected him to be: confident and assured and completely oblivious to what was happening right in front of him. How did he not notice the change in Eve? How could he not realize that something must have been bothering her? To me, it couldn't have been clearer in the slouch of her shoulders and the fidgeting of her fingers.

He made small talk with me and Claire as if nothing had happened, his dark eyes fixed on me in a way that felt a little too familiar. Eve's eyes were the same shade, and had the same habit of staring directly at me in a way that suggested people very rarely told her no. After what I'd just learned about her, that all made a bit more sense to me. There probably wasn't much that she'd ever been denied. Her money would have gotten her everything she ever wanted.

Numbly, I listened while Mr Stamer explained why Eve had been using a different name, and though I could understand his reasoning for while she'd been abroad, it didn't explain why she'd never mentioned it to me. We'd talked about her family, she'd shared stories about them and their likes and dislikes, and yet, she'd left out the single most defining thing about them.

Numb seemed to be the best word to describe the way I felt in general, at least until Claire piped up from beside me, much more talkative than usual, and commented about how Eve's billions would have made her a target.

The word 'billions' triggered a memory of Eve's disembodied voice from behind me as I sat on the chair in my living room, wearing my priest's robes. *I come from a very wealthy family. I don't have the exact figures... it's in the billions, though.*

Crisse. She'd been telling me the truth and I laughed it off because it sounded ridiculous; I thought it had been part of the roleplay. But she'd told me that she had something to confess to me, and she did once we started the scene. Her sudden departure made a lot more sense in that context, as did her reluctance to find time to meet with me that day. I'd offered to come and see her so she could tell me what she'd wanted to say, but she'd already told me. I just hadn't understood.

For the first time since we'd got to the table, Eve spoke. Though technically, she replied to Claire, it felt like her words were meant for me. "Sometimes, the money blinds people when they hear our family name. It can bring out the worst in people, or give them ideas about what we're like before they get to know us."

Was that why she'd kept it from me? I'd made no secret of the way I felt about wealth like hers. Did she think it would change the way I felt about her?

Did it?

"I'm sure it's tough." Claire's response sounded sympathetic on the surface, but a deep vein of sarcasm ran through it that I immediately picked up on. "It must have been especially hard when you were volunteering with those women struggling to feed their families, knowing that you could sell off one designer bag and support the whole village for a year."

Mr Stamer's expression immediately darkened, and I shot Claire a warning look. Yes, she and I had made comments like that to each other before, but not directly in front of the donors. Whatever else might be going on that night, we still needed to make a good impression on behalf of the charity. Normally, Claire would be the one keeping me in line, not the other way around. She seemed almost as thrown off by the revelation about Eve as I was.

"That's a challenge all of us face," I quickly jumped in, trying to smooth over the tension. "Finding a balance between helping one person and making more systemic change can be tricky. That's why events like this that help highlight the problems we're dealing with and providing ways for people to provide meaningful funding are so important."

Mr Stamer accepted my words with a curt nod, but I could tell he was still wary.

The other seats at our table quickly filled up and the conversation turned more general. Eve recovered her poise as she spoke to the two other couples who had joined us, both of whom I knew by name. They were some of Toronto's biggest philanthropists, and getting them on board as donors to the charity would be a huge coup. I had to keep my head in the game, no matter what my heart felt.

Especially when I didn't even know what I felt.

She had told me the truth, sort of. Eventually. But the way she had done it and even the way she had phrased it, made it clear she knew it would bother me, and that had been the reason she'd kept it from me as long as she did.

And it *did* bother me, I couldn't deny that. Looking around at the extravagance surrounding us, the fancy cuisine and the champagne, the glittering dresses and the elegant room, everything suggested excess. I despised everything about this world, and it was *her* world. She sat there, wearing diamond earrings that were probably real diamonds, laughing and talking with people who could afford to give away more money than most people would ever see in their lifetime, looking completely comfortable and at home. An expensive luxury watch graced her father's wrist, his suit of the highest quality. He was probably exactly what my own father looked like, wherever he was.

That thought suddenly brought back another memory: how Eve had asked me if my father had been a Stamer. I told her how the man abandoned me and my mother, and she thought it could have been someone from her own family. That told me even more about the type of people she associated with than her name or bank account did.

"Mr Labrecque can tell you much more about the charity's overall vision than I can." Eve's voice cut into my musings as she said my name. She hadn't actually called me Julien since I sat down. She hadn't even looked in my direction again. No one at the table would think we had more than a passing acquaintance with each other. "But as a volunteer on the ground, I can tell you that I felt very well supported at all times. The regional team members were wonderful and the local women that I worked with taught me so much. I think it would be an incredibly valuable experience for any young person who wants to get a better understanding of the world at large."

"Sounds like she's flogging her own proposal, not the charity," Claire muttered to me under her breath. "Maybe that's the point of all of this? She and her father are trying to buy the charity's support with their donation?"

Merde, I hadn't even considered that yet. Whether it was her intention or not, coming in front of the charity's board in a few days and asking them to support her proposal and essentially give her a job when her father had just made a large donation looked bad. At the very least, it gave the appearance of a conflict of interest, just as our own relationship did. I had declared it to the board, but they might reconsider their acceptance of it once her other connections came to light. I didn't think Eve had been using me since she hadn't even known who I was when we met, but to the casual observer, it might suggest impropriety when coupled with the matter of her family's name and influence.

It felt like everything was unravelling and sitting in that elegant ballroom, I couldn't see a way forward where we were ever more than just acquaintances again, and that literally broke my heart. The woman I'd fallen in love with over the last week hadn't been real. She'd been an illusion, partly of her own creation and partly of mine.

With the illusion lifted, she was only a stranger to me.

~Eve~

As the dinner progressed and my initial shock and panic receded, determination slowly took its place. The truth had come out. With no way to turn back the clock, dwelling on what I could have or should have done would be pointless. All I could control was how I reacted and what I did next. Hiding did me no good. I might have screwed up in keeping the truth from Julien, but I wouldn't have done it if he hadn't been so judgemental in the first place. My cowardice shamed me but my family didn't, and I wanted to make that distinction clear.

If he wanted to reject our connection based on the fact that I'd lied to him by omission, that would be a bitter pill to swallow, but I would take responsibility for it. I'd screwed up, and I would own that. However, if he planned to reject me simply because of who my parents were and how much money they had, that reflected badly only on him, not me. To me, it seemed no different than his father rejecting his mother because of *her* social status.

Honestly, I had no idea how he might be feeling. With my dad acting as a buffer between us, we didn't speak to each other directly over dinner. He had come to my defense, sort of, when Claire made her barbed comment, but he hadn't looked at me as he said it. He hadn't acknowledged me at all.

And if that was his plan, if he intended to simply ignore me and pretend that we had nothing to say to each other, maybe I could still get my point across while I had the attention of everyone in the room.

As the meal drew to a close, my dad stood back up, walking over to the podium to get everyone's attention again. "I hope you've all enjoyed your meal. Now, I'd like to invite Eve to come up and tell you more about why we're here tonight."

He gave me a warm, proud smile that helped to buoy me as I followed him to the podium, my heart drumming a slightly irregular beat but my mind clear. Dozens of faces looked back at me, all interested to hear what I had to say, and I didn't intend to disappoint any of them.

"Thank you all for coming tonight. I actually had no idea before I arrived that anything like this was planned for this evening. Some dads buy their daughters jewellery for Christmas but mine organizes a charity benefit. I'm sure you can all appreciate that Cole Stamer never does anything halfway."

Smiles met my words from around the room, other than from Claire, whose lips were tight, and Julien, whose head was down. If he reacted, I couldn't see it.

I carried on talking away. "I've had a blessed life by anyone's standards. I have amazing parents and a supportive big brother. I grew up in a gorgeous apartment in Manhattan, never knowing what it felt like to worry about money. I have wonderful friends. I went to the best schools, knew all the right people, and I had a job waiting for me when I finished college with one of the most recognizable hotel chains in the world."

My dad cleared his throat loudly, and I rolled my eyes before correcting my statement.

"Alright, *the* most recognizable hotel chain in the world."

That earned me a laugh from the room, but Julien's eyes remained down, his hands folded on the table in front of him. At least he seemed to be listening, though. That would have to be good enough.

"However, that life, as wonderful as it might be, never felt entirely comfortable to me. In a way, it felt like my whole life had been set out for me, choices made for me and assumptions made about me by virtue of the family I was born into. I knew, just like all of you here tonight do, that there are very few people in the world as lucky as I am, but living within that bubble for the rest of my life didn't sit right with me. I wanted to experience life from a completely different perspective, and that's why I signed up to volunteer for a year in South America."

The projector on the ceiling above me flicked on, and a quick glance over my shoulder confirmed that some of the photos I'd sent home to my parents were being displayed on the wall behind me. It got Julien's attention too, and he looked up, his eyes focused on the images behind me rather than on me.

"The year I spent there had its high points and its low points, there's no sugarcoating that. I got homesick. I cried myself to sleep over the way some of the women I encountered had been treated. I questioned what I was doing there and whether anything I did could ever make a difference when the problems went so much deeper than I could have ever imagined. But every morning, those women had to get up and face another day. They had nowhere they could run to, and so I didn't run either."

The eyes of everyone in the room flicked between me and the photos behind me, all except Julien, who continued to look only at the photos, his brow furrowed.

"I'm not saying this because what I did was extraordinary. It wasn't. What those women went through, what they overcame, *that* is extraordinary. What the charity does in supporting them and helping them to better their lives is extraordinary. That's the work that you can help them with through your donations."

I didn't want to get too much into what the charity actually did, knowing that Julien would be speaking next. Instead, taking a deep breath, I steeled myself for what I wanted to say next, the words that I hoped would make my case to one person in particular if not to the whole room.

"The lessons I learned there will stay with me through the rest of my life. I went there to try to help people, but in the end, they were the ones who helped me. Most of all, they taught me that the circumstances of someone's birth don't define who they are. The women I met there were some of the smartest, most resourceful, most determined people I have ever known. Their poverty didn't define them any more than my wealth defines me. We had much more in common than we did to separate us, and it's what we do with what we have that matters. You all understand that, and that's why you're here tonight. You want to make a difference, just like I did, and I can tell you that any donation you make to the charity's work *will* make a difference. To explain to you exactly how, I'm delighted to introduce the charity's Executive Director, Mr Julien Labrecque."

Warm applause filled the room as I made the introduction. Looking calm and collected, Julien joined me at the podium, leaning down to kiss my cheek. "Well done," he whispered, his breath soft against my skin. "Thank you."

He turned to the podium as I took a step back, my skin still tingling from his proximity even as disappointment filled me. Those were words he might have said to anyone, completely impersonal. What I'd said didn't seem to have made any impression on him at all, and as he began speaking, I took a seat back at the table next to my dad, trying to project an outward aura of calm, even if inside, I felt anything but.

~Julien~

I listened carefully to each word that Eve said. She didn't speak directly about the charity's work, speaking from the heart instead about her motivations for volunteering and the impact it had made on her. Coupled with the pictures projected behind her, it made a powerful statement, but what exactly she meant to demonstrate with that statement, I couldn't be certain.

Was it, as Claire said, a pitch for Eve's own program? It certainly wouldn't have felt out of place as one. Perhaps, if what she'd said was true and she really hadn't had any warning about the event, it made sense that she would default to the material she'd been preparing for that.

Or had it actually been meant to convey something else entirely, something far more personal? Had her words, spoken in front of the glittering crowd, been meant for me? In them, I thought I could hear an explanation for why she'd kept the truth from me, of how she'd chafed against what she viewed as the limitations of her gilded life, and how she believed it didn't define her.

I would have to respond to that somehow, and as I stood in front of the podium, all eyes in the room on me, it seemed like that might be as good a time as any.

"First of all, I'd like to thank Mr Stamer for arranging this event and for his personal donation to the charity's work."

The spotlight on the ceiling shone into my eyes as I looked back towards the table where Eve and her father sat, making me squint. Eve hadn't seemed bothered by the lights, but she was shorter than me, so maybe they hadn't hit her in the face quite the same way. Funny how two people standing in the exact same spot could see things so differently.

"And thank you to Eve for sharing her experience. In a similar yet different way, my own circumstances were also what inspired me to get involved in this particular charity's work."

Eve leaned forward in her seat curiously while Claire frowned on the other side of the table. Those weren't my prepared remarks, and she clearly had no idea what I planned to say. Neither did I, to be honest. I was making it up as I went.

"Unlike Ms Stamer, I didn't grow up in a wealthy family. I'm the only child of a single mother who worked long hours to support us both. Sometimes, we couldn't afford heating or we had to skip meals. When I made my first trip to the kind of community where Ms Stamer volunteered, I could see myself in the children of the women that the charity helps."

I tried to glance over at Eve again, but the lights blinded me once more so I turned away, focusing on the other diners instead.

"Just like my mother, those women didn't lack anything in dedication, determination or pure grit. What they needed was opportunity and support, and that's exactly what the charity provides. Working with local women who understand the cultural and bureaucratic challenges of each individual location, we help those who have been exploited or abused by their partners or their employers and give them the tools they need to build a sustainable life with security for them and their children, and the promise of a better future. This isn't just about money, though money helps, obviously; that's why we're all here tonight."

A soft chuckle rippled through the crowd, appreciating me stating the obvious.

"But millions of dollars of donations wouldn't matter without the drive and determination of the women who we help and the volunteers on the ground who make it happen. For a year, Ms Stamer left behind her comfortable life to dedicate her time and energy to making a difference in the lives of the women in Ecuador. She used her first-class education, her talents, and her natural leadership abilities to lift up those around her, and as much as the charity could use your money, what we could use even more is another dozen volunteers just like her."

Through the glow of the lights, I caught a glimpse of Mr Stamer's face, full of pride.

"That's why I couldn't be more excited that she's chosen our charity to trial a new program that would do exactly that: source volunteers just like her, sponsored by donors like you, to bridge the gap between the world of privilege that we're in tonight and the disadvantaged people the charity serves. I probably shouldn't be talking about it because the board still has to approve the program, but having spent some time with Ms Stamer myself, I have no doubt that she'll make it happen."

Claire's face had gone stony, from what I could see, while Eve watched me carefully, her expression somewhere between confusion and hope.

"I could give you all the facts and figures about the number of people we've helped and all the countries we operate in, but you can find all of that on our website. If anyone wants to know more about the actual impact, please, come and speak to me or to Ms Stamer. Thank you all for being here tonight, and I hope we'll get a chance to speak soon."

That certainly had to qualify as one of the most unusual speeches I'd ever given, but as I returned to the table among the applause of the crowd, I felt satisfied with it. Along with piquing the interest of the crowd in general, it should have made it clear to Eve that I still respected her and supported her proposal, no matter what had happened or would happen between us personally.

Mr Stamer gave me a nod of approval as I approached. "That was great: get them interested and leave them wanting more. We're going to clear away the tables in a minute so you can mingle, so if you want to take a quick break, this is the best time."

I appreciated the warning, and hopefully, it gave me time for the conversation that I really didn't want to put off any longer. "Thank you. Eve, do you have a moment?"

"Julien?" Still frowning, Claire tried to get my attention from across the table, but I shook my head at her.

"In a minute. I'll be back soon."

Without a word, Eve got to her feet and I followed her out of the room. Walking behind her, I couldn't help admiring the way the dress wrapped around her body, hugging each inch of her perfectly. She really was utterly exquisite.

Not stopping once we reached the hallway, Eve led us to a small meeting room that lay empty. Flipping the lights on, she walked in, leaving the door open for me, and I closed it behind me, not wanting to be overheard. Inside was a large, round boardroom-style table, and Eve went to lean against the edge of it while I stayed standing close to the door.

"Do you want to go first or should I?" she asked, giving me a rueful smile as we finally found ourselves completely alone.

Putting it off wouldn't make things any easier, so I volunteered. "I'd like to. I'm sorry, Eve. I'm sorry that I didn't realize what you were trying to tell me last night, and I'm sorry that the comments I made about wealth and privilege probably made you uncomfortable. Given how open you've been with me in every other way, I can only assume that my own behaviour is the reason you didn't feel you could be honest with me."

Eve took a deep breath, exhaling through her mouth as her shoulders relaxed. It seemed she might have been anticipating a fight, so my apology surprised her. She quickly matched it with one of her own. "I'm sorry too. I should have just told you. I had plenty of opportunities to do it but I didn't want to mess up what was happening between us. I thought if you got to know me better first, you'd see me as more than just a bank account. I was afraid, and fear isn't something I usually let control me. I'm ashamed that I gave into it this time."

With a nod, I accepted her apology. "I understand."

I did, and I accepted the responsibility for the role my own actions had played. I could see clearly how we had both contributed to the situation blowing up in our faces that evening.

"Thank you for what you said up there," she added, taking a step closer to me. "It means so much to me to have your support. I admire you so much, Julien: your passion about the charity's cause, your dedication to it, and the way you live your whole life without apology."

She wasn't just talking about the charity anymore. She meant my sexual preferences too, but unfortunately, that wasn't the only part of my life where I had firmly-established limits, and however much she suited me in some ways, what I'd learned about her that night made it clear to me that in other ways, we were completely incompatible.

"I believe in your vision for this program, Eve, and I'm looking forward to working with you on it. Professionally, I think we'll make a great team."

My words made her pause, not coming any closer as she looked up at me, her eyes searching mine. "Professionally?" she repeated, not missing a thing, as usual. I had used the word on purpose. "What about personally?"

My throat tightened around the words I had to say, but I forced them out anyway. "I think it would be best if we kept our relationship strictly professional from now on."

She took a step back, her eyes full of confusion. "Why? I thought... I thought you accepted my apology."

"I did. I do, but it doesn't change the facts of who you are. There's a distance between us, Eve, a huge gulf that I don't see how we can bridge."

"So, you still think that just because I have money, I'm a bad person? That I'm not good enough for you?" Her words were sharp, but their edges were jagged with her own hurt. I didn't take it personally.

"I don't think you're a bad person, but what I wanted from you, what I thought we could have, that kind of deep connection, just isn't possible given the difference in our circumstances. I would never fit into your world, Eve. I don't want to. It makes me uncomfortable. *Tabarnak*, even being here tonight is a bit like torture."

"You like torture," she reminded me, trying to make me smile. "I could reward you for it later."

"I'm sure you could." For just a moment, I was tempted, but as quickly as it came, the feeling fell away, melting into the pit of empty disappointment inside me. "But it wouldn't work, Eve. I would never ask you to give up your wealth or the world you live in just for me, and I can't do it for you either. This is who I am. And it doesn't mean I don't... love you."

I choked the words out, well aware that I hadn't said them before, and Eve's eyebrows drew together, her entire expression pained and unhappy.

"I think we would have been amazing together, actually. I've never felt the way I feel about you."

"Then why are you just giving up?" she demanded, stepping closer to me again, so close I could almost feel her breath as her words came out of her forcefully. "Why won't you even try?"

"Because it won't work, and the longer we drag it out, the more painful it will be. I'm sorry, Eve. I wish it could be different, but it can't."

With nothing else I could add, I turned out to go, but Eve caught hold of my arm. "Julien. Don't do this."

Her voice had that firm, commanding tone that turned me on so much, and against my will, my body reacted to it as it always did. But in this situation, I had to listen to my head instead, and so I turned back to her and whispered the one word I knew would end the conversation for good.

My safeword.

As soon as I uttered it, Eve let me go instantly, stepping back again and nearly tripping over her high heels in her surprise. Every instinct I had wanted to reach out and steady her, to support and comfort her, but I simply couldn't. I had to walk away while I still could, and so I turned and went out the door, leaving her there on her own.

Chapter Thirteen

The Root of the Problem

In the silence that Julien left behind, I could almost hear my heart splintering.

I thought I'd been prepared. When I decided the night before to tell him the truth, I thought I could handle it if he decided my deception meant he couldn't trust me or if he couldn't look past the fact of my wealth in the first place. I'd told myself it would be better to know rather than to live with the uncertainty and feeling the sword hanging over me, waiting for the moment of discovery.

Now, I knew that had been a lie. I only thought it would be better because deep down, I hadn't believed he would throw away what we had. I thought we would find a way through it. With the benefit of hindsight, I realized the guilt I'd felt over keeping my secret from him had been better than the bereft emptiness I felt after his departure because at least then, I'd still had hope.

When he used his safeword, he took that hope away, crushing it under his heel and leaving my heart broken along with it.

That word had been the most devastating one he could have used at that moment because of what it symbolized: I'd gone too far, pushed past his limits, and for his own protection, he needed to withdraw. Like the scar his previous domme had left upon his skin, he seemed to be telling me that I'd permanently wounded him too.

I never meant to.

And what about what he'd done to me? He had put his full trust in me and then withdrawn it for reasons I didn't fully understand. He didn't like my wealth but why did that outweigh everything else we had felt and shared together? I wasn't royalty. He didn't have to give up his life and live in a palace with me. Why wouldn't he even try to find a way to compromise and make it work? The fact that he could walk away just like that, like it had never meant that much to him in the first place, hurt me most of all.

Had I only been fooling myself all along?

Gradually, as the seconds ticked by, my initial shock began to recede. As much as I wanted to run away and hide, to nurse my wounds and my pain, I couldn't. A room full of people were waiting for me, wanting to talk about the charity and, now that Julien had mentioned it in his speech, my own project too. Maybe all the roleplaying we'd done that week had been worthwhile, since to get through the rest of the evening, I would need to put on the performance of a lifetime, acting as if I were having a wonderful time and not like everything had just fallen apart.

In the end, I was a Stamer, and Stamers didn't back down from a challenge. My parents had both gone through their own heartbreaks when they were my age and they'd survived. I would too, no matter how much it hurt that night. After checking my makeup in my compact mirror, I straightened my shoulders and walked back into the ballroom, my head held high.

"Is everything okay?" My dad cornered me as I went to get myself a drink from the bar.

I fixed my most serene smile on my face. "Of course. Why?"

"Julien looked upset when he came back from talking to you, and he went straight into an intense conversation with his assistant."

With his head, he gestured over his shoulder, and I glanced over to see Julien and Claire standing together, separate from anyone else but close to each other. It certainly didn't look like a happy discussion, but I had no idea what they would be arguing about. I supposed it no longer concerned me.

"I'm not sure what that's about, but I would like your help, Dad. Who should I focus on first? Which of the donors are the best bets?"

He gave me a nod of appreciation as I slipped into business mode, and with his typical directness, he introduced me to a couple who had two college-age children and were particularly interested in my proposed program. The rest of the evening passed in a blur of names and faces and questions. Julien kept his distance, working one side of the room while I did the other. I praised him whenever the opportunity arose, and several people mentioned to me that he had said complimentary things about me too. As far as anyone could tell, we made a great team.

Only he and I knew the truth.

After finishing one particularly in-depth conversation, I excused my-self to go back to the bar, my mouth feeling dry. Once again, my dad found me there. "You've done great, Eve. Whenever you want to disap-pear, feel free. I can finish things off here."

As surreptitiously as possible, I glanced around the room, but I couldn't see any sign of Julien or Claire. "Where's Julien?"

"He left a few minutes ago. He told me to say goodbye since he didn't want to interrupt your conversation."

He left without even speaking to me. It seemed any hopes I might have had that he would regret his earlier action were unfounded. As the pain of his rejection hit me again, I gave my dad a nod. "In that case, I think I'll go too. Thank you for tonight. It means so much to me to have your support."

"You'll always have it."

His complete, unconditional love made the contrast with Julien's behaviour even stronger, and I quickly excused myself before my facade started to crack.

Back in my room, I did my best to ignore the morose face looking back at me from the mirror as I removed my jewellery and unzipped my dress. When I bought it that afternoon, I had imagined Julien seeing me in it; not that night, but eventually. I had imagined his hands running up beneath my skirt and the way he'd get down on his knees and beg for the pleasure of making me come while I was wearing it.

That would never happen, not in that dress or any other. In less than a week, I'd found my ideal man and lost him again. Would I ever have that level of innate understanding with anyone else?

Lying in my bed, I tried to convince myself that I would be better off without him. Why would I want to be with someone who wouldn't fight for me? My mom and dad had refused to let each other go. Olivia fought for my brother, and Noah pulled out the stops to win her back after being an idiot. Aaron made it clear to Noelle that his feelings had changed once he realized she was the one he wanted all along. Even Noelle's parents often told the story about how they had each been on their way to make a grand declaration of love to the other, and nearly missed each other until they got on the same train at Grand Central Station.

But that came later, I remembered as I thought it over. At first, Holly had been insistent that she didn't want a relationship with Jackson because she couldn't be what he needed. Somehow, he'd convinced her otherwise, and though it wasn't exactly the same thing as my current situation, it felt the closest. Before I could change my mind, I picked up my phone and called New York.

"Eve? This is a nice surprise." Jackson's voice on the other end sounded as warm and cheerful as usual. "Are you back home?"

"Not yet. Dad and I are still in Toronto but we'll be heading home in a few days. How are you?"

Jackson chuckled. "I'm good, but I don't think you're calling this late on a Sunday night just to chat. What's up?"

He knew me almost as well as my dad did, so I answered him bluntly. "I was wondering if you could give me some relationship advice."

"And you don't want to go to Cole for this?" he teased me gently, knowing as well as I did that my dad's definition of romance differed from most people's.

"Actually, I'd rather he didn't know about this. Not yet, anyway."

"Sounds serious." I could hear his sofa creaking through the phone as he settled in. "What's going on?"

With as few specifics as possible, I told him about the situation with Julien. When I'd finished, I summed up with the question I wanted answered most of all. "I know we'd be good together but he's convinced himself it won't work. Should I let it go, or do you think there's something there worth fighting for?"

A pause followed, letting me know Jackson was really thinking it over by responding. "You're the only one who can answer that, but the fact that you're asking makes me think you're not ready to let it go. You really like him, huh?"

I couldn't hide it. "Everything other than his irrational hatred of people like me. But who's perfect?"

Jackson laughed again. "Well, my first thought is that his aversion probably isn't as irrational as it seems. When Holly and I first started seeing each other, she told me she was never going to fall in love with anyone. I thought that was pretty irrational too, but sometimes, we get these ideas in our head, usually branded there through some kind of pain, and after a while, we get so used to them, we can't see them logically anymore. They become part of the fabric of who we are and blind us to the truth that's right in front of us."

That described Julien's prejudice pretty well. "What did you do? How did you convince her she was wrong?"

"There's no simple solution," he told me apologetically. "It took a while, but eventually, she opened up about what made her feel that way, and as best as I could, I showed her that I wouldn't ever treat her the way she'd been treated. It didn't happen all at once, but eventually, she believed me, and she let go of that belief that held her back."

I groaned in frustration. "That all sounds good, but I don't have that kind of time. He won't even talk to me and I'm leaving the country in a few days."

"Maybe he's already given you some clues," Jackson suggested. "If you can figure out what the root of the problem is, maybe you can find a way to address it in a way that will actually get through to him."

As much as I wished he could solve my problem for me, I knew he couldn't. He'd given me some things to think about, at least. "Thanks, Jackson. I really appreciate your insight."

"Anytime, Eve. And I'd be remiss in my surrogate dad duties if I didn't add one more thing: if he truly can't see what an amazing woman you are, rich or not, then he doesn't deserve you."

That was easy to say, but a lot harder to convince myself of. "Thank you. Goodnight."

After hanging up, I lay down again, but sleep still wouldn't come. I kept returning in my head to the day Julien had told me about his dad and why his dislike of rich people had started. There had to be more to the story than he'd told me, maybe more than he even knew.

There was one person who *would* know, one person who had been there and whose description of the events would have shaped Julien's view of them.

One person who might not like talking to anyone in English, but who would find it hard to ignore me if I showed up at her door.

Maybe it would be overstepping, but honestly, he'd already rejected me. How much worse could things get? If I really wanted to get to the bottom of things, Julien's mom seemed like the best place to start.

~Julien~

My house felt colder than usual when I returned home after the benefit. I'd looked around for Eve before I left, catching sight of her in deep conversation with a potential donor, looking at them in that way she had of making it seem like she'd never heard anything more interesting than whatever they were saying. She didn't see me, and I didn't want to interrupt her. What would I say, anyway? I couldn't add anything to what I'd already said, so I passed my goodbye through her father instead, retreating into the cold winter's night alone.

In the space of one evening, I'd managed to disappoint two different women in different ways. Aside from everything that happened with Eve, Claire also left the event not speaking to me.

When I returned from my conversation with Eve, feeling empty and numb at the loss of what I had built up in my imagination into the great love of my life, Claire cornered me almost immediately.

"Why would you hype up her program? The board hasn't even agreed to it yet."

"They will," I replied dully, unable to summon the fire needed to match her tone. The ache in my heart was too strong. "It's a great idea and now it has the Stamer name behind it."

"You told me that you could see her without compromising your impartiality. It doesn't feel that way right now."

She had really gotten herself worked up about this. I didn't understand why, but I had a pretty good idea how I could shut it down. "Well, you don't need to worry about that. Eve and I are no longer seeing each other."

That stopped her cold, her eyes going wide with surprise. "You broke up?"

"That's what I said, isn't it?" In a way, Claire had been right when she warned me about Eve the day before. She had hurt me, just not in the way Claire thought she would.

"Oh. Well. Good." Claire didn't seem to know what to say, but the word she settled on managed to cut through my numbness as a flash of annoyance went through me instead.

"Good? Why is it good?"

Claire's cheeks flushed as she looked down. "Well, because of the conflict of interest. Now, you don't have to worry about it."

I stepped closer to her, lowering my voice, my eyes narrowed. "You're lying. Why do you really think it's good, Claire? Why do you care?"

Normally, I didn't seek out confrontation that way. My submissive side didn't like it, but at that moment, Claire's behaviour and the way she had been talking Eve down all night had started to wear on me. I didn't want any more backhanded comments; I wanted the truth.

"She's just not right for you," she stammered in response, and I almost laughed at the ridiculousness of that assertion. Not only did Claire have no idea what I wanted in a partner, she also couldn't have been more wrong. I'd never met anyone better suited to me than Eve, other than that one fatal misalignment.

"And who would be? You?" I spat the words out without fully thinking them through, and when her cheeks flushed deeper, the truth finally hit me. Inadvertently, I'd stumbled upon the actual root of Claire's dislike for Eve, a far simpler one than I'd realized: jealousy.

"It's not such a crazy idea," she mumbled as more and more pieces began to fall into place in my head. The way she always took care of little personal tasks for me, even going so far as to cook for me and decorate my Christmas tree. The way she'd come over to my house earlier that week when I got back from my trip. Even the way she'd invited herself along as my guest for that evening. It all made complete and utter sense in the context of her trying to earn not only my approval as a boss but my affection too.

And I had completely missed it, because I knew, far better than she did, that Claire would never be what I needed.

"I didn't know you felt that way, Claire." I softened my tone to try to make the words more palatable, but I didn't see the point in beating around the bush either. "I'm flattered, but it wouldn't work."

"Because we work together? I could find another job. I've had offers, in fact. I..."

"No, that's not why." I cut her off before she could offer her resignation right there on the spot. It looked like I would need to be even more blunt. "The kind of woman I would fall for isn't the kind who would wait months to tell me how she felt."

She finally looked me square in the face again, her expression full of dismay. "That's not fair. You're not the easiest person to talk to. You're always so busy."

It had nothing to do with being busy. Eve didn't wait until I had time for her. She demanded my attention, right from that first night in Quito. *That* was what I found sexy.

Claire could hardly put all the blame on me, anyway. "What about yesterday when you came to my house? You had no trouble talking to me then, trying to get me to doubt Eve. And can you really still pretend you didn't have any ulterior motive in telling me what you saw?"

It all became a lot clearer to me, the more I thought about it: Claire had been doing her best to cause trouble, but in the end, she hadn't had to. My relationship with Eve had fallen apart without her help.

"I think you should go, Claire. I can manage the rest of the evening without you."

What I would do about her at work, I hadn't decided yet, but at that moment, I didn't want to have to worry about her offending any other donors the way she'd offended Eve's father. Her eyes started to water as she turned away from me and hurried out the door, leaving me well and truly on my own.

Eve had returned to the ballroom while Claire and I were talking, and my eyes were immediately drawn to her, her red hair and her red dress, elegant and beautiful as she spoke to a group of men and women. She looked poised and sure of herself, as confident as always, and nowhere near as heartbroken as I felt. Gritting my teeth, I did my best to put all the evening's arguments behind me and do my best to sell the charity, since that was the reason I'd gone there in the first place.

After a fitful, unhappy sleep, I dragged myself to the office on Monday morning. Everyone greeted me with their usual smiles, other than Claire, who sat typing at her computer, pretending she couldn't see me as I walked by.

It didn't really surprise me when I found her resignation letter sitting on my desk.

For a brief, wonderful moment, I imagined what it would be like to work with Eve, not as boss and assistant but as partners, making plans together, solving problems, travelling on rickety buses or horse-drawn carts down remote mountain roads, nothing easy but everything worthwhile because we were together.

As quickly as it came, the image faded. That wasn't Eve's world. She belonged to the men in suits and the women in diamonds from the night before, drinking champagne beneath crystal chandeliers. The life I'd imagined for us, without even realizing I'd done it, would never exist.

With a sigh, I called the human resources manager into my office to pass on Claire's resignation and ask him to work on getting me a replacement as soon as possible. She'd stated in her letter that she would work until Christmas, which didn't leave us with a lot of time.

The thought of Christmas made me think of Eve again. On my phone, I had a photo I'd taken of her at Casa Loma, looking up at the tree with an expression of awe and delight on her face, and I pulled it out when I was alone again. She hadn't even known I'd taken it, but it was one of the few things I had left from our week-long relationship, one of the few things to prove to me that it had really happened at all.

The feeling of loss as I stared at it was so strong that I was tempted to delete it too, to try to forget the way she'd made me feel since I felt so awful in comparison, but in the end, I simply turned the phone off again, tucked it back into my pocket, and got back to work.

~Eve~

My dad's eyebrows raised curiously at me over breakfast. "What's in Québec City?"

I had just told him I planned to fly there that afternoon. I would have to stay overnight because of the available flight times, but I would be back the next day, in plenty of time for my presentation to the charity board on Wednesday. Luckily, the Stamer hotel in Québec could make room for me.

I hated lying to my dad, but I could hardly tell him the whole story either, not at that point. "Someone related to the charity lives there. Meeting with them might help my pitch."

That had a whiff of truth to it, at least. First thing that morning, I'd been on the phone to Noelle's fiancé, Aaron, asking him to help me track down Julien's mother.

"Just because I wear glasses doesn't make me some kind of computer hacker," he grumbled as Noelle woke him up to talk to me.

I didn't let his Monday morning grouchiness throw me off. "Can you do it, though?"

After a moment's pause, he conceded. "Probably. When do you need the info?"

"As soon as possible."

By the time I met my dad for breakfast, I already had her full name and Aaron was working on narrowing it down further from the five people with the same name he'd managed to find in the city.

"I have a feeling there's more to it than that," my dad mused as he took a drink from his coffee. He'd always been good at reading people, so it didn't surprise me he could tell I had held something back. The fact that I'd managed to keep it all a secret as long as I had was a bit of a miracle. "But if you don't want to tell me, I assume you have a good reason. Do you need anything?"

"No, but thanks, Dad." I appreciated that he hadn't pressed me on it, and I *would* tell him eventually, once I knew for sure how it would all end.

By the time I landed in the snowy Québec capital, Aaron had sent me two addresses: one for Julien's mom's house and another for the corner store where she worked, the one Julien had told me about. *I hope this guy's worth it,* he texted me when he sent the information.

I hoped so too.

Given that it was still early afternoon when I arrived, I had the taxi take me directly to the store. I could ask there if Madame Labrecque was working that day, and if not, I'd try her at home next.

"Bonjour," a friendly voice called out as I walked into the tightly-packed convenience store. The voice belonged to a young man standing behind the counter of the shop that felt similar to a bodega in New York with an array of pre-packaged food and essentials, though the aisle full of wine took me by surprise.

"Bonjour," I answered back in awkward, accented French. "Je cherche Emilie Labrecque, s'il vous plaît. Est-elle ici?"

I've practiced that phrase most of the plane ride and asking if Julien's mother was there pretty much exhausted the whole of my French knowledge.

The man, younger than me, tried not to laugh as he answered me in flawless English. "Sure. Just a minute, I'll get her."

So much for trying to make a good impression.

As he headed through a small door in the back, I looked around the store. Although the shelves were worn and weathered in places, everything was neat and clean. I tried to imagine Julien there as a young boy, stopping in to see his mother at work. It would have been a different experience, certainly, than when I visited the Stamer Hotel headquarters to see my father. We did come from different backgrounds, but I would never presume to know anything about him based on that. Why couldn't he do the same for me?

"Oui?" I'd been so distracted by my own thoughts that I hadn't heard the door reopen or anyone come out. As I spun back around, a middle-aged woman stood in front of me, probably around my mom's age though she looked older. Strands of grey wove through her brown hair, the same shade as her son's, and deep lines at the corners of her mouth made her look unhappy even when her expression should have been neutral.

"Madame Labrecque?" I felt sure it must have been, but I didn't want to make any assumptions.

"Oui. Je peux vous aider?"

Perhaps the young man hadn't told her about my terrible French, but I couldn't begin to explain what had brought me there in her language, so I had to switch to mine. "My name is Eve. I was hoping I could talk to you..."

"Je ne vous comprends pas. Parlez en français." She cut me off, claiming she couldn't understand me, and asking me to speak in French instead.

"I'm sorry, my French isn't good enough, but I think you can understand me, Madame. You understood your son's father well enough."

Her eyes widened in surprise, making it entirely clear that she *did* understand me perfectly well. Her eyes darted over to the young man who had stepped back behind the counter, pretending not to listen, but in the small space, he must have been able to hear us. When she spoke again, the words were English, clipped and heavily accented. "Follow me."

She turned around and walked back through the small door at the rear of the store while I hurried after her. There, I found myself in a large storage area, and to one side, where she headed next, sat a small office with a desk and a computer and a few filing cabinets. As soon as the door to the office had closed behind me, she spun around and addressed me again, her voice simmering with repressed emotion.

"Who are you? One of his girls?"

I blinked in surprise at both her tone and her question. One of Julien's girls? Did he have so many? As I struggled for a response, a moment of clarity hit me and I realized what she actually must have meant: *one of her ex-lover's girls.* A daughter, maybe? That made much more sense.

"I know your son, Julien, Madame. I don't know his father at all."

That surprised her perhaps even more than my initial statement. "Julien is here?"

Her eyes glanced back over at the door in anticipation, as if he might walk in behind us, and I had to disappoint her. "No. He's in Toronto. I came here alone to see you. I'm sorry if this feels like an ambush but it's important to me. Please, can we sit down?"

There were two chairs in the office, one behind the desk and one in front of it, and she rounded the desk to take a seat while I lowered myself into the one closest to me, unzipping my winter coat now that the chill from outside was fading.

"Julien doesn't know I'm here," I admitted to her first. If I expected honesty from her, I would need to demonstrate it too. "We were seeing each other but he broke up with me last night."

Her eyebrows shot up in surprise, much like my dad's had that morning when I told him about my trip. Her eyes were hazel, not like Julien's warm brown ones; those must have come from his father. "And you think I can convince him to take you back? I didn't even know about you."

She might have thought that would offend me but it didn't, especially since I hadn't told my dad about Julien either. It didn't make my feelings for him any less real. "I don't expect or want you to speak to him on my behalf. I just came to try to understand. The reason he gave me for why we couldn't be together doesn't make any sense to me and I thought you might be able to explain it."

She still looked confused, understandably. "What is the reason?"

Again, I answered with complete honesty. "I'm from a rich family. Very rich. That's the only reason. In every other way, we suit each other perfectly, but apparently, that's a dealbreaker for him and I think it must stem from what happened with his father. If I can understand that, maybe I can understand why he rejected me."

"Why does it matter so much to you?" Her expression had turned pained, her confusion clearing but her hesitance still strong. "Why would you come all this way?"

There could only be one answer to that. "Because I'm in love with him."

Chapter Fourteen

No More Secrets

~**Eve**~

The look in Julien's mother's eyes when I told her I was in love with her son didn't give me a lot of hope. "Look, I'm sure you're a very nice girl..."

"Woman," I interrupted. Maybe she used the word because of a linguistic difference, but at twenty-four, I didn't consider myself a girl with all the connotations of inexperience that word carried. I was a woman who knew exactly what I wanted and exactly what I'd come there for.

Madame Labrecque's brow furrowed. "Yes, fine. A woman, but you are not the first to have a man break up with you. If he already told you what happened with his father..."

"He told me what he knows." Again, I interrupted her, refusing to let her put me off, but in the next sentence, I did my best to soften my tone with sympathy. "I want to hear it from you. I understand this man broke your heart. It couldn't have been easy for you raising Julien on your own and you probably kept some things from him to protect him. I promise, anything you tell me here will be kept in confidence. I won't tell Julien anything you don't want me to."

The woman across the desk from me sighed, probably realizing that she wouldn't be getting rid of me easily. "You are very determined."

"Yes, I am. Your son likes that about me."

She almost smiled. I could tell she was tempted to, the corners of her mouth twitching even though she tried to hide it, and though she didn't smile in the end, at least she gave in to my request. "Alright. You want to know my sad story? I will tell you."

With her accent thicker than Julien's, I had to pay close attention to catch every word, and I leaned forward eagerly, not wanting to miss anything.

"I was twenty years old when he came to the city with his father. They were staying for three months to work on a new business project. A friend of mine who spoke better English than me got hired to translate for them. Over lunch one day, Julien's father mentioned that he wanted to meet some people his own age, away from his father, so she brought him to a house party and that's where we were introduced. I don't know if you have ever seen someone and felt an immediate connection with them, not quite love but stronger than lust?"

Understanding her perfectly, I gave her a nod of encouragement to continue. That described exactly how I felt with Julien on that night in Quito.

"We fell hard and fast. Or I did, anyway. We spent all our free time together. My English wasn't great but he helped me improve. I taught him French but he was terrible at it. He used to joke that I would teach our kids and we could all talk about him right in front of him and he wouldn't know what we were saying. He said things like that all the time, things that made me think he wanted a future together as much as I did."

I had to agree it certainly sounded that way.

"There were signs, though. Things I should have noticed. He never introduced me to his father. He would joke about how his father wanted to control his life and make all his choices for him, but I didn't think much of it. I thought in the end he could make up his own mind, but I didn't fully understand the situation, not until I found out I was pregnant."

Julien had already told me some of this part, but again, I wanted to hear it in her own words, so I kept quiet and waited for her to continue.

"We didn't plan it. We used protection sometimes but not always. We could have been more careful, but I honestly believed we were going to be together forever, so when I told him, I wasn't even that nervous. I thought he would be surprised, but we would deal with it. However, that's not what happened."

She fell silent for a moment, no sound in the small office except the ticking of the clock on the wall above her head as she sat there, lost in her memories.

"He said he needed some time to 'think things over', whatever that meant, and the next thing I knew, both he and his father turned up at my door."

I winced instinctively, imagining her surprise and dismay. "That was the first time you met his father?"

"Yes. And as soon as he came inside, he started accusing me of sabotaging my birth control so I would get pregnant and trap his son into marrying me."

Again, Julien had told me that part. Everything she said lined up exactly with what he'd told me, but hearing the pain in her voice, thirty years on, made it feel even more real.

"I kept waiting for him to stand up for me, to tell his father off for speaking to me that way, but he didn't. He just sat there and nodded whenever his father asked for his agreement. When I tried to make eye contact with him, he looked away. His father insisted that I get an abortion, and again, he said nothing. At that moment, any love I ever had for him completely disappeared. He wouldn't stand up for me and he wouldn't stand up for his own child."

I honestly couldn't imagine how that must have felt. It hurt me badly enough the night before when Julien gave up on us, and her situation would have been even worse.

"I said no. I told them I would keep and love my baby all on my own, and so his father wrote me a cheque, said I would get nothing more from them, and whatever I did, not to name the baby after the child's father. Those words particularly stuck in my head, they seemed so unnecessarily cruel. I wouldn't have even thought of it if he hadn't mentioned it."

A moment of clarity hit me. "So, you did, didn't you? Just to spite them?"

Her lips curled upwards again. "Almost. His father was Julian. He's Julien. It sounds different enough in French that it doesn't remind me of him, but on paper, it looks almost the same."

Petty, perhaps, but I could see the appeal.

"Of course he commented on it when he got in touch with me again. He thought I did it because I still had feelings for him. Il est rien qu'un petit connard."

She lost me when she switched to French, but I imagined whatever she said wasn't very complimentary. Meanwhile, my heart had already started beating faster by what she said just before that: *when he got in touch with me again.* Julien told me she'd never seen his father again after the day he tried to pay her off. Certainly not after Julien's birth, as far as he knew.

"How old was Julien when he got in touch with you?" I tried to keep my tone interested but not too much so, not to give away that I didn't know this part.

"The first time? About five. He'd just had his first child with his wife, a rich young woman from a good family, and apparently, it brought out some kind of paternal instinct in him."

The first time. So he had been in touch more than once, it seemed, yet Julien didn't seem to know about it. "What did he want?"

"He asked why I never cashed his cheque. He wanted to know if we were 'doing okay'. And he asked if he could meet Julien."

No, Julien *definitely* didn't know about that. "And you said no?"

"Of course I said no." Her eyes flashed with indignation. "After five years, he wants to come and meet him? For what? It would have still been a secret. His father didn't know he was contacting me. Neither did his wife. He was still just as weak as he'd always been, and if he'd disappeared again after meeting Julien, he would have broken my boy's heart. Better that he never got his hopes up."

I could understand that, sort of, though I didn't think letting Julien think his father had never shown any interest was fair either. "But he got in touch with you again? You said that was the first time."

Madame Labrecque gave an almost impressed huff, not having expected me to catch that. "Oui. Julien's grandfather died when Julien was eight, so now, his father didn't have to worry about his disapproval. His wife had just given birth to their second daughter, and he got in touch to ask about joint custody. Can you imagine? He wanted to bring Julien into his family now that he was in charge, make him his little heir since he didn't have a son yet, to make him grow up under his thumb just like he had been under his father's, letting this other woman have my son just as she had my lover."

It felt like she was projecting a lot of her own biases onto her former lover, in the same way Julien had let his prejudice influence his opinion of me. At least now I could see where he got it from.

"What should I say? Yes, please take my son and give him expensive things I can't give him, teach him that he deserves more than other people just because of the blood in his veins, teach him to look down on people like me. If he went to that world, he would not come back the same boy. I wanted him to have a real life, not one where he would tell people one thing and do another. And before you ask, I don't regret it. Julien is a good, decent, honest man. He does good in the world every day, and he would not be that man if his father had raised him."

"So, you never told Julien that his father wanted to get to know him, but you told him all these other things: about how rich people like his father are different, that they don't care about other people, that they live in a 'different world'?"

Finally, I could clearly see where Julien's ideas had come from, taught to him and reinforced from early childhood, internalized before he even knew what they meant. Those childhood biases stayed with us for a long, long time, influencing the way we interacted with the world around us, and though they didn't fully excuse his prejudice, at least I could understand where it started.

"I told him only what is true," his mother declared, sounding just as frustratingly pigheaded as her son did.

"No, you told him what made you feel better. I understand that you had your heart broken, and I agree that what Julien's father did to you was terrible. Should he have stood up to his father? Yes, of course. But people make mistakes. He tried to make amends. He tried to support you and Julien, and you wouldn't let him. That would have spoiled the story you'd created, with yourself as the star. You made him the villain, but that doesn't make you any better than him."

She looked offended, as I expected. My words had been offensive. "You don't understand..."

"No, you don't understand what keeping this from Julien has done to him. Growing up thinking that his father never thought about him once? You didn't think that would affect him? Not to mention the animosity you fostered in him against people with money. Last night, your son stood in front of me and did just what his father did. He told me we couldn't be together because my background didn't match his. He said because my family has money, we wouldn't work, even though he loves me. You might not have been standing beside him like your lover's father was, but I can hear you in his words."

In frustration, I got to my feet, the chair squealing against the floor as I pushed it away from me.

Julien's mother looked up at me, her expression more startled than anything. "He loves you? He said that?"

"He did, but apparently, love isn't enough for him. He needs to be a martyr too. I wonder where he got that from."

Again, my words were intentionally sharp, and she grimaced beneath their assault. Maybe they would give her something to think about, but at that point, I didn't believe it would change anything. For thirty years, she'd nursed her grudge, holding onto her pain as some kind of badge of honour, and teaching her son to do the same.

It seemed clear to me that I wouldn't get any help from her, but at least I had the full story. "Merry Christmas," were my last words to her as I turned and left the store. Just as Julien's father had before him, Julien was going to have to make a choice about whether he wanted to stay stuck in the beliefs his mother had instilled in him or whether he would fight for us. I couldn't make that choice for him. I could only hope he would come to his senses before I had to cut my losses and go.

~Julien~

The name that flashed across my phone screen as I ate dinner in front of the TV that night took me by surprise. Usually, my mom would email me before she called to make sure what time zone I was in, and since I would be seeing her soon for Christmas anyway, I didn't expect to hear from her at all.

"Bonjour, Maman. Y a-t-il un problème?"

It said something about how often she called unannounced that my first instinct was to ask if something was wrong.

"No, there's no problem," she assured me as we carried on speaking in French. "At least, not with me."

What did that mean? "Is that a riddle?"

"If it is, maybe we can solve it together."

That didn't make things any clearer and I clicked the TV off to focus on her completely. "What's going on?"

She cleared her throat, sounding almost nervous. "Have you been spending time with a young woman named Eve lately?"

Very little she might have said could have surprised me more, and just the mention of Eve's name brought her image to the front of my mind and sent a pang of loss through my whole body. "How do you know about Eve?"

My mother and I lived very different lives. Aside from the woman I rented the house from, who knew nothing about Eve, I couldn't think of any other mutual acquaintances who might have told her.

"I'll take that as a yes, then." She gave a soft chuckle, but I could still tell she didn't feel completely comfortable. "Have you spoken to her today?"

Apparently, though she knew something about Eve, she didn't know the whole story. "No. We're not seeing each other anymore. Maman, who told you about Eve?" I found it rather disconcerting that details of my private life were spreading across the country.

Although I couldn't guess what her answer would be, the one she gave me still managed to take me completely by surprise. "She came to see me today."

"What?" She must have been joking. How would that even be possible?

As quickly as the question formed in mind, an answer appeared to it: with enough money, just about anything was possible. Not only possible, but acceptable, even though tracking down my mother seemed rather extreme. What had she been trying to accomplish?

"She came to my work and insisted that I talk to her," my mom continued. "She's very pushy."

That almost made me smile. I supposed people might use that word for Eve, but I never saw it as a bad thing. Her assertiveness was one of things I liked best about her.

"What did she want to talk to you about?" It must have been about me, but I couldn't imagine how that conversation would have gone or what Eve had hoped to get out of it. Had she actually gotten my mother to speak to her in English? I didn't think Eve spoke much French.

"She wanted to know why you hate rich people so much. She said you broke up with her only because she is rich. Is that true?"

That felt a little simplistic to me, but I couldn't refute the basic details behind it. Besides, my mother, of all people, would understand how I felt. "She's not just 'rich'. She could buy herself a whole country if she wanted to. She's a whole other level of rich."

"But do you love her?"

"It doesn't matter."

"Julien." There was an emotion in her voice I hadn't heard for a long time. Disappointment? Recrimination? *Self*-recrimination? I couldn't be sure. "Of course it matters."

Frustration built up inside me that the one person I thought would understand my decision without question seemed to be disagreeing with me. "Not enough. I told you: she's from a completely different world."

"It's not so different," she argued. "You are a successful, independent man. People admire and respect you. If she loves you too, she will see that."

Her words utterly baffled me. "That's what you thought, remember? You thought love would be enough, but you know it wasn't. In the end, she would never be satisfied with someone like me."

Those words came out of my mouth before I even realized I meant to say them and they stopped me short. Did I really believe that? I hadn't consciously been aware of thinking those thoughts before, relying instead on my conviction that our backgrounds and beliefs made it impossible for us to be compatible, but maybe deep down, that fear had always existed. Did I simply push her away before she had a chance to prove me right?

"Merde." My mother's blunt curse cut through the silence that followed my declaration. "Maybe Eve was right."

"Right about what?" My voice had lost its fight as I struggled to come to terms with what I had just involuntarily revealed, both to her and myself.

"That you not having a relationship with your father affected you more than I realized. You think because he didn't accept you that she won't either?"

She'd talked to Eve about my dad? This conversation kept getting stranger and stranger. "Maybe it did affect me, but it's not like you could have done anything about it. He made that decision."

Through the phone, I could hear my mother's shaky breath, and it set my whole body on edge. My mother rarely got nervous or unsure of herself. If she hesitated to tell me something, it had to be something big.

"Maman? What is it?"

"It's not... entirely true that he never wanted a relationship with you."

What on earth was she talking about? "Not *entirely* true? Which part isn't true?"

"He did make contact with me a few times, wanting to meet you, but I refused to let him. I didn't want him to think he could buy your affection after abandoning us."

Those kinds of comments were very familiar to me from my childhood, about how wealthy people could smooth over their indiscretions and mistakes, paving the road to redemption with a sprinkling of cash. I never realized she'd been referring to my father's overtures at the time.

"Why did he want to meet me?" It made no real difference at that point but I still wanted to know. Would I have simply been a curiosity to him or did he actually have a change of heart?

"He... he mentioned shared custody at one point," she admitted as my jaw dropped in disbelief. She had never given me *any* indication that had happened. "He wanted you to go and live with him and his wife and their daughters in their mansion in New York so he could send you to a private school. He had it all planned out."

Daughters? I had half-sisters? I'd had no idea, and I honestly couldn't imagine what it would have been like if my mom had agreed. My life would have been completely different. Maybe I even would have crossed paths with Eve's family at some point if they moved in the same circles. The irony of it wasn't lost on me.

"The last time I heard from him was when you were sixteen," my mother continued, each revelation surprising me even more than the last. "He wanted to invite you to come and spend the summer in the Hamptons with him and his family so he could get to know you. I told him you already had plans to volunteer in Belize and that you were interested in helping people, not exploiting them. He didn't call again after that."

In her words, I could hear all my own arguments I used about why I had no time for wealthy people. I'd never realized just how deeply they were rooted in my mom's attitude and the way she'd taught me to think about my father, a way that now didn't seem to be entirely fair if he hadn't completely forgotten about me the way she always said he had.

I couldn't say exactly what his motivations would have been for spending time with me, but he *had* wanted to. Knowing that lifted a weight off of me that I hadn't even realized was there. Suddenly, it seemed a little bit easier to breathe.

"Did you tell Eve all of this?" I still didn't quite see how she fit into everything my mom was telling me.

"A lot of it. She said she wouldn't tell you what we talked about, but I don't know if she's someone who keeps her word so I thought it would be better if you heard it from me. Maybe I didn't make the right choice in keeping him from you, but I did what I thought was right to protect you, Julien. I knew what it felt like to have him look me in the eye, tell me he loved me, and then leave me behind. I didn't want you to have to go through that."

I could understand that when I was a little boy, but at sixteen, she might have told me. In all the years since then, she could have said something. Would she have *ever* told me if Eve hadn't gone there?

As if she heard my thoughts, my mother continued. "It isn't only because Eve might tell you that I decided to tell you myself. She said something that has been stuck in my head all day, ever since she left."

"What is it?" My voice sounded detached as I struggled to sort through all my thoughts, trying to decide how to feel.

"She said that you breaking up with her because of her wealth is no different from your father leaving me because of my lack of it. I tried to raise you to be proud of who you are and where you come from, but maybe I went too far. I don't know, but I don't want you to lose your chance at happiness. If you really love this girl, maybe you can find a way to accept everything about her, even this."

"If I didn't know any better, I would think you liked her." My mom was usually very tough to please.

"She knows her own worth and she insulted me to my face rather than behind my back," my mom replied, sounding almost amused. "I can understand her."

That might be the highest compliment she could give, but my head was still spinning with everything she'd just told me. "I need to think about all of this."

"Of course, but don't put it off too long. When your father refused to fight for me, I lost my respect for him. Even if he had come and begged me to take him back after that, I wouldn't have. I believe Eve is the same. She won't wait forever. You need to decide what you really want, Julien, and if it's her, then swallow your pride and tell her so."

Hearing my mom encouraging me to pursue someone like Eve had to be the most surreal thing of all. I still had to sort through how I felt about my dad wanting to be in touch with me and my mom preventing it, but at the moment, all of that paled in comparison to the bigger question on my mind: was I letting my past hold me back? Did I only push Eve away because I was afraid she'd leave me like my father had?

And if I decided that I had made a mistake, could I find a way to make it up to her, or had I missed my chance for good?

~Eve~

Québec City at Christmas time could hardly be more magical. With nothing else to do that evening, I wandered through the streets of Old Québec, along snow-covered lanes and squares and through the German Christmas market with the regal Château Frontenac high on its hill keeping an eye on all the activity below. It felt like Europe, not only because of the centuries-old architecture but because of the French being spoken all around me, and yet, there were plenty of distinctively North American touches too.

The only thing that would have made it better would be having Julien there with me.

I would have loved to hear his stories about growing up in those streets, or at least visiting them as a child. He would have explained the history, translated for me, laughed at my jokes and innuendos, just as he had when we went sightseeing in Toronto. Was it possible to be homesick for someone you'd only known for a week? That was the best way I could describe how I felt, like in him, I'd found a place where I belonged, perfectly and completely, and away from him, I felt adrift, like I didn't quite belong anywhere.

At a little market stall outside the Notre-Dame-des-Victoires church, I bought a small replica of the church for Julien's stocking. I didn't know what the odds were that I would actually give it to him. Maybe I would take it with me to the charity office and leave it for him after my presentation as a parting gift, something to remember me by. It just felt important for him to know I'd been thinking of him there.

Men smiled at me as I walked, a few of them saying hello in French or English, or both, but although I smiled back, I barely even registered their presence. No man bold enough to approach me on the street would be the type of man I truly craved. After my time with Julien, I understood that in a way I hadn't fully known it before. But in that case, how else was I supposed to find someone? With Julien, it had all happened so naturally, both of us understanding in a matter of minutes that we each provided the missing piece that the other one needed.

Love stories didn't always have happy endings, though. Julien's mother's story offered proof of that; she had been in love longer than I had and just as deeply, and it didn't work out. Would mine and Julien's story end the same way? It felt out of my hands at that point.

I'd made my position clear to him and I'd done everything I could to try to understand his concerns, but although I had a better grasp of the wider picture after speaking with his mother, I couldn't do anything to change the fundamental disconnect between us. I couldn't change my past or my family, and when all was said and done, I didn't want to. I loved my family. My parents worked hard to give me the things they had, and I would do the same to help my own children find their place in the world someday, while encouraging them to be good, responsible people.

My family *were* good people, no matter what Julien believed.

In the end, I wasn't about to beg. He had made his choice, and although I didn't like it or agree that he'd made the right decision, I had to respect that he'd made it. Somehow, I would just have to find a way to move on.

Having come to that rather unsatisfying conclusion, I returned to my hotel for the night.

My flight the next morning arrived back in Toronto early enough that I could meet my dad for lunch between his meetings. "Do you want me to come to your pitch tomorrow?" he asked, checking his schedule on his phone as we ate. "I could move some things around if you want me there."

"It means a lot to me that you would come, but no, I don't think it's necessary. I also don't want them to feel like your support for the charity depends on them agreeing to launch my program. It's probably better if we keep the two things separate."

He understood that, as I knew he would. "We'll have breakfast tomorrow, then, for good luck. I've got one last dinner meeting tomorrow evening and I'll be ready to fly out Thursday morning. Your mom can't wait to see you."

I was excited to see her too, and Noah, and Noelle, and all the family and friends I'd been away from for the last year. I had a whole life waiting for me back in New York, I had to remember, no matter how much it felt like I might be leaving behind when we left Toronto.

"What about dinner tonight?" I wondered. "Are you free?"

"I'll send you a note later."

A note? That sounded odd, but my dad liked his surprises, so I didn't push for any further details. I felt pretty certain it wouldn't be another charity benefit, at least.

Alone in my hotel room, I spent the afternoon reviewing all my slides and my presentation for the charity meeting the next day. When I was sure I'd made it as good as it could be, I emailed the final copies to Claire, as she'd requested. She would make sure everything got loaded and would be ready to go when I got there. I hadn't had a chance to speak to her directly at the benefit dinner, and I had no idea if Julien had told her anything about what happened between us, so I didn't say anything and she didn't bring it up either. Our correspondence remained completely professional.

As the afternoon sky darkened, a knock on the door pulled me away from work, and I opened it to find one of the hotel's uniformed staff with a folded note on a silver tray. Apparently, my dad really hadn't been kidding about sending me a note.

"Thank you." I gave him an amused smile as I took the paper from the tray, and he smiled back, telling me to have a good evening as I took the note into my room to open it.

You can't leave the city without going skating. I'll meet you in Nathan Phillips square at five. Don't wait for me if you get there first, I'll find you on the ice.

My dad had always enjoyed skating, so the activity itself didn't surprise me, but the secrecy around it did. Why wouldn't he have just told me we were going skating? With a shrug, I grabbed my coat, gloves and scarf and headed out the door.

Although I'd been to the square in front of City Hall already during my visit, I hadn't been on the ice yet, and lit up beneath the coloured lights and the dark sky, it looked wonderfully Christmasy. I couldn't see my dad when I arrived, so I did as he suggested and rented my skates, changing from my boots on the benches at the side of the rink before stepping out onto the smooth, icy surface along with the other skaters. A few wobbles sent a spike of adrenaline through me as I tried to keep my balance, but soon, the muscle memory kicked in and I was gliding around the ice as if I did it regularly, starting to relax more and more with each lap.

"Is there anything you're not good at?"

The question didn't take me by surprise nearly as much as the voice that asked it, and as I turned back to look at the figure behind me, wondering if my ears were playing tricks on me, my blade caught an edge in the ice and I stumbled awkwardly. I had visions of falling flat on my face, the wipeout seeming inevitable, but a pair of strong arms caught me before I could injure myself.

"Julien?" The sound of his voice, the smell of his cologne and the feel of his arms were all so familiar, but I didn't understand how he could be real. "What are you doing here?"

"I said I'd meet you here in my note." He let go of me once he seemed certain I had my balance back, shoving his hands in his pockets almost sheepishly.

"*Your* note?" I took a step back as skaters flew past us. "How did you know where to find me? I thought that was from my dad. I'm supposed to be having dinner with him. I thought..."

"Eve, calm down." He offered me a small, tentative smile. "Your dad knows you're here with me. I didn't know if you would agree to meet with me if you knew I was the one asking, so I went through him instead."

His words confused me even more. "Wait... when did you talk to my dad?"

"This morning. About... twenty hours after you talked to my mom, I guess."

So, he knew about that? He didn't seem upset about it, but I still felt completely thrown off. "I think I've missed something."

"Then let me explain." With his gloved hand, he gestured to the flow of skaters around us. "Shall we?"

Chapter Fifteen

THE PITCH

~Julien~

As nervous as I was, I still found Eve's consternation a bit amusing. At least she got a small taste of just how thrown off I'd been the night before to find out that she'd gone to Québec to see my mother. In comparison, meeting with her father had been relatively simple. Tracking down one of the richest men in the world didn't take too much effort, but explaining myself to him had been a little trickier.

"Mr Labrecque." Cole Stamer stood up to shake my hand as another member of staff led me into his office first thing that morning. "What can I do for you?"

"Thank you for seeing me at such short notice." When I'd called the hotel, I really had no idea if he would have time for me, but I made a point of saying it had to do with Eve and he found room to squeeze me in.

"You said you wanted to talk about Eve," he dove in, wasting no time as he sat back down behind his large, solid desk, appearing to be in his natural habitat in an expensive suit and wearing the same watch I'd noticed on his wrist the night of the benefit. Meanwhile, I wore a sweater over an Oxford shirt and dark grey dress pants, dressed up by my standards but downright casual compared to him. "Is it about her presentation tomorrow?"

"No. It's more personal than that."

As much as I'd tried to prepare myself for the conversation, my heart still pounded as he raised his eyebrows curiously. "I don't usually interfere in my daughter's personal life."

I could have guessed that. As a confident, capable, independent woman, Eve could take care of herself. "Well, think of it as interfering in my personal life, then."

Leaning forward with his elbows on his desk and his dark eyes fixed on me, Mr Stamer gave me his full attention. "Let's hear it."

I told him as much as I could without exposing anything Eve might not want me to. Most importantly, I told him I'd screwed up with her and wanted a chance to redeem myself. When I asked for his advice on how to approach her, he answered as bluntly as he did for everything else.

"Be honest with her. Tell it to her like it is. I have a feeling it's a message she's open to hearing."

That gave me hope, and when he offered to help me arrange a time to meet with her, my hopes lifted even higher.

"What did your mom tell you?" Eve asked as we rejoined the other skaters on the ice. The cool evening air nipped at my nose and lips as we glided along, but the way my hands shook had much more to do with the conversation we had to have than it did with the weather.

Intuition told me that Eve didn't care what my mom had said about their conversation; she wanted to know if I knew about my dad, so I gave her that answer. "She told me about my father trying to make contact and how she kept it from me. I can't quite imagine how you got all of that out of her, and in English too."

In saying that, I attempted to both compliment her and turn the conversation back to her, but Eve still wanted to talk about me. "That's a pretty big deal, Julien. How are you feeling?"

"Honestly, I don't know. It changes nothing and everything at the same time. Does that make sense?"

She nodded in understanding, though what I said barely even made sense to me. "Are you angry with your mother?"

"Anger isn't productive."

Eve snorted, her dark eyes reflecting the Christmas lights above us as she looked up at me. "Productive or not, you can still feel it."

I supposed I could, but in this case, I really didn't. "The other emotions are bigger, I guess."

"Which other emotions?"

"I feel a sense of loss over what might have been between me and my dad, and over this whole other family that I have and didn't even know about. Most of all, though, I guess I feel sorry for my mom."

"Sorry for her? Why?" Her eyes were so focused on me that Eve nearly ran into another skater who had come to a sudden stop, and she laughed as she apologized to the other woman.

Although she seemed surprised about me not being angry, she didn't seem angry either, though she also had every right to be. Maybe she had decided it wouldn't be productive either.

As I glanced over at her, I was struck yet again by how utterly gorgeous she was. Even without the effort she'd put into her appearance for the benefit, she shone. If anything, she actually looked better beneath the glowing lights than she had with her diamond earrings on.

And as intuitively as always, she had hit on the heart of the issue by asking me why I felt sorry for my mother. "I guess I can sympathize with her because she thought she was doing the right thing. She convinced herself of it, and in doing so, she made things harder for herself. She never wanted my dad's money because she thought accepting it would make her weak, but there were times we could have really used it. She thought she had to stick to her initial convictions, no matter what. She never saw the big picture."

"Sounds like someone else I know." Eve didn't miss the parallels, and neither did I. I had drawn them for her intentionally.

It had occurred to me the night before while I weighed everything over in my head, examining not just my relationship with Eve but the whole of my life and the beliefs I held. I had not only absorbed many of my mother's attitudes towards the wealthy based on her experience with my father, I'd also inherited some of her intransigence too. Maybe I couldn't change that, but I could recognize it and try to find ways to compromise. That was what I really wanted to talk to her about.

"I can admit when I was wrong, Eve, and when I pushed you away at the benefit, that was wrong."

She glanced up at me, a new hope sparking in her eyes before she looked ahead again, not wanting to run into anyone else. "I'm listening."

She had no idea how much I appreciated that. "Rather than just saying we wouldn't work, I should have given you an opportunity to tell me how you think we could. You knew how I felt and you wanted to be with me anyway, so you must have some ideas about how we could reach a compromise."

I'd hoped she would go first, but she put the ball immediately back in my court. "I'm curious to hear your ideas too. What have you been thinking?"

"Well, there are some things that aren't going to change. I'm never going to be comfortable with excessive spending or really lavish lifestyles, but your dad told me that you've always been reluctant to take part in those things anyway."

The mention of her dad made Eve smile again. "I still can't believe you talked to him. Most people find him a little terrifying."

He definitely wasn't the warm and fuzzy type, but I had dealt with more than my share of dominant people. In a way, I spoke their language.

"He also told me how you'd turned down a six-figure salary to work on your charitable project."

"I want to help people," she reminded me. "Just like you do."

"I know. I should have put more value on that side of you. I shouldn't have let one thing derail our entire relationship. And really, when I weigh up all the pros and cons, all the positives and negatives, one drawback, even a big one, doesn't have to cancel out all the good things about you. As long as you don't want that lifestyle for yourself, I can learn to live with the rest of it."

Based on her reactions to what I'd said so far, I expected that to earn me another smile, but Eve frowned instead.

"You can 'learn to live with it'?" She repeated my words back to me like there was something wrong with them.

"Well, maybe not right away, but eventually. If the charity accepts your proposal, you'll be based here, right? You'll travel; maybe we'll even travel together. We definitely won't live in New York."

Her frown grew even deeper. "My family is in New York."

What did that have to do with anything? "And my mother is in Québec, but it doesn't mean I want to live there. You don't want to live in New York, do you?"

Eve glanced over her shoulder, making sure no skaters were coming up behind her before heading to the side of the rink, the movement taking me by surprise. "I don't want to live there right now, necessarily, but I don't want to feel like it's not an option either."

I followed after her, dodging a few slow-moving skaters. "You're upset but I don't know why."

This conversation had started better than I expected, with Eve being open and willing to listen to me, but it had just taken a turn for reasons I didn't understand.

Eve, however, was willing to lay them out for me. "I'm upset because you're making it sound like it would be some grand sacrifice for you to be with me. You'd compromise your principles to be with me. You'd *settle* for me."

She hopped off the ice, heading back to the bench where her boots were waiting, and again, I trailed behind her, trying to keep up.

"I never said that..."

She didn't let me finish, spinning back to face me with fire in her eyes. "You didn't have to. It's underpinning every word out of your mouth.

I'm not exactly what you wanted, but you're willing to overlook my irredeemable flaws? How very generous of you."

I honestly hadn't meant it that way. "You must have things about me that you're not thrilled about either."

I meant it to lighten the mood, but it didn't seem to improve her mood at all. "The only thing I don't like about you is this blind spot you have around your own prejudice, but honestly, that might be too big a drawback for me. I'm not sure I can 'learn to live with it'."

All the anger that had been missing in her before was on full display by that point as she pulled the skates off forcefully and shoved her feet back into her boots. My fingers fumbled over my laces as I tried to keep up.

"Eve, wait. That came out wrong, obviously. What I was trying to say is that I want to be with you. I want to give us a chance..."

She got to her feet, her eyes still blazing. "On *your* terms, where I'm supposed to feel ashamed every day for who I am. Well, you know what, Julien? I'm not ashamed, but maybe you should be."

Things were completely falling apart and I still didn't fully understand why. "Eve, tell me what you want me to say and I'll say it. Tell me what you want me to do and I'll do it."

She shook her head, a look of regret crossing her face along with the anger that still burned there. "I'm not your domme anymore, remember? You have to figure it out on your own, but honestly, I'm not holding my breath. Goodbye, Julien."

I had just finished getting my skates off as she turned and walked away, quickly disappearing into the crowd of people, leaving her skates behind as well as all my hopes of a reconciliation. Somehow, after all my efforts, we felt even further apart than before.

~Eve~

I honestly didn't know which was worse: what Julien had said, or the fact that he couldn't see anything wrong with it.

Once I got over my surprise at finding him at the rink instead of my dad, my hopes quickly rose. The fact that he had gone out of his way to plan a rendezvous for us, even working with my dad to arrange it, seemed to suggest that he had realized the error of his previous decision and wanted to make it right.

When he told me he knew that I'd spoken to his mother *and* that she had told him the truth about his father, my optimism continued to grow. If he accepted that his father had never been the complete monster that he'd been raised to see him as, maybe he'd reevaluated his feelings about the selfishness of the upper classes in general. Maybe he was willing to accept that money or status didn't automatically define a person as good or bad.

But when he started to actually outline what he saw our relationship looking like going forward, I quickly realized that I'd assumed too much. Yes, he missed me and yes, he wanted me back, but his fundamental objections hadn't changed. He'd just decided he could 'live with' the disappointment of having fallen for a woman who, by his very nature, he despised.

That wasn't going to work for me. I wanted to be with someone who loved me just as I was, who wouldn't prefer that I was different in some way. I made no claim to be perfect, but I wanted someone who could love all those less-than-perfect things.

In short, nobody settled for Eve Stamer.

When I met my dad for breakfast the next morning, I could see the curiosity in his eyes, wondering how my evening had gone though he respected my privacy enough not to ask me directly. Now that Julien had let the cat out of the bag regarding our relationship, though, I would have to tell him something.

Sitting back with my cup of coffee, I broached the subject as neutrally as possible. "I understand Julien came to see you yesterday."

My dad had a world-class poker face, giving me no idea what he was thinking. "He did. I didn't realize you two knew each other that well."

"We only met a week ago."

He shrugged, taking a drink from his own coffee. "A lot can happen in a week."

He had that right, and I knew he spoke from his own experience too. He and my mom had a pretty immediate connection. He proposed in less than a month and they'd been together almost thirty years. It could definitely work out; time didn't necessarily dictate the strength of someone's feelings.

But sometimes, it *didn't* work out. "Did he tell you why we argued?"

"Not the whole story, I'm sure, but he told me a few things. He said that he didn't know who you were until the night of the benefit and that it threw him for a loop. I didn't realize I'd outed you that night."

I didn't blame him for that. "I actually tried to tell him before that. I knew he wouldn't be thrilled about it. He's pretty anti-capitalist, or at least anti-wealth."

My dad's face melted into a very uncharacteristic look of confusion. It looked so out of place on him that I almost laughed. "I don't under-stand."

Of course he didn't. My dad had never known any other world, nor did he see anything wrong with his. "Well, I do, somewhat, but he's taken it farther than that. He sees my wealth, my status, and even my name as disadvantages and I'm not sure we can move past that."

The usually unflappable Cole Stamer still looked befuddled. "But you're using your wealth, status and name to bring attention to the very cause he supports."

"That's how I see it, but apparently, he doesn't. There's more to it: there's a whole situation with his parents and I don't want to get into the whole thing right now, but basically, I don't think it's going to work."

Although I'd left an awful lot out, my dad accepted my summary. "I trust you to make the right call, Eve, but I'm sorry. I actually kind of liked him. I always thought I'd need to watch out for the men who wanted you for your money, not the other way around."

"Trust me, I'm aware of the irony."

We shared a small smile; not a happy one, but one of commiseration, and he wished me luck with my presentation before heading to his own meetings for the day.

My meeting with the charity board was scheduled for eleven o'clock that morning, so I showed up ten minutes early to be safe. Wearing a tailored deep blue suit with a light blue blouse underneath it, my hair down and some understated, elegant jewellery on, I looked professional and confident. I felt confident too; no matter what had happened between me and Julien, I believed in my proposal and I couldn't see any reason that the charity's board would pass up the opportunity to be involved.

"Ms Stamer? They're ready for you." The receptionist gave me an encouraging smile as she pointed me towards the boardroom.

Eleven people made up the charity's board and they all sat around a large oval table, including Harold Measner, the chairman I'd met while on my date with Julien on the weekend. He looked much more focused on business than he had that evening, shuffling his papers in front of him rather than making eye contact with me. Julien sat near the front of the room, and he gave me a nod, his expression neutral, while Claire sat next to him with a notepad in front of her, ready to take notes.

"Thank you for joining us, Ms Stamer." It felt strange to hear Julien using my real name, but he managed to say it without wincing. "We're all excited to hear about your proposal this morning. Please, go ahead when you're ready."

With the opening slide of my presentation already projected on the wall behind me, I stepped up to the small podium holding the laptop computer and gave the entire room a confident and, hopefully, engaging smile.

"Thank you all for having me. In the invitation to this meeting, you all received a short summary of the work I did over the last year in Ecuador along with a brief overview of my proposal, but today, I'm going to give you all the nuts and bolts about how it will work. So, let's dive right in. First, I'm going to…"

As I clicked the mouse to advance to the next slide in my presentation, the screen in front of me went completely black. Quickly, I glanced over my shoulder at the screen there, but it had done the same, nothing but a large black box remaining.

"I'm sorry, it seems to have turned off somehow. Does someone know…"

Julien leapt to his feet before I could finish my question. "Let me take a look. Sometimes, it can be a bit tricky."

His cologne hit my nose as he stepped close to me, and I took a step back to give him better access to the computer, doing my best to take the unexpected diversion in my stride as the members of the board began to whisper to each other.

"That's strange," Julien mattered, jabbing at buttons on the laptop to no avail. "It's completely dead. Claire, can you send a message to…"

Before he could finish, she held up her phone. "I've lost the network connection."

"We're sorry about this, everyone." Julien did his best to sound reas-suring as he addressed the rest of the room. "I'll go get my laptop instead. It will only take a minute."

This was hardly the impression I wanted to make, but since I couldn't do anything about it, I did my best to diffuse the situation while Julien left the room, leaving the door slightly ajar behind him. "While we're waiting for Mr Labrecque to return, maybe I can answer any questions you have about my own experience or background."

"I have a question." Claire stuck her hand up to draw attention to herself, despite it being completely unnecessary. "Have you ever accomplished anything in your life that your father didn't pay for?"

"Excuse me?" Her question stunned me so much, I could only ask for clarification as I tried to figure out exactly what she meant.

Claire seemed happy to explain it to me. "He made a large donation to the charity just last week and hosted a benefit for it on the weekend, and now, you're here asking for a position and to put the charity's name behind your project. Are we meant to ignore that rather convenient timing?"

A quick glance around the room showed me that no one else was about to come to my defense. If anything, several of them seemed to be agreeing with her, or at least waiting to hear my response.

I answered her truthfully. "My father didn't know about my project until after the donation had been made and the benefit planned. I didn't know about either the donation or the benefit until the evening of the benefit."

Though that was true, I could tell it didn't sound particularly convincing, so I tried some plain logic instead.

"If it had been our intention to bribe the board with a donation, why would he have made it *before* my presentation?"

"To try to avoid suspicion, I would guess," Claire suggested, and to my frustration, I saw one of the women in the back nodding.

"That's ridiculous." I did my best to keep my voice calm and authoritative despite the anger racing through my veins. "I brought this proposal to this charity because I respect its work and want to help further it. My father donated for the same reason, but the two things are completely separate."

"Just like your relationship with Julien?"

Was *that* where this all came from? Was she really just jealous? Maybe Julien hadn't told her we'd broken up? I couldn't believe she would let her personal feelings interfere with her professional life that way. She was completely out of line, and surely, I couldn't be the only person who noticed.

Before I could say anything in response, however, Claire turned to the rest of the room. "Just in case daddy's money didn't do the trick, she decided to seduce the charity's director. Obviously, Eve Stamer only cares about herself. Is this the kind of woman you want representing this charity to the world?"

Through my fury, I could see all my plans and preparation going up in smoke. Though there wasn't an ounce of truth to what she said, I could see how it made for a compelling conspiracy theory. It would sow some doubts, if nothing else. She'd completely undermined me.

Again, though, I didn't have a chance to respond. A different voice spoke instead, one usually soft-spoken and polite but in that moment, laced with an anger I'd never heard from him before.

"What the hell did you just say?"

~Julien~

No matter how much I'd tried to prepare myself for seeing Eve again that morning, the sight of her still took my breath away. As soon as she entered the room, everyone else seemed to disappear until all I could see was her.

I'd spent the night trying to figure out where I went wrong in my apology. There didn't seem any point in going after her until I knew how to fix it, but try as I might, I couldn't see what had made her mood change so abruptly. At the benefit, she accused me of not being willing to compromise to make our relationship work, but then she did the same thing, disappearing into the night when I tried to lay out my initial thoughts.

It didn't help that my mom had also sent me my father's name, after all this time, and the last contact number she had for him. She couldn't confirm he'd definitely be there, but even if his number had changed, it wouldn't be hard to track him down. A quick internet search gave me his company details and several photos, including one of him and his wife and his two daughters. The picture was a few years old, when my half-sisters were in their late teens. The older one would probably be close to Eve's age when I adjusted for the passage of time.

Overall, I thought I probably took more after my mom, but I could see some similarities in the pictures of my dad. His eyes were the same colour as mine and his lips the same shape. Would we have anything in common besides that? I really couldn't imagine how.

By that morning, I'd come no closer to deciding what to do about either Eve or my father, so I tried to put both things out of my mind as I went into the office. No matter what happened between Eve and me, I still believed in her project and hoped that the presentation went well. I would back her up any way I could, and so when the presentation disappeared just as she got started, I immediately got to my feet to try to help.

Unfortunately, the extent of my technical knowledge amounted to turning something off and back on again, and when the laptop in the boardroom didn't respond in any way, I went to grab my own laptop instead, hoping we could access Eve's presentation on there instead.

Outside of my office, a few people had gathered. "The network seems to have crashed," one of them told me as I ducked inside to grab my computer off my desk. "Nobody can access email or any of the share drives."

Tabarnak. In that case, my laptop might not be of much use, since I didn't have Eve's presentation saved directly on it. Maybe Claire had another idea, though, so I took it back to the boardroom anyway. Just as I reached the door that I'd left open, I heard Claire say my name. Pausing outside the door, just out of sight, I listened in disbelief as she accused Eve of using both me and her father's money to win approval for her project.

"Obviously, Eve Stamer only cares about herself," she tried to claim.

Before she could spout any more of her bitter, ridiculous nonsense, I strode into the room to confront her. "What the hell did you just say?"

All eyes moved to me, all except Eve's who still stood at the front of the room, facing the table, her back to me. Her shoulders were tense, her muscles tight, and though she hadn't said a word, I could tell she was livid, and rightfully so.

Claire's eyes widened at my sudden appearance, but it only took her a second to regain her composure. She seemed to have no intention of backing down. Perhaps she'd decided she had nothing left to lose.

"It sounds like you heard me. Don't look so shocked, Julien. You were saying the same thing at that benefit. She was supposed to talk about the charity and she spent the whole time talking about herself and her own project, winning the donors over for herself rather than for the charity."

At last, Eve turned back to face me, but rather than anger in her eyes as I might have expected, I saw only hurt there. Was she really going to take Claire's words at face value? I hadn't said anything like that; those were Claire's words, not mine. Did Claire assume I agreed because I hadn't contradicted her at the time? And did Eve really believe I was on Claire's side in this?

Maybe she did. Maybe my actions had led her to believe I would think the worst of her because of who she was, but hearing those spiteful words from Claire suddenly made things a lot clearer to me.

Claire cared only for herself. She'd given up her job because I made it clear I had no personal interest in her, and she did her best to sabotage Eve's presentation despite it clearly being in the best interests of the charity. Being from a similar background to mine and working for the charity didn't make her a good person, just as having money and coming from a place of privilege didn't automatically make Eve selfish. Eve cared about the people we helped; I'd seen that in the glowing reviews I'd had from her time in Ecuador. She cared about me, as she showed the night before when she took the time to ask about the situation with my father even after the way I'd treated her. And she cared about her family too, enough that she would give up what we had together rather than accept the way I viewed them.

Calisse. When I thought about it like that, I finally understood her reaction to what I said the night before. She didn't want me to accept her only if she suppressed part of herself. She wanted me to accept all of her, including her family, including her past and her upbringing and to love her *because* of who she was, not in spite of it.

It felt like someone had finally switched a light on and I could clearly see just how hurtful I'd been to her without even realizing it. In Claire's ignorance, I saw myself, and I really didn't like the view. Hopefully, I wasn't too late to do something about it.

I started with my soon-to-be-ex-assistant. "Claire, your resignation is now effective immediately. I'll have security escort you out as soon as I'm finished here. The only person in this room I wouldn't want to represent this charity a moment longer is you."

A tiny bit of the tension left Eve's shoulders, but not enough. Not nearly enough, so I kept talking.

"Ladies and gentlemen of the board, I can only apologize for my former assistant's completely inappropriate comments, but I trust that you're all intelligent enough to make up your own minds. Eve has no need to bribe or seduce her way into anything. She is an intelligent, dedicated woman who has a passion for this particular project, a project which we would be lucky to work with her on. Yes, Eve and I have spent time together on a personal level. I declared that to Mr Measner ahead of today's meeting simply to avoid any appearance of impropriety, but our relationship has nothing at all to do with this project. When we first met, I had no idea she was a volunteer, and she didn't know who I was either. And in the interest of full disclosure, Ms Stamer and I are no longer seeing each other, but I still support this project whole-hearted-ly."

One of the men at the back spoke up, a rather sour man always looking for an excuse to find fault with everything. "Be that as it may, it still looks bad, Mr Labrecque. It makes me question not only her judgement, but yours as well."

That was exactly what I'd been afraid of when Claire walked in on Eve in the first place, but that morning, after everything Eve and I had been through in the meantime, I no longer cared. "I decided to date a beautiful, kind, smart, funny woman, and you're questioning my judgement? Surely, my sanity would be called into question if I *didn't* want to date her."

That made a few of the others around the table smile, but I could tell there were still reservations, so I carried on.

"This project that Ms Stamer is proposing *will* be a success. It's going to work because it's a smart, well-thought-out idea, and because the woman behind it is incredible. She doesn't need our support to make it work. What she's offering us is an opportunity to be a partner in it, to bring a level of awareness to the charity that we could only dream of without her, and she's doing this as a favour to us because she enjoyed her experience as a volunteer. If this board has any sense at all, you will give her your full support and thank her for the opportunity to do so."

I dared to glance over at Eve who watched me with a completely inscrutable expression on her face, but somewhere in those deep, dark eyes, I thought I saw a glimmer of desire as she caught my allusion to our sexual dynamic. I had always been happy to please her and to thank her for letting me do it. No one else would have caught the parallel, not knowing our relationship, but I felt almost entirely certain she did.

I'd never been particularly impulsive, but in those eyes of hers, I could suddenly see our future clearer than I ever had, and I spoke the words out loud without hesitation. "In fact, if she were to offer me a place, I would gladly go to work for her myself."

That would entwine my life with hers even more firmly, not to mention making her my boss. She would be able to tell me what to do on a daily basis, and the idea sent a shudder of desire through my whole body as I held her gaze, waiting for her response.

Chapter Sixteen

STOCKINGS

~Eve~

Nothing about my presentation had gone to plan. Between the computer dying and Claire's accusations, it could hardly have gone worse. However, as I stood at the front of the room listening to Julien firmly and passionately defend me, it didn't seem like a total disaster. He called Claire out on her extremely unprofessional behaviour and he contradicted everything she'd said about me. He gave my project the strongest possible endorsement and then, to cap it all off, he offered to come and work with me.

Did he really mean that? He wouldn't be embarrassed to work for a Stamer? That morning, I wouldn't have believed it, but as he'd been speaking, something seemed to shift, the look in his eyes and the tone of his voice altering just enough that I was left wondering. Maybe he *did* mean it? Maybe he'd changed his mind?

With a roomful of people watching us, I had to keep my answer as impersonal as possible and move us along to what I had actually gone there for. "I would be happy to discuss ways we might work together, Mr Labrecque, but for now, could I give my presentation?"

I gestured to the laptop in his hands, the one he'd brought in with him but hadn't done anything with yet since he'd been so occupied with shooting down Claire's allegations.

Julien grimaced as he looked down. "I'm afraid the whole network seems to be down and I don't have your presentation downloaded."

From the corner of my eye, I caught the look of satisfaction on Claire's face, and the realization hit me with complete certainty: she did it on purpose. She sabotaged the computer and my entire presentation, I would bet anything on it. If it weren't so utterly devious and completely short-sighted, I would almost be impressed.

If she thought it would break me, though, she had truly underestimated me. As Julien had just said, and as I'd learned through my conversations with the donors at the benefit on Sunday evening, the interest in a project like mine went beyond one charity. I had thought that aligning with the charity would give me some legitimacy, but perhaps if Julien was serious about coming to work with me, his presence along with the robustness of my plans would be enough to let it stand on its own, without any particular charity's backing.

I had the capital to start a foundation on my own, and after what had just happened, I was more motivated than ever. By thwarting my presentation, Claire had simply spurred me on to even more ambitious plans.

"Well, perhaps this is a sign to reevaluate how the pilot project should be rolled out. Julien, are you still interested in discussing a position within my organization?"

"Mais oui." His eyes shone as he answered me in French. "There are some things I need to take care of here but I can meet with you this afternoon. May I send you a time and place?"

It sounded like he already had something in mind, though how he could, I didn't know. I'd literally just suggested it.

Claire was obviously one of the 'things' he had to take care of, and her expression soured as she realized that not only was I not upset about the presentation not working out, but she had pushed Julien and I even closer together.

"That sounds great. I'll see you soon, Julien. Ladies and gentlemen of the board, I'm sorry this didn't work out, but I wish you all a very merry Christmas."

With my head held high, I walked out of the room and back out onto the Toronto streets.

A message already waited on my phone from my dad, checking in to see how things had gone. There would be no easy way to explain it over text, so I simply replied that I would tell him about it later, and I returned to the hotel to have lunch, change into more casual clothes, review my plans for my pilot project to see how they could be adapted to function independently rather than attached to the charity, and wait for Julien's message.

When it came, he apologized that he would be held up longer than he originally hoped, but he asked me to meet him at 4:30 outside the former Maple Leaf Gardens, almost halfway between his house and my hotel. Trusting that he had a plan, I did as he requested, turning up there almost exactly on time to find him waiting for me beneath the Art Deco awning of the former hockey arena. A small black backpack was slung over one shoulder as he kept his hands in his pockets to keep them warm, his breath swirling up above his head in the chilly late afternoon air.

"Eve." His brown eyes looked hopeful as I walked up to him, and he leaned down to kiss my cheek. "Thank you for coming. I'm so sorry about today."

"I don't blame you. I think we both know exactly who's to blame."

His expression immediately hardened, his lips tightening in disapproval. "Yes. I can't prove that she crashed the network, but I'm sure of it anyway."

He'd obviously reached the same conclusion I had. "I'd rather not waste any more time on Claire. Where would you like to go to talk?"

He gestured down the street. "It's just a few blocks this way, if you don't mind."

He had me curious, so I agreed, and we walked together down the street with Christmas light fixtures attached to the street lights overhead. The sky had already turned almost completely dark, and when we reached a park and he turned to head into it, I looked up at him in surprise.

Julien laughed even though I hadn't said anything. "Trust me."

In spite of everything, I did, and soon, a set of greenhouses appeared, soft light glowing from within them, and when we stepped inside, the sight took my breath away. Candles lined the path through an indoor botanical garden, with poinsettias in red, white, pink and various combinations of the three stretching ahead of us. I could only make out a handful of other people within the glass structure. "What is this place?"

"This is Allan Gardens. They do the candles every year for Christmas, but it hasn't quite hit the tourist radar yet. It's also free to get in. It's one of my favourite spots in the city."

I certainly hadn't heard of it, and the peaceful, warm ambiance felt perfect for a private talk while still enjoying something special together.

He'd chosen perfectly.

"So, I don't think that's a board meeting anyone will be forgetting anytime soon," I joked as we began to walk down the greenhouse path, taking our time as we looked at all the winter flowers on display.

Julien didn't seem to be in the mood to laugh about it yet, though. He shook his head angrily instead. "I can't believe she would do that. After I had her escorted from the building, I spoke to the board for a while longer. They're quite nervous that you're going to poach me from them."

I could imagine. Julien was very good at his job, and they wouldn't want to lose him. "If you were anyone else, I would say you could use it to negotiate for a raise, but I know you're not interested in that."

"No, I'm not." He came to a stop, turning to face me. "I also explained to them that the words Claire put in my mouth were never mine. I didn't say anything at the benefit about you using it to promote yourself. She made all of that up."

That didn't surprise me in the least, but it relieved me anyway. No matter how he felt about my money and my family, it cheered me to know that he didn't think I would stoop to that level.

Julien took a step closer to me, close enough that I couldn't see anything other than those intelligent brown eyes looking straight into mine. "Eve, I owe you an apology. Another one, a bigger one. When I heard Claire saying those things about you today, making judgements about you without getting to know you, it made me see how I'd been doing exactly the same thing. Maybe not as overtly or as crudely, but the same nonetheless. I let my preconceived ideas about wealth and the wealthy blind me to the woman right in front of me. I see it now, though. I see how awful I've been and how I hurt you, and though I know simply saying I'm sorry isn't enough, I'll say it anyway. I'm sorry, Eve. I..."

I couldn't wait any longer. With every word, I could hear his conviction and his understanding, the things that had been missing during our conversation the night before, and though it didn't make up for everything, it was a start. At last, it felt like we were back on track, and with that in mind, I wrapped my hand around the end of his scarf, using it to pull his face down to mine, and kissed him hard.

~Julien~

I still had a lot more to say, but when Eve's kiss cut me off, every other thought immediately left my head. She took charge, just as I liked, and her actions showed me that even though I still had work to do to make it up to her, she would be willing to give me a chance. Relief flowed through me, filling my body from head to toe with the realization of just how close I'd come to losing her forever and never getting to feel her perfect kiss again.

"Maybe we should move this conversation somewhere a little more private," Eve suggested as she loosened her grip on my scarf, though not entirely letting go.

I didn't want her to let go. She could lead me around by it as much as she wanted.

"As beautiful as the gardens are, I'd rather be alone."

I couldn't agree more. I'd brought her there in case things didn't go well, in case she didn't accept my apology, but I'd hoped we could eventually move somewhere a little more intimate. I'd brought the backpack along with me in that hope.

When I nodded my agreement, Eve smiled. "Your house?"

Just as quickly, I shook my head. "I thought we could go to your hotel room, if it's okay with you."

Understanding dawned in her eyes as she immediately picked up on why I suggested it. I wanted her to know I would be proud to be seen with her in her own world. I wouldn't make disparaging comments about the expensive hotel or try to make her feel bad about staying there. She didn't have to hide anything about herself in order for me to want to be with her.

My feelings about the excesses of personal wealth weren't going to disappear overnight, but my feelings for her were stronger, and I was willing to listen and learn from her. I would try to see things through her eyes because I wanted to understand her on every level, not just the ones that were easy for me.

I had to tell her all of that, and more, but from the look in Eve's eyes, I knew she had already picked up on a lot of it just from me suggesting we go to her hotel. She could see me, *truly* see me, like no one ever had before.

On the walk to the Stamer hotel, we stayed close to each other as I told her more about what happened at the office after she left. The human resources manager came to escort Claire out of the building, but before she left, I thanked her.

"For what?" Claire looked understandably confused by my gratitude considering the way she'd just behaved in front of the board. I should have been furious, and though I still vehemently disagreed with everything she'd said and done, I recognized that without her over-the-top behaviour, I might not have had my moment of epiphany in time.

"For making me see everything I stand to lose." It might not have been her goal, but she'd saved me from making the biggest mistake of my life, so long as Eve agreed to give me another chance.

I told Eve about looking my dad up online the night before and how conflicted I still felt about whether or not to make contact with him. I also shared with her the thoughts I'd had about how we could have grown up in the same circles, if things had been different.

"It's possible," she had to admit. "What's your father's full name?"

"Julian Ribar. He has two daughters: Maribel and Crystal."

Eve's head snapped up to look at me, her eyes wide with surprise. "Are you serious?"

Why would I be kidding about that? "Yes. Why?"

Shaking her head, she let out a disbelieving laugh. "I do know Maribel Ribar. She's engaged to a guy named Corey who I dated very briefly a couple of years ago."

It really was a small world, but after the way Eve and I had met in Quito, I couldn't really doubt it. "Are you telling me that you've slept with my half-sister's fiancé?"

"Yes?" She gave me a sheepish shrug. "Is that weird?"

"It's not not-weird."

We laughed together, and the cold December air seemed a little bit warmer because of it.

At the hotel, she led me through the lobby to the elevators, and I shared my impression of it from the night of the benefit. "I thought this place would be really stuffy and ostentatious, but I was wrong. It's very classy and understated."

A bit like Eve herself, actually.

My assessment made her smile. "I'll tell my mom you thought so. She designed it."

I hadn't put that together yet about Eve's mom being an architect and her dad building hotels, but it made sense. I supposed they made a perfect couple, their interests aligning perfectly just like mine and Eve's did.

Other people got on the elevator with us, so we stayed silent until reaching Eve's floor. The room she led me into was spacious and elegant, a king-sized bed along one wall facing a large, wall-mounted TV on the other. A fireplace sat in one corner and a desk in the other, and a small kitchen area took up the space nearest to the door, beside the door to the large bathroom.

I couldn't imagine what it must normally cost to stay there, and while I looked around, I could feel Eve's eyes on me, waiting for my reaction.

"The bed looks comfortable." That seemed a safe observation and one designed to move her thoughts in the direction mine were already straying simply by being in the same room with her and a bed, and it seemed to work. Eve smiled at me, her shoulders relaxing.

"It is. Now, what's in that bag you're carrying? I've never seen it before and it's been driving me crazy."

With a grin, I placed it down on the table as I began to remove my coat and all my other winter accessories. "Well, we said we would exchange stockings after the board meeting, before you go home. I didn't know if you would want to open it with me, but I wanted to give it to you anyway."

Unzipping the bag, I pulled out the stocking inside, filled with little individually wrapped gifts for her.

"The whole point was that no matter how angry we might be with each other, they should remind us of the deeper feelings we have, and when I suggested it, I couldn't have imagined how necessary that would be."

Eve took a step closer to the table. "I have yours as well. I was going to send it to your house in the morning."

We truly were on the same wavelength. In so many ways, in the ways that truly mattered, we were a perfect match.

"May I open yours first?" I was desperate to know what things would have reminded her of me and what things she felt symbolized our relationship.

Eve raised an eyebrow at me in that completely irresistible way of hers. "If you can prove to me you've earned it."

I knew exactly what she meant: she wanted me to work for it, and I deserved that. I deserved more than that, and I would be happy to try to make it up to her.

"What can I do to please you, Madame E?" Bending my head to her in submission made my heart beat faster, the blood rushing through my body and to my cock in anticipation. I could hardly believe after the last few days that we could slip into our roles so comfortably again, that I got to hear that tone from her and offer my service to her.

"You can get on your knees, to start."

Immediately, I dropped down in front of her, thrilled to have the chance to prove myself.

"Take off your shirt."

Again, I did as she ordered without question, but when I tossed it aside, Eve surprised me by walking behind me and reaching down to the scar on my back, the one she had noticed the first night we were together.

"I want to know the story of how you got this. Will you tell me?"

~Eve~

That morning, I never would have imagined that I would have Julien on his knees, half-naked in my hotel room before supper time. Since then, he had apologized and sworn that he wouldn't make the same mistake again, and after the way he stood up for me at the board meeting and especially after he suggested that we come to the hotel rather than going to his house, I believed he meant it. It might not be easy for him, but he would be willing to try, and I couldn't ask for more than that. I was far from perfect, but I would try too.

We could try together, with no more secrets between us.

So when I asked him about the scar on his back, I did it not simply out of curiosity, although I had been curious about it ever since I first saw it ten days earlier in Quito. I did it because I wanted to understand what happened in his previous relationship when there had been a breach of trust. Even if it had only been a sexual relationship and not a romantic one, it felt like it might help me to understand him better. What happened to lead up to it, and what happened afterwards?

"Of course I will tell you if you want to know." Julien's head remained bowed, his eyes on the floor as I walked back around in front of him. "Her name was Elouise. She is the domme I had the longest and she taught me many things about myself and about how to be a good sub."

"What did you like about her?" If they were together for a long time, there must have been a lot that appealed to him.

Even with his head down, I could see the smile that flashed across his face. "Many of the same things I like about you; her confidence and her imagination, most of all. She was older than me and I wasn't her only sub. We didn't have any relationship outside of our play."

Though I'd never had a long-term relationship that remained purely sexual, I certainly didn't judge him for it. As long as everything involved consented and understood the relationship the same way, they both got their needs met and it didn't hurt anyone.

At least, not until it hurt him.

"She hit you as part of your scenes?"

Julien nodded. "Impact was her favourite kind of play. I hadn't done much of it before her, but I'm open to trying new things. Some of it I did enjoy and still do, but other parts were too intense for me. The whip that gave me the scar, it sat right on that edge when she used it normally."

"But that time was abnormal?" I didn't want to put words in his mouth, but I wanted to be sure I understood it.

"Oui. When I arrived at her house that day, we argued. I had a trip coming up for work and wouldn't be able to see her for several months. While some dommes like to treat their subs, she liked me to buy her things instead, just everyday things like clothes and groceries, things she needed. I was happy to do it while we were in an active domme/sub relationship, but with me going away, she would lose those benefits. She got quite upset about it, acting like I'd done something wrong even though we never promised anything to each other, and it made me feel like she only cared about the money and not me. The argument got quite heated. I don't know if you've noticed, but I can get a little passionate on the subject of money."

Since he obviously meant that as a joke, I responded in kind. "You don't say."

My deadpan response made Julien smile once more, only for a second before he continued his story. "Eventually, we reached a compromise where I offered to give her some money to cover some things while I went away, and we decided to go ahead with the scene but really, we shouldn't have. We were both still on edge and not in the right frame of mind."

He seemed to be accepting part of the blame, but it seemed to me that the person holding the whip should be the one in most control of their emotions.

"The feelings from the argument carried over into the scene. I'm not usually a brat, but I pushed back more than usual and she punished me in return. It stopped feeling sexy pretty quickly and I used my safeword."

Immediately, my mind flashed back to the argument we had at the benefit and how he had used his safeword then to walk away.

"I'd never used it with her before, but instead of stopping, she hit me again, not harder but with less control, and that's the one that scarred. I could tell immediately that she regretted it, probably when she saw the skin split open."

I winced instinctively. "What did you do?"

"I had to go to the hospital and get stitches. She offered to go with me but I said no. I didn't feel safe with her anymore. I had to tell the doctor what caused it, and while I travelled, I had to regularly go to small medical clinics in the middle of nowhere to have the dressing changed and the wound treated. It wasn't much fun."

"Shit." I knew it wouldn't be a good story, but it hurt my heart to imagine him being subjected to that, *especially* after he'd used his safeword.

"Yes," Julien agreed, his eyes glancing up to meet mine for the first time since he knelt down. "It taught me an important lesson. Everyone gets angry at times, but you can be angry without hurting the person you're angry with. You can still respect their boundaries. And that's what you did, Eve, when I used my safeword with you. I know you had more to say to me that evening, but when I told you I couldn't face it, you accepted that without question. It showed me I could trust you, even more than I already did."

I appreciated those words more than I could say, but I wanted to be honest with him too. "I thought you used it because you *couldn't* trust me anymore. I felt like I'd failed because you had to use it."

"No, not at all." Concern lined his face and I could see him fighting to remain in position, fighting against his instincts to come and comfort me. "The only failure would be not respecting it. I use the word when I'm overwhelmed, and that's how I felt that evening, but by letting me go, you gave me the space to think things over and to, eventually, come to the right conclusion. You did exactly the right thing."

With a deep breath, I let go of any remaining guilt or hurt I felt from that evening. As hard as they had been, maybe the past few days did prove that we could weather a storm when it came, as they were bound to do in any relationship. The fight we'd had wouldn't be our last, but hopefully with a deeper understanding of each other, it would be the last to cut quite so deeply.

At the very least, Julien had earned the right to see his gifts. "Your stocking is in the gift bag by the fireplace."

His head immediately turned towards it. "I can open it now?"

Laughing at his eager tone, I gave my permission. "Yes, go ahead."

He looked exactly like a kid on Christmas morning as he got to his feet and went to grab the bag. Holding it in his hands, he took a seat on the bed while I sat down on the other side to watch him, both nervous and excited to see what he would make of the gifts.

"This is lovely," he commented as soon as he pulled the stocking itself from the bag. "Where did you get it?"

I told him about the stall at the Distillery District market and he smiled as I mentioned it came from a fair-trade vendor.

"You do know me already." First from the presents inside, he opened the key I'd bought, and he turned it over in his hand a few times, trying to guess what it might be for. Just when I thought I would have to explain it, he made the connection. "It symbolizes the cage?"

"Yes. For the trust you put in me."

Julien's warm smile turned to laughter when he unwrapped the smoke detector that had reminded me of our night in Quito. "I know exactly what this is for. I never hated a smoke alarm so much as I did that night."

I'd bought him a nutcracker to symbolize the ballet we attended together, and a book with a pop-up globe. "Because you care about people all over the world," I explained when he gave me a questioning look.

When he opened the small replica of the church in Québec City, he seemed lost for words for a moment. His voice sounded tight when he did speak again. "I know this church very well. You went there?"

I nodded in confirmation. "I did, and I wanted you to know that you were in my thoughts while I was there."

"Even after the things I said to you?" He shook his head in disbelief. "Eve, these gifts are perfect. You have put me to shame."

"I'll be the judge of that." Giving him a wink, I stood up to get the stocking he'd brought for me from the table and carried it back to the bed as he gathered all of his gifts carefully back into the hand-made stocking.

The first thing I opened was a 'World's Best Teacher' ornament that made me laugh out loud, remembering our roleplay at his house. Next, there was a handmade necklace that I recognized immediately as being Ecuadorian. "Where did you get this?"

"I bought it at the airport in Quito. I saw it and thought of you."

"In Quito?" I repeated in surprise. That was long before we had agreed to do the stocking exchange.

"I didn't know if or when I could give it to you, but I felt optimistic," was all the explanation he would give me.

There were a few more little souvenirs from Toronto, one of Casa Loma and one with the subway logo. One present contained my underwear from our night together in Quito, the panties I had accidentally left with him after the fire alarm.

"I forgot you still had these," I said with a laugh as I held them up. "You don't want to keep them?"

"I would be happy to, but I also wanted you to know that anything you give me is safe in my keeping."

When I pulled a large package from the bottom of the stocking, Julien shook his head.

"Save that one for last."

Obediently, I put it aside and pulled out the other remaining gift instead. Inside was a small, flat, circular silver container.

Julien smiled as I looked at it in confusion. "Read the other side."

Turning it over, I found the words: 'the world's most beautiful smile'. "I don't understand."

He chuckled softly. "Open it."

I had missed the small latch before, but flipping it open, I found myself looking into a small compact mirror. It took me a second, but eventually, I realized what it meant, and I had to smile, the mirror reflecting the image back at me.

"You see?" Julien's brown eyes were full of admiration. "Beautiful."

"It's very sweet, thank you." I tried not to blush as I put it away. I'd never really been the sentimental type, but even I had to admit he'd charmed me. "Now, can I open the last one?"

Julien's expression shifted, becoming almost nervous. "Yes. This gift is a little different. It's something that I hoped we might do together. It doesn't have to be tonight, but you said on your checklist that you would be interested in trying it, so I bought it for you."

On my checklist? That got my full attention, wondering exactly which of the items on that list had stood out to him the most. There had been so many things on that list I hadn't tried yet, and a lot of things I had said I would be interested in trying with him. Which one had he chosen?

I couldn't wait to find out.

Chapter Seventeen

The Last Gift

~Julien~

The curiosity and excitement in Eve's eyes as she began to open her final present from me had my whole body on edge, a rush of anticipation filling me. I honestly hadn't wanted to assume anything when I put the gift in her stocking that day. I knew she might not give me another chance, and even if she did, she might not want to jump straight back into sex. Knowing all of that, I decided to give it to her anyway, since based on our conversation back when she filled out the checklist, she didn't seem to know that these items existed.

Her pleasure and enjoyment would always be paramount to me, so even if she never tried it with me, I wanted to share my knowledge and experience with her.

A white box greeted Eve when she had the wrapping off, completely plain with no indication about what might be inside. Raising her eyebrows at me, she lifted the lid and immediately let out a surprised laugh.

"Well, I'm glad I didn't open this in front of my family."

The thought made me shudder as I tried to imagine her serious, no-nonsense father getting a glimpse of the strap-on vibrator and dildo I hoped to use on his daughter. "So am I, though I would have warned you if you decided not to open it with me."

With her usual curiosity and confidence, Eve lifted the silicone shaft out of the box, leaving the lube and bullets in the box. Soft and sleek, it had two large rings attached to it and one smaller one. Eve turned it over to examine it from all angles, slipping her fingers through the attached rings. "I haven't seen one quite like this before. How does it work?"

Although I hoped she would give me the chance to demonstrate it at some point, for the time being, I stuck to a verbal explanation. "Well, in case you didn't already guess, this is for double penetration. It attaches to my cock here." My fingers joined hers through one of the larger rings. "The other ring goes around my balls. The rings help to prolong my erection, giving me more opportunity to focus on you."

"So, your cock would be inside me as usual, and this is for my ass?" She ran her fingers over the six-inch silicone shaft molded with a defined head to resemble a cock, though not as thick as mine.

"Exactly." I grabbed the bullets out of the box to complete the demonstration. "These both vibrate. One goes inside the shaft while the other goes through this last loop, above my cock, for your clit."

Eve shivered at the last piece of information, her fertile imagination already working overtime. I could picture it too, and my cock had already started to stiffen in anticipation. Even so, I would never want to rush her into anything. "We don't have to use it today. It's completely up to you, but I wanted you to have it so that you can try it when you're ready."

She didn't respond right away, turning the shaft over in her hands a few more times before she raised her eyes back to mine. "Actually, I think I would like to use it, but not in the way you just described."

Though I had no idea what she meant, excitement raced through me anyway at the thought of being intimate again with her in any way at all. "What would you like to do?"

"I'll tell you when you need to know."

Taking control of the situation, Eve swept all her gifts off the bed onto the side table. She seemed to appreciate everything I'd gotten her, understanding the meaning behind each one just as I understood her gifts. None of them were things we would show off to the rest of the world. They were simply for us.

"Take off the rest of your clothes."

"Oui, Madame." With the state of my cock, getting my pants off came as a relief, and once I was completely naked, I stood next to the bed to await her next instruction.

"On your hands and knees, facing away from me," she ordered, pointing to the bed, and again, I followed her command without question. Facing the room's large window, I had no idea what she might be doing behind me, but she soon gave me a clue. "You mentioned the checklist, and there's something on your form that you said you liked that I haven't done before."

That didn't narrow things down very much. There were a number of things that she hadn't tried. "Which one?"

The touch of her hand on my ass made me jump in surprise, but the surprise quickly melted into pleasure as she trailed her fingers over my skin. "You said that you enjoy anal penetration."

I had indeed said that. Something about a strong, sexy woman taking full control and fucking me rather than the other way around turned me on more than I could possibly explain, and as Eve's hand ran over my naked behind again, I finally understood what she meant by using the strap-on I'd just given her in a different way. It was my turn to shiver as all the blood in my body rushed forcefully to my cock.

A moment later, Eve's hand came down on my ass with a sharp sting. "Don't ignore me."

Crisse. I'd been so focused on my arousal I hadn't realized that I hadn't said anything, and the fact that she would spank me to punish me for it turned me on even more, leaving me nearly dizzy with desire. "Oui, Madame. I do enjoy it. From you, I would."

When Eve spoke again, her voice had turned softer. "You'll tell me if I do something wrong, right? I haven't done this before."

"Of course. I trust you, Eve."

Those seemed to be the magic words, and while I knelt there on the bed on my hands and knees, my cock fully erect, I could hear the snap of the lid on the lube bottle as Eve opened it. Soon, she touched me again, but not where I expected. One hand reached between my legs to stroke my cock, drawing a deep groan from my chest.

Having successfully distracted me, the pressure of the silicone cock against my asshole took me by surprise. Heavily lubed, it rubbed up and down a few times, circling the hole before she began to push it in, all the while continuing to stroke me.

Taking a deep breath, I forced myself to relax to make it easier for her as she pushed the thicker head of the cock inside me. The first time a domme had done that to me, we had to go a lot slower as my body got used to the unfamiliar sensation, but since I already had some experience, Eve's pace was perfect. She had me completely and utterly at her mercy, one hand around my cock and the other impaling me with her own version of it.

As she got more confident that she wouldn't hurt me, her pace increased, thrusting the shaft into me quicker and faster, and when she praised me, I nearly came right there and then. "You're doing so well, taking all of that in for me."

"Calisse," I swore beneath my breath. "Eve..."

My need grew stronger than ever, rising quickly to the edge, but just before my orgasm hit, she suddenly stopped, dropping her hand that held my cock and pulling the dildo out of my ass.

"I don't think you deserve to come yet."

Disappointment washed over me as I gulped in a deep breath. "Non?"

"No. You can wait a little longer. I'm getting hungry."

My head dropped in both frustration and no small degree of admiration. I completely agreed with her: after the way I'd treated her, I didn't deserve any kind of reward, and if she wanted to eat, I would do as she said. Some people may have found it cruel, but for me, it came part and parcel with giving up control. My body belonged to her. She made the rules, and if I disagreed, I could always use my safeword, but I had no intention of using it then.

No matter how long it took, I would prove to her that I was ready to give myself to her fully, body and soul.

~Eve~

I left Julien naked on the bed while I grabbed the room service menus, giving him a moment to recover. If I thought for a moment that he would be truly unhappy about being left without an orgasm, I wouldn't have done it, but from both his checklist and the conversations we'd had, I knew that orgasm denial actually turned him on. It worked as both a punishment and a reward at the same time, just as spanking him did.

Using the toy on him had been something completely new for me, but I had to admit I liked the feeling of power and control it gave me. It also brought to mind the regular strap-on dildo I'd seen in the supply room at his house, and the idea of wearing one like that and fucking him not just with my hand but with my body appealed to me more than I'd ever imagined it would.

He'd taught me so much about myself already.

Julien's eyes widened at the price of the items on the menu when he looked it over, but to his credit, he didn't comment on it. When he'd made his selection, I offered some information I hoped would help him feel better.

"I won't be charged the menu prices. Everything for my room is billed at cost. As for the prices the other guests pay, the hotel restaurant also has a program that provides jobs, training and scholarships for young people from low-income households, so some of the profits it makes goes towards that."

"And you just happen to know this?" he asked curiously. "I mean, I don't think you're making it up, it's just... you have a lot of hotels."

He was right about that, and I smiled to let him know I didn't take offense to him questioning it. "It's actually a standard policy at all Stamer hotels around the world."

His raised eyebrows suggested both surprise and approval. "Did you have something to do with that?"

I specifically hadn't mentioned that, not wanting it to look like I had brought it up to try to win his praise, but when he asked me outright, I answered him honestly. "I suggested it when I was in middle school, and my dad assigned someone from the company to work on it and make it happen."

Julien nodded thoughtfully. "I suppose when you have the resources, you can make more of an impact."

That was exactly my hope. "In that vein, I've been thinking that it makes more sense for me to run my project from an independent foundation. Maybe we can talk about that over dinner. How are you feeling?"

I ran my hand lightly over his legs, smiling as goosebumps formed.

"I'm good," he assured me. "A little frustrated, but good."

That was just where I wanted him. "In that case, why don't you go and clean up while I order the food? Take my present and wash it too. Maybe we can use it again later."

Excitement sparked in his eyes again even though I didn't say exactly how we would use it. To be honest, the idea of him using it on me both excited and scared me, but I trusted him enough to want to give it a try. There was no one else I trusted more to push my limits in a safe and mutually enjoyable way.

By the time the food arrived, Julien had come to sit on the sofa with me, wearing one of the hotel's bathrobes. As we ate, we talked over my project plans and what it might look like to do it independently rather than through the charity as I'd originally been envisioning.

"I won't lie: it will be a loss to the charity to miss out on the chance to do the pilot exclusively," Julien told me. "However, I think that working with multiple charities broadens your appeal and your reach. Rather than working for me, you'd be your own boss, and you could make changes to the program more quickly without needing to go through the charity. You'd have complete control."

That brought us back to what he'd said earlier, what I hadn't been able to stop thinking about since he said it: "Would you really consider coming to work with me?"

"That depends."

My fork froze halfway to my mouth, his answer taking me by surprise. "On what?"

He wouldn't care about the salary or hours or travel requirements, so what would be the dealbreaker for him?

"On whether we're going to have a relationship too."

My stomach sank as I lowered the fork back to my plate. "You don't want to work with me if we're dating? Why? It wouldn't be against the rules. It's my foundation, I would get to make the rules!"

His warm chuckle sent a delicious shiver through my body. "You always make the rules, Eve."

For a moment, the heat that passed between us felt so intense, I thought we might have to skip the rest of our meal, but he dropped his eyes to continue his thought as he took another bite.

"It's actually the opposite: if you decide that you aren't interested in a relationship, then I'm not sure I could work with you. Having to see you with someone else would be a kind of torture I'm not interested in."

"Seriously?" The sentiment was kind of sweet, but also completely irrational. "What if we start off seeing each other and we break up? Are you going to just quit?"

He also put his fork down, giving me his full attention. "If you give me another chance and I screw it up again, then I'll deserve that pain and I'll deal with it. But if you tell me now that you don't see a future between us, then I will wish you the very best and respectfully decline your job offer."

He sounded completely serious. "Julien…"

"I can be submissive and possessive at the same time," he pointed out before I could complete my objection. "And I know myself. *For* you, I will learn to compromise, but when it comes *to* you, I never will. I've had a taste of what we could be, Eve, and I won't ever be satisfied with anything less."

Well, *fuck*. So much for dinner. "Take that robe off right now."

Without any argument at all, Julien stood up, abandoning his meal and discarding the robe, leaving him once again naked in front of me, his cock visibly twitching as the blood rushed back to it in anticipation of whatever I had in mind.

And what I had in mind was to show him that even though I was the one in charge, I could still belong to him, if he truly wanted me to. "You're going to show me how your gift works."

"Oui, Madame." Immediately, he went to the bathroom to retrieve it while I quickly removed my own clothes, my body already throbbing with excitement.

It had been four days since he touched me, four long days since our misunderstanding during the roleplay, and I craved him as if I'd been in withdrawal, my body aching with need.

Julien put the strap-on on the table next to the bed and picked up the lube bottle instead. "It would be my honour to get you ready. Will you let me?"

"Yes. I'll go as you were, on my hands and knees."

He bowed his head in agreement and I climbed up onto the bed, facing away from him just as he had for me, spreading my legs enough that he would have a good view. I'd had anal sex a couple of times before and though I hadn't hated it, I hadn't particularly enjoyed it either. Maybe it was one of those things that just wasn't for me, but Julien seemed pretty certain he could make it enjoyable for me, so I would give him a chance to try.

When he lowered his mouth to my pussy to start with, I certainly couldn't complain. All the desire for him that had been building all day, the frustration of our separation and the anticipation of having another chance, all of it melted into the perfect feel of his mouth on me, and I exhaled in satisfaction as my whole body relaxed.

He didn't seem to be in any hurry to get to my ass. Apparently, he wanted me feeling both good and needy first, and he did a great job of it, his tongue working my clit as his hand reached up to cup my breast, his fingers flicking across my nipple to mimic the action of his tongue. Craving more, I leaned back towards him, my body issuing a silent demand that he understood perfectly.

Only when he had me close to the edge did he gently start to circle the rim of my asshole with a well-lubed finger, gently pressing against it but not in yet. When I felt my orgasm coming, climbing the peak fast, he slid his finger inside, and I came hard with his finger buried in my ass.

"Parfait," he whispered from behind me, speaking in French as he often did when we were intimate. At least I knew that the word meant 'perfect', and as he started to slide his finger slowly in and out, letting me get used to the sensation, it felt a lot less awkward than I remembered it with other men.

Maybe it had to do with knowing that I had full control to stop it whenever I wanted. For the time being, at least, I didn't want to.

"I'll try the toy in a moment," he let me know. "Tell me if it's too much."

I promised to, and again, he took his time. With his finger still in my ass, his other hand slid into my wet pussy, fingering me in both holes at the same time. The slight taboo of it and the fact that he was entirely focused on me helped to make it even more enjoyable than the actions would have been on their own.

When he had me writhing again, ready for more, he finally replaced the finger in my ass with the toy. Slowly at first, just as I had with him, he pushed the head of it in while his other hand went to my clit, doing its best to distract me. It mostly worked too, and soon, he had the toy all the way in. Already, I felt full, and I knew it would feel a lot fuller when his cock got involved.

"Shall we try the whole thing?" he asked, his voice tight with desire as he pulled the dildo slowly out of me.

He hadn't let me down so far, so I gave my permission. "Let's try it."

Flipping over onto my back, I watched as he fit his cock and balls through the rings of the strap-on, leaving the toy beneath his cock to line up with my ass when he was inside me. From the box, he grabbed the bullet vibrators and put them both in place.

"I'll switch them on when we're ready," he promised. "Please, lay back. Let me please you."

Resting my head on the pillows, I spread my legs for him, smiling as he crawled towards me on the bed. "You look like something from a sci-fi romance book with your two cocks."

"There's a reason those books are popular," he teased me. "Let me show you."

I had no intention of stopping him, but just as he had himself lined up against both holes, he hesitated.

"I forgot the condom, tabarnak. Let me just..."

"No." That one word stopped him instantly. "It's alright. You don't need it."

After everything, I trusted him more than ever before, and I wanted to feel him that night. I wanted us both to get as much out of the experience as we possibly could, and in Julien's eyes, I could see how much it meant to him. He understood me perfectly, as he so often did.

With how wet I already was, his cock needed no lube and the strap-on still had plenty. He went very slow the first time, his eyes watching me carefully as he slid inside both my holes at once.

"Fuck. That's... different," I managed to gasp. I had never felt so full.

He immediately stopped for clarification. "Good different?"

"I'm not sure yet. Not bad, at least."

He understood that as my permission to keep going, and the more I relaxed, realizing that I *could* handle it, the better it felt. Even after his own denied orgasm earlier, Julien's focus was entirely on me. He would do whatever it took to make me happy, and that was the biggest turn-on of all.

"Are you ready for the vibrators now?" Julien asked when I started to moan in pleasure.

Shit. I forgot about the vibrators. I could barely think already, so what was one more stimulation? "Yes, go ahead."

The one in the shaft in my ass didn't do much for me, but the other one, attached above his cock at its base, connected with my clit when he was fully buried, and Julien rotated his hips against me to make sure it hit me perfectly.

"Oh, fuck, yes."

With him completely filling me and the vibrator giving my clit the attention it craved, it didn't take long for me to come again, and one more time after that, once I gave him permission to keep going. As the final waves of pleasure washed over me, Julien finally let go too, his much-delayed orgasm hitting him deep inside me as he muttered in French, his body trembling from his powerful release.

I'd had some good presents in my life, but that one might have just jumped to the very top of the list.

I had no idea how we were going to top it, but at the same time, I had absolutely no doubt that Julien would find a way. He'd accepted me in every way, and with us finally, completely on the same page, nothing could stand in our way.

Chapter Eighteen

A FAMILY CHRISTMAS

Ten days later

~Julien~

Stepping out of the door of the arrivals lounge at JFK airport in New York just before noon, I scanned the waiting crowd, looking for the sign with my name on it. Eve had said she'd arrange for a driver to meet me since she had an appointment with her lawyer scheduled for that morning, so when my eyes landed on her distinctive red hair and stunning smile, I almost dropped my bag in surprise.

"What are you doing here?" I asked as I walked over to her, drinking in the sight of her after ten long days apart. After I spent the night with her at the hotel in Toronto, leaving only when I absolutely had to go back home to change the next morning before work, she flew home to New York as planned, but not before extracting a promise from me to come and visit her over the holidays. I had the week between Christmas and New Year's off from work, and after spending Christmas Eve and Day with my mom, talking a lot more about my dad and Eve and everything that had happened, I flew to New York on the 26th.

"It's nice to see you too," she teased me, wrapping her arms around me and giving me a firm kiss, completely unbothered by all the people around us.

"Of course it's good to see you. You just surprised me." I pulled her tighter to me, inhaling her familiar scent and savouring the warmth of her breath against my skin. "Happy birthday. Merry Christmas."

I'd spoken to her on both her birthday and Christmas, but I wanted to repeat those wishes in person, and she smiled as I did. "Thank you. Joyeux Noël to you, too. The meeting with the lawyer got moved up an hour, so I was able to make it here after all. I literally arrived less than five minutes ago."

"You didn't have to come." She must have had better things to do than travel back and forth from the city to meet me.

"I know," was Eve's response, her dark eyes shining with amusement. "Now, let's stop wasting time and go."

"Oui, Madame." The words were meant to be teasing as she took charge the way she always did, but I noticed the shiver that ran down her spine, letting me know she'd been missing me just as much as I missed her.

In the back of the car on the way into the city, we talked about our Christmases and families. I would be meeting the rest of her family when we arrived, which was intimidating enough, but she let me know that some additional guests had also been invited. "My best friend, Noelle, and her fiancée are coming, and Noelle and Liv's parents too."

Liv was Eve's sister-in-law, and the sister of Eve's best friend, Noelle. I was starting to figure it all out, though meeting them all in person would probably make things a lot clearer.

"My parents' place is pretty luxurious," she warned me as we drew nearer to the Upper West Side apartment building where they lived. "There are some expensive pieces of art. I know it's not your thing, but…"

"I won't say anything," I promised. "I'll try not to even think about it."

In the time we'd been apart, I'd done some research on my own into the Stamer family. They were every bit as wealthy as I assumed, but they also sat firmly in the lists of the biggest philanthropists in the world, partly through personal donations and partly through their company.

Mr Stamer had a taste for the finer things in life, quite clearly, but he was also generous, and the pace of the family's giving had picked up significantly over the past ten years. I had to believe the responsibility for that fell at least partly to the woman next to me.

I'd looked up information about her too. There were photos online of her at New York events, looking stunning in evening gowns and heels, but there were other articles too, about an initiative in high school where she gathered the previous season's clothes from her classmates at her exclusive private school to be donated to raise funds for earthquake support in Asia, or about a food bank program she sponsored at her college for students who needed it, not taking any credit for it until someone had outed her as the donor behind it.

It began to annoy me that in every article, it always came back to talking about how much money and influence the Stamers had, as if that made her actions any better or worse than anyone else who would have done the same. Why did her family name and position need to define her?

And yes, I understood the irony of me feeling that way. Eve had opened my eyes to a lot of things.

Inside the elegant apartment building, we took the elevator up and the doors opened straight into the entrance hall as the Stamers' apartment took up the entire floor. "We're here," Eve called out as we took off our coats and shoes.

Only a few seconds later, a beautiful, older woman came around the corner, and there could be no doubt who she was: her red hair was just the same shade as Eve's, and if it weren't for her bright green eyes, they would have looked almost like two versions of the same person.

"Julien." She greeted me with a hug, her British accent still strong even after thirty years of living in New York. "I'm Gemma, Eve's mum. I've heard so much about you."

"I've heard a lot about you too. Eve has promised me an architecture lecture before I leave."

Gemma laughed, her laugh also a near copy of Eve's. "We'll see about that. Please, come on in, we're all in the living room."

Eve took my hand in support as we followed her mom into a huge room, beautifully decorated for Christmas. The pine scent of the real tree hit me as soon as we walked in, a fire crackled in the fireplace, and Eve tugged on my arm as she pointed upwards.

"Mistletoe," she whispered. "It's a whole thing for my parents. Don't stop underneath it."

The other men in the room started to stand up as we walked in, but Eve instructed them to sit back down in her usual commanding, confident tone. "Don't all attack him at once. I'll introduce you from here. Julien, you already know my dad."

Mr Stamer gave me a nod from behind his glass of whiskey, sitting in an armchair next to the fire.

"This is my brother, Noah, and his wife, Olivia."

"Call me Liv," the beautiful blonde woman told me while her husband, a younger, green-eyed version of Eve's dad, gave me a nod that subconsciously mirrored his father's almost precisely. They sat on a sofa across from the Christmas tree where Gemma sat down next to Olivia.

"This is Noelle, and her fiancé, Aaron."

Despite Eve's instructions to stay seated, Noelle got up anyway, coming around the large corner sofa where she'd been sitting to give me a hug.

"It was touch and go there for a while," she whispered in my ear. "I didn't know if you'd make it."

Obviously, she and Eve didn't have any secrets from each other, so I didn't pretend not to know what she meant. "I didn't know either, but I'm glad I'm here."

"Me too." She gave me a warm smile before returning to sit down next to Aaron. As the other outsider in the group, I hoped to have a chance to get to talk to him one-on-one later.

"And these are Noelle and Liv's parents, Holly and Jackson."

The last couple in the room also said hello before Eve and I took our seats on the sofa next to them. Holly was an older version of Olivia, the two of them resembling each other almost as much as Gemma and Eve did, while Jackson leaned over to whisper in my ear as I sat down. "If you need any backup with Cole, just let me know. We can work out a code word or a hand signal or something, and I'll come rescue you."

I really hoped that wouldn't be necessary, but I thanked him for the offer anyway, feeling at ease with him right away.

The afternoon flew by as we all sat and laughed and talked. Everyone was curious about my work and the plans that Eve was making for her foundation. When Jackson suggested that she should try to poach me from my current job, we played dumb. Although we had talked about it, nothing would be official until she had the foundation created. That was what she'd been meeting with the lawyer about that day, and I was excited to get a chance to speak to her about it when we were alone later.

First, though, we had one more big meeting to get through, and as the gathering began to wind down in the late afternoon, Eve turned to me. "Are you ready to go?"

I really didn't know how to answer that. With her support, I'd made contact with my dad by email and let him know that I would be in New York if he wanted to meet. I had no idea what the response would be after all those years, but he wrote back almost immediately to invite me to have dinner with him and his family. I set it up for the day I arrived, not wanting to have it hanging over me for the entire trip, and when I asked Eve if she would go with me, she agreed without hesitation.

"I guess I'm as ready as I'm going to be," I answered her, and after saying goodbye to her family, we headed back out into the city together to go and meet mine.

~Eve~

Julien handled himself very well with my family. Not only did he not seem uncomfortable or say anything to indicate he might be, he actually seemed to enjoy himself. To start, he chatted easily with Jackson, which wasn't too difficult to do. Jackson put everyone at ease. Noah and my dad were tougher nuts to crack, but Julien held his own. Over the course of the afternoon, all the women in the room found a way to tell me that they thought his accent was sexy, which I couldn't argue with.

Overall, it couldn't have gone much better, and I hoped the dinner with *his* dad would go just as well. From the way his knee bounced in the back of the cab as he looked out the window at the New York streets, I could tell just how nervous he felt about it.

Placing my hand on his knee, I leaned close to him. "If it gets too much for you, if you want to go, just use your safeword. I'll make an excuse and take care of it." What good was a domme if not to protect him and make him feel safe?

Julien gave me a grateful smile, understanding my message perfectly. "I will. Merci."

The Ribars lived in an elegant brownstone house in Brooklyn Heights, decorated with pine boughs on the railings leading up the stairs and a beautiful wreath on the door. A large, decorated Christmas tree stood in the window to the left of the door, the picture of a happy family home. Julien took a deep breath as he faced the door, and I squeezed his hand for support before he knocked.

Only a few moments later, the door opened to reveal a familiar face, at least to me. "Hi, Eve, nice to see you. You must be Julien."

Maribel Ribar held out her hand to her half-brother and he shook it politely, giving her a nod of greeting as I quickly introduced them. "Julien, this is Maribel. We went to the same college."

"Eve mentioned that to me before," Julien confirmed, his eyes still on his half-sister. They didn't share much in common looks-wise other than the shade of their hair. Maribel must have taken more after her mother. "She said she knows you and your fiancé."

I tried not to wince at the mention of Corey and our short-term, ill-fated fling, but Maribel laughed it off. "He's here too. Everyone else is inside and they're all freaking out a little. Crystal and I had no idea you existed until a few days ago."

Crystal was her younger sister, who I'd never met, but I noticed that Maribel didn't say Julien's existence came as a surprise to her mother, making me wonder how long she'd known and what she felt about her husband's first child.

She ushered me and Julien inside, taking our coats before leading us down the hall to a large sitting room at the back of the house where the rest of the family had gathered. As soon as we appeared in the doorway, the older man sitting on the end of the sofa got to his feet, his expression a mix of curiosity, trepidation, and disbelief.

"Dad, this is Julien," Maribel introduced him, stepping away to go and sit down next to Corey, who gave me a friendly smile. We hadn't seen each other for quite a while since I'd been away in South America, but he looked happy in his new circumstances.

I wondered if he thought the same about me.

Mr Ribar stepped closer to us, examining his son's face as closely as Julien regarded him in return. Between the two of them, I could see the similarities much more clearly than I could between Julien and Maribel. He didn't resemble his father as much as Noah looked like our dad, but the resemblance was there.

"Julien." His father did his best to pronounce the name with a French accent, distinguishing it from his own name. "Thank you for coming."

Julien nodded, his body still a little tense. "Thank you for having me. This is Eve Stamer."

All eyes in the room moved to me and I smiled in acknowledgement but kept silent, not wanting to take any attention off the reason we'd come.

Mr Ribar looked unsure about what to do next but he offered Julien his hand, and after a moment's hesitation, his son shook it. "I'm not sure what changed your mind about getting in touch, but I'm glad you did."

Julien threw a glance my way, and I nodded in encouragement. He hadn't said anything to his father in his email about his mother's omission, but I thought his father should know and he had agreed. "Actually, I only found out two weeks ago that you had tried to make contact with me. Until then, I thought you never had."

While he kept his eyes on his father, I cast a sweeping glance around the room to see everyone else's reaction to that news. Maribel and Crystal were both leaning forward, not wanting to miss a thing, their expressions curious and interested, but Mrs Ribar's nostrils flared. Was she upset on her husband's behalf, as I had been on Julien's when his mother told me, or did she not believe Julien's story? Would she welcome Julien in or see him as a threat to her own children? It could honestly go either way.

"Let me introduce you to everyone else." Mr Ribar said, still looking a little overwhelmed. "You already met Maribel at the door, and this is Crystal, my youngest daughter."

Probably around 20 years old, she stayed seated but gave her new half-brother a slightly awkward wave and a friendly smile.

"And Michelle, my wife."

Unlike her daughter, Mrs Ribar got to her feet and came over to Julien. His shoulders tightened as he watched her, probably wondering the same as I did what her reaction would be. Her expression was curious as she got closer, no doubt looking for similarities to her husband the same way I had looked for them in Mr Ribar. She seemed to find what she was looking for, since she surprised both him and me by pulling him into a hug a moment later. "It's so nice to finally meet you."

"Thank you." I could hear the tinge of confusion in his voice as he returned her embrace.

Mrs Ribar turned to me next. "Lovely to meet you too, Eve. I know you by reputation, of course. How did you meet Julien?"

He and I exchanged glances again, that time with a hint of amusement. The story of how we actually met was a little too risqué for polite company, so I stuck to a half-truth. "Julien is the director of a charity I volunteered with."

"Julian told me about the charity. It sounds like a wonderful cause." She beamed at both of us, as proud as if we were her own children. "Dinner is ready, why don't we all go sit down and we can get to know each other better while we eat?"

The others all got to their feet and we followed Mr and Mrs Ribar into a large dining room with a crystal chandelier above the oval mahogany table. Everything in the room looked expensive and old, but Julien didn't seem to notice, keeping his eyes on his new family instead. He and I sat on one side of the table with Maribel, Crystal and Mrs Ribar across from us. Mr Ribar sat at the head of the table next to Julien, and Corey sat at the other end, near me.

Over dinner, the Ribars asked Julien about his work and Mr Ribar told us about his own business. It didn't sound like something Julien would have any interest in, but he asked polite questions anyway. Nothing further was said about Julien's mother until dinner ended and Mr Ribar asked if he and his wife could speak with Julien privately.

Immediately, Julien's body tensed again, and I slid my hand onto his knee beneath the table, letting him know I would do whatever he needed me to. The gesture was tiny, but I could see the comfort that it gave him. "Perhaps Eve could stay as well?"

"Certainly." Mr Ribar gave me a curious look as his daughters and Corey left the room, giving us some privacy. "What exactly is your relationship, if you don't mind me asking?"

Julien and I exchanged smiles. That was a good question, one that we planned to discuss during his visit, and he answered for the both of us. "We're still figuring that out, but Eve has spoken to my mother. She knows the whole story, so you can speak frankly in front of her."

He seemed to be assuming that his father wanted to speak about the past, and he was quickly proven right.

"Leaving your mother was the biggest mistake of my life," he started bluntly, his wife taking his hand for support just as my hand remained on Julien's knee. "Obviously, I love my family and my life now, but I truly regret the way things ended between us, and I especially regret that I never got to know you."

"Was it really just about the money?" Julien asked. "It meant more to you than she did?"

He minced no words, but his father accepted the summary. "The idea of being cut off terrified me. My father threatened to leave me penniless and I thought my life would be over if he did, so I sat there and let him accuse your mother of things I knew weren't true. I hated myself that day, and I don't blame her for the hatred she has for me."

Every word from his mouth sounded sincere, and I hoped Julien could hear it too. His expression was impossible to read. "When did you find out that I existed?"

"I knew which church she attended, and I checked the website until I saw the notice of your baptism. When I saw she'd named you after me, or so I thought, I nearly got on a flight right then, but two things stopped me: the first being my father, and the second was the thought that she'd turn me away."

Based on what Madame Labrecque had told me, she might well have, but I couldn't say that for certain. I'd given Julien another chance; maybe she would have done the same for the elder Julian if he'd taken the chance.

"Julian told me about you on our second or third date," Mrs Ribar interjected. "He wanted me to know about you in case he was ever able to have a relationship with you, which he wanted to. He didn't want there to be any friction between us because of it. You were always on his mind."

From the way Julien's lips tightened, I could tell that meant something to him, even after all those years.

"There's a trust fund in your name," Mr Ribar added, almost nervously. "It's all the money I wanted to give your mother over the years but she never accepted. I know you're a grown man now and you don't need it as you once did, but it's entirely yours. I can't take it back even if I wanted to. It has no strings attached to it, I simply want you to have it."

How ironic that Julien Labrecque should have a trust fund. Somewhere inside, he probably found it a little amusing too, though his face betrayed no sign of it. "How much is it?"

The question surprised me, since I couldn't imagine why he cared, but Mr Ribar answered him without hesitation. "Five million dollars."

I hadn't expected it to be that much, and obviously Julien hadn't either. His eyes widened just a little, enough that I noticed but the people sitting across from us might not have. "And I can do whatever I want with it?"

Mr Ribar nodded. "It's yours, as I said. I can send you all the information, there's no rush to claim it. It's been sitting there almost thirty years already."

We talked a little longer, Mr Ribar asking tentative questions about how Julien's mother was doing. He seemed genuinely disappointed to hear that she'd never married. I suspected it had a lot to do with the bitterness she'd carried with her for so long, but now that Julien knew the truth and had moved on, maybe she finally could too.

When we stepped back onto the Brooklyn street more than two hours after we'd arrived, Julien exhaled deeply. "That went pretty well."

"I thought it went *very* well," I agreed, and as he smiled, I couldn't resist the chance to tease him. "And you're a millionaire! Who knew?"

His eye roll made me laugh, but as he put his arms around me, the mood between us shifted. My laughter died away as heat rushed through my body, the heat of ten days of longing and dreaming of him. "Let's go back to your place."

"Avec plaisir." I put on my best French accent, and Julien smiled in appreciation. "Is it as sexy when I say it as when you do?"

"Everything you say is sexy, Eve. Thank you for coming with me tonight."

"I'll always be there when you need me." We got a taxi in a matter of minutes and headed back into Manhattan, back to my parents' apartment, where we could finally have some time alone to talk about what came next for the two of us.

~Julien~

As we rode the elevator back up to the Stamers' apartment, it felt like I had reached a turning point, one of the truly pivotal moments of my life. It started with Eve that night at the benefit and how she made me confront my biases, carried on with learning the truth from my mother about my dad, and led up to meeting him and his family that evening. From my dad and his wife, I got no hint of hard feelings, at least towards me. A bit of sadness lingered over all the time we'd lost, and I felt it too, but they wanted a relationship going forward. They'd left the door wide open.

It felt like the door was open with Eve too. We had chosen to leave the conversation about our future, both personal and professional, until we were reunited and could discuss it in person but I had been thinking about it a lot and I suspected she had too. Although I'd already made up my mind, after the visit with my father's family, things had become even clearer to me.

When we reached the apartment, I expected Eve would want to go and have that conversation immediately, just as I did, but she surprised me by leading me to the kitchen instead. Her parents were both there, talking together over a glass of wine. They both looked over as we walked in, Gemma giving us a smile and Cole acknowledging us with a nod.

"I'd like to show Julien your locked room," Eve stated bluntly without even saying hello first. "Could you let us in?"

Gemma looked over at her husband in surprise, but he simply shrugged, taking another drink of his wine. "Go ahead."

Completely confused about what was going on, I followed Gemma and Eve back into the hall, to a door that had a fingerprint scanner next to the handle and Gemma pressed her index finger against it to unlock the door.

"Try not to move anything around," was all Gemma said before walking away. "Your dad has everything where he likes it."

Promising she wouldn't touch anything, Eve pushed the door open, and I didn't even get a half-step forward before my jaw dropped in surprise.

Some of my previous dommes had their own playrooms, but I'd never seen anything to compare to the one in front of me. It had everything I could think of: equipment, toys, screens, mirrors, and more accessories than I could count. Walking slowly into the centre of the room, I turned around, looking up and down to make sure I hadn't missed anything though I could barely take it all in.

"Tabarnak," I finally muttered when I could collect my thoughts again. "I guess being rich does have some benefits."

Eve's warm laugh filled the air. "That's the only benefit you can think of?"

"It's the only one I've ever been envious of." I wouldn't even have a clue where to start in a room like this, but I would be willing to figure it out.

"I believe you." Eve shook her head in amusement and affection. "Well, maybe we can have our own version someday, but that's not the reason I'm showing it to you."

"What is the reason?" My attention immediately went to her, tuning everything else out. Though I didn't understand what her words meant, it sounded important.

Just as focused on me as I was on her, she explained her thinking. "My parents have always embraced their kink. They don't flaunt it; this door stays locked most of the time, but they don't hide it either. You said that you've never had a relationship with a domme that was romantic as well as sexual, and I just thought this room is a good reminder that it's possible to have both. My parents are best friends, they're business partners, and they're lovers who still can't get enough of each other, even at their age."

She said that as if they were ancient, but I knew what she meant: decades had gone by, and they still enjoyed playing together in a room like this. She found it inspiring, and so did I.

"They raised me to believe I could have it all too," Eve continued. "To go after what I want and never settle. And I know what I want now: I want you, Julien."

"I want you too, Eve. I want..."

"Did I say you could speak yet?" Her raised eyebrows were stern, but the corner of her mouth curled up, letting me know she was teasing.

I bowed my head to her, playing my role. "Non, Madame. Please, continue."

Her tone immediately softened as she carried on. "I've thought about things over the last ten days, like we said we would, and I've come to one conclusion: I've never met anyone who suits me as well as you do. There's the sexual side, naturally, but it's more than that. We care about the same things, and I admire your passion, even if I don't always agree with its focus. You bring a different perspective and challenge me in good ways. When I think about the future, I want that passion. I want us to build a true partnership together. I want you to come and work with me, and I want you to trust that I will always have your back. I want... well, I guess that's about it, really."

Her final summary made me smile because she had been so confident and sure of herself throughout her whole speech, but at the very end, I caught a hint of the vulnerable woman I knew existed within her: the one who had been nervous to tell me the truth about her family name and her background, the one who had been uncertain when we went over the kink checklist together.

The one who desperately wanted me to say that I saw things the same way she did.

Luckily for us both, I had no intention of disappointing her ever again.

"As you said, I've never had a relationship with my domme before. I didn't think finding someone who fulfilled me on every level would be possible, but when I saw you at that bar in Quito, you spoke to me in a way that something deep in my soul recognized. You're dominant in all the right ways but you also have a caring, compassionate side, and it's the mix of the two, the way they contrast and complement each other that really made me fall for you. It wasn't easy for me to accept that the woman who enchanted me so much came from a world I disagree with on principle, and it was even harder to accept that I was wrong about so many of the preconceptions I had about that world. But you challenged me to, and you made me see it. I almost lost you, and I never want to do that again."

Her dark eyes had been filling with happy tears, her lips pressing together to keep her emotions in check as I laid out all the reasons I wanted to be with her, but the last thing I said snapped her back to practical matters in an instant.

"I also want to donate the money my father put aside for me to your foundation."

Her eyes widened and her lips parted in genuine surprise. "You don't have to do that. That money is yours."

"To do what? There's nothing I need or want more than to help you succeed. I want us to be equal partners in the foundation. That's why I gave my notice at the charity three days ago."

Her eyes widened even more. "You quit? Already? But I hadn't even told you what I wanted to do."

She looked bewildered by my confession, but in my mind, it made perfect sense. "If you weren't certain or you had changed your mind, I would have done whatever I could to convince you. My father said tonight how he almost got on a plane to see my mother after I was born, and I don't want to be another 'almost'. I got on the plane, Eve. I came here to offer myself to you, professionally, personally, as your partner, as your sub, however you want me, because I love you. It's really as simple as that."

I'd never said those words to another woman before, but they came out as easily and as naturally as if I said them all the time.

It could only be because they were true.

"I love you, too." She was in my arms almost before I could blink, both of us moving towards each other at the same time, and as I kissed her, the taste of her sweeter than ever now that I knew she felt the same as I did, her hands slid across my chest and she groaned into my mouth. "You're wearing it."

"I promised I would."

The 'it' referred to the corset beneath my clothes, the one I'd been wearing ever since she left Toronto. I told her I wanted a reminder of her while we were apart but she thought the cock cage would be too intense for ten days. She suggested the corset instead, though she still hadn't seen me in it. I was allowed to remove it to sleep and shower, but every time I got dressed in the past ten days, I put it on underneath my clothes, a secret only she and I knew about. Every time it hindered my movement or momentarily cut off my breath, it reminded me of the discomfort of our separation, and the relief that awaited me when we were reunited.

"Let's get out of here," she ordered, her dark eyes filled with desire. "I can't wait to see it, but not in my parents' playroom."

That was fair enough.

Back out in the hall, she called to her mother in the kitchen to say we were finished in the room and that we were going to bed. It wouldn't leave them in much doubt about what we intended to do there, but it wouldn't have taken much imagination for them to figure it out anyway.

The room Eve took me to had been her room growing up. Pictures still hung on the pinboard, her old books on the bookshelf, and I couldn't wait to explore all of it, but first, I had to fulfill my domme's request: she wanted to see my corset and I would happily obey.

My fingers tripped over the buttons of my shirt in my impatience as I tried to get them undone as fast as I could, and when I finally got them all open, I pulled the shirt off to reveal the silver garment underneath the midnight blue shirt I'd been wearing. Tight against my skin and cinched at the waist, it provided just the right amount of pressure: firm, but not painful.

Eve's eyes travelled over it slowly, taking in every detail, circling me as she made her inspection. Though she didn't know it, though she wouldn't know it until the next Christmas, I had ordered a miniature version of the corset to go into her stocking the following year. I would add to that pile of gifts whenever an idea hit me, every time we made an enjoyable new memory, so that no matter what might be happening in our lives by the time December came around, we would have the reminders of the good times to look back on.

Hopefully, the next year, there would be no question about whether she'd accept it from me or not. We were on the same page, on the same side, with no more need for a standoff between us ever again.

Sliding her fingers beneath the laces on the back of the corset, she pulled them even tighter, making me gasp at the sudden constriction.

"You've been so good wearing this for me, and I think you've earned your reward."

With another tug, she undid the laces, and I took a deep, cleansing breath as the pressure eased.

"I want to ride you sometime while you're wearing that," she warned me, still standing behind me as she placed the corset down on her dresser. "You look hot as hell in it, but not tonight."

"What do you want tonight? What can I do for you, Madame E?" The eagerness in my voice was impossible to miss.

Eve walked back around the front of me, sliding her hands down the newly-exposed skin on my chest, her touch feeling all the better after its long absence. "I want you to make love to me. That's all."

That, I could certainly do, that night and every night, for as long as she wanted me to. From the first time I saw her, and that night more than ever before, I belonged entirely to her.

~~THE END~~

IF YOU ENJOYED THIS...

The final book in the series, *Eggnog Experiment*, revisits all your favourite couples one more time.

Turn the page for a preview from the first chapter!

EGGNOG EXPERIMENT

~Gemma~

Cole's voice in my ear still had the power to make me shiver, even after more than thirty years together. "That seatbelt is such a tease. I can't wait to get you properly restrained when we land."

His words conjured so many memories, all the way from that Christmas when he first wrapped his ties around me to much more recent adventures in our personal dungeon at home.

As much as I wanted him to tie me up that night too, we had to be realistic. "We have the welcome dinner tonight with Julien's family, and jet lag is bound to catch up with us. It might have to wait."

"I'll be thinking about it until it happens," he murmured before settling back in his seat and turning his attention back to the others in the plane with us. Grey strands streaked through his dark hair these days, but it only made him look more distinguished and possibly even more handsome than he had in his youth. I barely noticed the lines on his face, and he certainly never commented on mine. "Are you alright, Olivia?"

Our daughter-in-law sat across from us on the other side of the table on our private plane, next to our son, Noah. I hadn't noticed how her hand had gone to her mouth, but Cole picked up on it. He didn't usually miss much.

Olivia swallowed, tucking her blonde hair behind her ears as she lowered her hand. "My stomach is a little queasy but I'll be fine. I can't remember the last time I got motion sickness on a plane."

"You should eat something," Noah suggested, taking his wife's hand supportively. At times, he looked so much like his dad, it felt like being in a time machine when I looked at him. He wore his dark hair differently than Cole had, and his green eyes came from me, but otherwise, they had everything in common. "You hardly ate any dinner."

"I'm not hungry," she assured him, looking like she'd rather be talking about anything else. "It's probably just the long flight."

None of us could argue with that. It *had* been a long flight. Even with a shortened refuelling stop in Hawaii, we were coming up to 24 hours since we left New York, and no matter how nice the Stamer private plane might be, we were all anxious to arrive.

"I'll feel better when we're on the ground," Olivia insisted even as Cole and Jackson exchanged pointed glances across the aisle.

Our best friends, Jackson and Holly Hanmer, also happened to be Olivia's parents, and I knew exactly what Cole and Jackson were both thinking even though neither of them said a word. Unbeknownst to our children, their fathers had a secret wager between them about which of them would be a grandfather first.

They were both a little chagrined that it hadn't happened yet. Noah and Olivia had been married for almost three years and together for six years before that. Olivia's sister, Noelle, had been with Aaron for three years, though they only got married earlier that year. It had been at their wedding that Cole and Jackson made the bet in the first place, enjoying the evening with a drink or two, and the young couple sat across from Jackson and Holly on the plane, completing the group of us making the trip together.

Our daughter, Eve, met her fiancé, Julien, the previous Christmas, and we were all travelling to Australia that December to celebrate their wedding, the last one in our extended family group.

Holly and I tried to explain to our husbands that many young couples chose to wait to start a family.

"Just because you knocked Gemma up the week you met her doesn't mean everyone should do it that way!" Holly told Cole bluntly when we overheard the men talking about it one day. "They'll have children when they're good and ready to."

"It's all in fun," Jackson protested, shrugging his shoulders sheepishly even though Cole remained unmoved. "We'd never put any pressure on them. It's just a silly rivalry between us. And if Olivia and Noah are the first, we both win."

We left it there, but I could read in their eyes as we started our descent into Sydney that they were both wondering if Olivia's nausea had anything to do with a potential baby. I would love for Noah and Liv to start a family *if* they both wanted it, but they hadn't said a word to me about it, and if Olivia talked to Holly, Holly hadn't mentioned it.

In the end, unless they asked me to get involved, it wasn't really any of my business.

"Tessa's going to have a car waiting for us?" I asked Olivia to help change the subject.

She threw me a grateful smile. "That's right. Our baggage will all be brought separately, we can go on ahead as soon as we're finished with immigration. Everything's taken care of. We're getting the VIP treatment, even more than usual. Tessa pulled some strings for us."

"It's lucky that she knew the owner," Jackson piped up. "I took a look at the resort online and it looks beautiful."

"Yeah. It's a lucky break for all of us," Noah agreed, giving Olivia a smirk that I hoped Jackson didn't catch.

When Olivia enlisted her college friend, Tessa, to help plan Eve and Julien's wedding, I expected something classy but not too showy, keeping in line with the less extravagant lifestyle that my daughter and her fiancé led. Maybe a historic house outside of New York, or maybe even something close to where Julien grew up in Québec.

So, when we had a video call with them in October where Eve shared their plans with me, Cole, and Noah, their chosen location took me completely by surprise.

"Australia? In December? But... *why?*"

They might as well have said they wanted to get married on the moon for all the sense it made to me.

"Julien and I are really busy," Eve reminded me. After spending two months in Africa in the late summer, they'd moved on to Asia and the Pacific islands to meet with charities who might be interested in joining Eve's new international internship program. Her charity matched young, ambitious college graduates, the companies in the United States who were interested in hiring them, and charities around the world who could benefit from some extra help. The young people got some real world experience and perspective, the companies benefited from that when their new employees joined the workforce, and the local charities got dedicated, hard-working, well-educated volunteers.

Although they'd just started, the program already had a waiting list of people wanting to apply, and so Eve and Julien had gone to recruit more charities and vet them in person, to make sure the experience would be a safe and successful one. Their travel plans had them booked well into the new year, but they had agreed to take a week off at Christmas to get married.

"With such a short time available, by the time we flew back to North America and got over the jet lag, we'd only have time to get married and turn right around again," Eve explained. "I know that you all have three weeks off over the holidays, so if you come to this side of the world, you can make a real vacation out of it and we'll all get to have Christmas together."

That part appealed to me, as she knew it would. Christmas had always been my favourite time of year, and I'd never had one apart from my children yet.

There was just one little problem. "It's summer there! How is it going to feel like Christmas in the summer?"

Everyone laughed as if I'd been joking. "It'll feel like Christmas because we're all together, Mom," Noah promised. "And I'm sure if you want it to snow, Dad'll pull it off somehow."

A glance at Cole made it clear he was already considering how he might do that, so I quickly nipped that in the bud. "I don't need snow. But how are you going to plan all this in two months in another country?"

"Tessa's one of the best wedding planners in the city," Noah piped up. "She'll pull something amazing together, I'm sure."

"I don't know if 'amazing' is necessary," Julien piped up warily. He sat next to Eve on our computer screen, the two of them wearing cool, loose clothing in the Vietnamese heat. "We were just planning to go to the local registry office, nothing fancy."

"She'll make sure everyone's happy," Noah promised, and as soon as we hung up with them, he turned to me and his dad, his eyes sparkling. "I know just the place. An acquaintance of ours opened a resort in Australia a couple of years ago. Their ethos is to literally provide whatever their customers want. It won't be cheap but it'll feel as low-key and casual as they want it to. As long as Eve doesn't see the bill, it'll be perfect."

"Will they have availability on such short notice?" I wondered.

"They will if the price is right," Cole remarked. "How do you know this 'acquaintance'?"

Noah didn't mince words, being as honest with us as usual. "I met him in the voyeur scene. There's a private club attached to the hotel too, for any kind of kink you can imagine, but it's extremely discreet. Unless you're specifically looking for the place, you'd never know it's there."

I had to ask the obvious question. "You're not suggesting we have your sister's wedding there just because you want to try this sex club, are you?"

Noah laughed, taking that as another joke. "Of course not. I really think this place would be perfect. The club is a bonus, and not just for us. I'm sure they've got BDSM rooms too."

Although I loved that our children felt comfortable talking to us about anything, every now and then I had to imagine what my own father's reaction would have been if he could hear half of the things that were said around our dinner table.

Cole seemed to be onboard, at least to consider it. "Let's see a proposal and we can go from there. But if we decide to go with it, whatever you do, make sure nobody tells Jackson about this club."

We all remembered Jackson's reaction to finding out about some of Noah's kinks, so we readily agreed it would be best to keep the club a secret from Olivia's dad. By the time the plane touched down in Sydney, no one had let the cat out of the bag yet, and thankfully, he didn't seem to notice the look Noah gave Olivia when he said how lucky we were to be going to the resort.

We had so much to look forward to over the next three weeks, I hardly knew what to get excited about first. It wouldn't be like any Christmas I'd had before, but I knew it would definitely be one I'd never forget.

~Cole~

Even by my admittedly exacting standards, the service we received from the hotel impressed me from the start. A concierge waited for us outside immigration and ensured we were comfortably settled into two air-conditioned SUVs, one for the older generation and one for the younger, before we left the airport and headed south to the city of Wollongong where we'd find our resort destination.

When I first shared the plans with him, Jackson asked why we didn't hold the wedding at one of the Stamer hotels in Australia. It certainly would have been simpler, but my reasons were twofold: first, it would be harder to keep things quiet if we held it in one of our own hotels. One small leak to the press and Eve would have photographers lurking outside just like there had been at my own wedding. I hadn't been happy about that and I knew she wouldn't be either. She didn't want anyone making a fuss, which led directly to my second reason: although Julien had made significant progress towards accepting that wealth didn't have to be a negative thing, she still didn't want to flaunt it, and having her wedding in a hotel that she technically owned wouldn't help.

In short, I tried to see things from her point of view, and my gut told me my daughter would rather not get married somewhere with her name above the door.

The resort Noah suggested looked ideal. A short distance out of the city, on one of the many beaches that lined the coast, it had something for everyone. The younger crowd could go surfing or swimming in the ocean, while Gemma and Holly had been eyeing some of the hikes in the surrounding forests and hills, along with the top-of-the-line spa within the hotel itself. It definitely didn't feel like Christmas when we arrived, even with the decorations in the airport, but I had a plan to help counter that.

As I said, the hotel staff were very accommodating.

The drive went quickly as we all enjoyed the scenery and talked about what the next few weeks might bring, and further into the future as well. In the new year, I would be scaling back my hours at Stamer Hotels and officially passing the reins to Noah. Gemma liked to remind me that I had been running the business for many years by the time I reached Noah's age, and in the eight years he'd been working with me, he'd proven himself a capable leader and shrewd businessman. I knew the business would be in good shape with him at the helm, but that didn't make it any easier to accept the fact that I wasn't needed anymore.

"You're not falling asleep on me, are you?" Gemma teased, leaning into me and taking my hand as the Hanmers chatted to each other in the seats behind us. I must have zoned out for a moment looking out the window. "I thought you had big plans for tonight and here you are napping."

"I wasn't 'napping'. I don't need to nap." My reply came out more tersely than I meant it to, since I knew damn well that Gemma didn't mean it that way. It just rubbed a nerve after all the talk of retirement and getting older. When I saw the confused look in her gorgeous green eyes, I immediately apologized. "I'm sorry. I'm just feeling my age today, I guess."

"I understand," she quickly assured me. "Our baby's getting married. It's kind of hard *not* to feel it. For some reason, it's different than with Noah."

I had to agree. Eve had been able to take care of herself for a long time already, but I still liked being the one she could turn to if she needed help. Now, she had Julien for that. Both of our kids were moving on with their own lives and the business would move on without me too. It felt a little bit like we were getting left behind with no real direction anymore.

However, Gemma was the last person I wanted to take any of that out on. If anyone kept me feeling young, she did, especially when I imagined all the things we might get up to in that club later on. At least for a little while, we'd be able to forget all about getting older.

At the hotel, another member of staff greeted us and showed us to our rooms. Each of us had a large suite, not unlike the one I'd been staying in when I first met Gemma in London. The whole wing of the hotel was reserved for Eve's wedding guests, so we would have plenty of privacy.

"Oh, hello, everyone." As we approached our rooms, the door to one of the other rooms opened to reveal a man I'd known in passing for several years but would likely be seeing more of from now on: Julien's father, Julian Ribar. He gave me a warm smile in particular. "Nice to see you, Cole. How was your flight?"

"Fine. When did you arrive?" We'd offered to fly the Ribars down with us on our plane, but they thought it might be awkward to be cooped up for that long with Julien's mother. Although Julien had made peace with his father's family, apparently things between his parents were less amicable. In the end, Julien's mother didn't come with us either, not wanting to accept our 'charity'. We hadn't even met the woman in the flesh yet.

"Last night," Julian replied. "Everyone else is out on the beach already, I just needed to grab a few things. Will we see you out there?"

An afternoon of lying in the sun might actually put me to sleep after the long flight. "Probably not today, but we'll see you at dinner tonight."

He said goodbye to everyone and headed out while I opened the door to our suite, letting Gemma go in first. She hadn't taken more than two steps when she gasped.

"Look at it! It's Christmas!"

Her squeal of delight drew the attention of everyone else in the hall who were still getting their keys sorted out, and they all peered in to see what was happening.

"It's gorgeous!" Noelle exclaimed.

"Is our room like this too?" Olivia asked.

"I don't think so," Noah replied, shooting me an amused look. "I think this is 100% Cole Stamer."

He was absolutely right. I'd requested that the curtains be closed when we arrived to give the full effect. Coloured lights were strung around the room and wrapped around the tall, thick, real Christmas tree in the corner, next to the fireplace. Stockings hung from the mantle, boughs of garland were draped around the table, and, of course, a sprig of mistletoe hung above the door.

"Cole." Gemma gave me a look that was part reproach and part delight. "You didn't have to do this."

"You said you didn't need snow, but you didn't say anything about the rest of it. Does it feel like Christmas now?"

"It does," she assured me, planting a sweet kiss on my lips. "Thank you."

"Alright, to your own rooms now," I ordered everyone else. They all left still exclaiming over the decorations, making Gemma smile again as I closed the door behind them.

Our luggage hadn't arrived yet, but the hotel had left us a welcome package with everything we'd need to freshen up in the meantime. A brochure highlighted all the resort's attractions, and tucked behind it, another small pamphlet gave us the information we'd need for the club. Noah told me that everyone in our travelling party would be getting one except for Jackson and Holly.

The club was called Paradise, and though the brochure didn't give too much away, it promised that its patrons would find their own version of paradise within its walls. If visitors wanted to have sex with other patrons, there were some hoops to jump through, but since Gemma and I only wanted the playspace, we didn't have to do much other than pay.

The blood pumping through my body as I let my imagination take over definitely made me feel like a much younger man, and when Gemma announced that she wanted to take a shower before dinner, my dick practically leapt in anticipation.

"I'll join you."

I didn't phrase it as a question, and Gemma immediately slipped into her natural submissive role, responding to my tone. "If you like, Mr Stamer."

Our clothes hit the bathroom floor in near record time, and soon, I had her with her back against the wall in the large walk-in shower. "Hold your hands above your head, like they're cuffed there," I commanded. Without question, she obeyed, and I took the opportunity to run my hands over every perfect inch of her. My fingers slipped over her puckered nipples, across her stomach and along the curve of her waist, down her thighs and back up again, ending between her legs where they made her gasp in pleasure as they rubbed her clit before thrusting into her.

So many men my age, people that I'd worked with or competed with or those who were mere acquaintances, had ended their marriages and wound up with much younger women, but that thought never even crossed my mind. Even if I looked at things from a purely sexual point of view, no one would ever suit me as perfectly as Gemma did. No one else would excite me the way she did when she moaned my name, or look at me with such pure surrender and need.

She came on my fingers, trembling around me with her arms still held above her head, but when she asked if she could return the favour, I declined. "If you want me to come, you'll have to go to the club with me tonight."

"You drive a hard bargain," she teased me, still catching her breath. "Let's get through dinner first and then we can decide."

"In that case, I'll be choosing what you wear tonight."

The heat in her eyes told me she knew exactly what I had in mind, but she didn't refuse.

The night ahead looked very promising indeed.

MORE FROM THE AUTHOR

<u>Contemporary Romance – New Adult/Clean</u>

It Figures duet
It Figures
Figuring It Out

<u>Historical Romance – 18+</u>

Lady in Waiting Series
Lady in Waiting
King in Training
Princess in Hiding

<u>Paranormal Romance – 18+</u>

Standalone
Out of My Depth

Cold Lake Pack Series
The Curse and the Prophecy
The Spell and the Legacy
The Dream and the Destiny

Mismatched Mates Series
Mismatched Mates
Misguided Motives
Mistaken Meanings

Serena's Story
The Alpha's Second Chance
The Returned Mate
The Vampire's Consort

Sacrifice Series
Blood Donor
Life Giver

Paranormal Romance – New Adult/Clean
The Alpha's Prey

KEEP IN TOUCH

Daily updates from my works-in-progress, bonus chapters and more can be found on my Ream account, Chilli & Chocolate, along with Emma Lee-Johnson:
https://reamstories.com/chilliandchocolate

You can find and follow me on Facebook at:
facebook.com/melodytyden

Join the Facebook group Melody's Romance Corner for fun games, interaction with the author and exclusive news and excerpts.

You can also sign up to my newsletter at www.melodytyden.com for all the latest news.

www.ingramcontent.com/pod-product-compliance
Lightning Source LLC
Chambersburg PA
CBHW071134180726
48291CB00007B/2167

9 781915 869210